I0582496

NEVER CRIED WOLF

BRIANNA RAE QUINN

Never Cried Wolf

Copyright © 2023 Brianna Rae Quinn

Hardbound ISBN: 978-1-7356362-7-6

Paperback ISBN: 978-1-7356362-8-3

eBook ISBN: 978-1-7356362-9-0

For Kale --
the only person who might be more excited
about this book than I am

Never Cried Wolf

PROLOGUE

Mona. Two years ago.

It happened in an instant. His lips crashed into mine, pressing so hard and desperate, as though any space between us would stop his breath immediately and he'd drop dead right there in front of me-- in front of everyone.

I felt my eyes widen in shock as I stared pointedly at his eyelids, which squeezed tightly shut. Why was it so... wet? Did he *just* lick his lips? Why did it feel like a lifetime before he finally pulled away, licking his lips (again, probably)?

Brianna Rae Quinn

My eyes held his, still wide in horror. Did that just happen? How? Why? And just before the words "What the hell!?" roared from my gut, he grasped my hand and whispered, "We'll finish this later," before ascending the staircase behind him, making the most jaw-dropping exit from a party I'd ever witnessed. It almost felt rehearsed.

Gross.

Time is truly fascinating. It's insane how a short kiss that perhaps lasted two or three seconds tops felt like a lifetime, but the two or three second processing time between being kissed by (who you thought was) your best guy friend and every other person you collectively knew jumping down your throat for answers you couldn't give felt impossibly short. I wasn't certain Samuel had even left the house.

"Mona!" Leta called from the couch to her left, her short, blonde curls bouncing as her head moved back and forth, looking between me and where Sam had just disappeared around the corner. The room was silent. "Honestly, what the fuck!?" she shouted, not angrily, as Leta never really seemed to get angry, but wholly confused.

Then the floodgates opened. Once Leta had started, the barrage of questions couldn't stop.

"Since when were you two dating?"

"How did this happen?"

"I thought you were into someone else?"

And most importantly, "I thought Sam was gay!"

Truthfully, so did I. I'd never push him to admit it, and I'd never judge him for it-- I just assumed he wasn't ready to come out yet, but he was into me. He had kissed me, and just walked away.

"No, no. We're not dating! I have no idea what that was!" I looked over my shoulder to the stairwell. Sam had definitely gone.

Correction: he'd run away, leaving me to field all of the questions. What exactly did he think was going to happen? I couldn't think straight, let alone deal with the snickers and teasing I which surrounded me. If he could run away, so could I. It wasn't too far to walk home, it was only about a mile. A little darker than I'd like, but it'd certainly give me the quiet I needed to process these last five minutes.

I quickly said my goodbyes, and booked it out the basement, following the same path up the stairs, through Leta's kitchen, and out the front door in the foyer that Sam had likely taken only minutes prior.

The blue light of my phone illuminated my furrowed brows as I stalked out of Leta's neighborhood, heading toward my own off the main street.

Mona

What the hell was that?

I stared intently at the screen. The three dots didn't take long to appear, though they seemed to type for a while. It was about a minute before the words finally revealed themselves.

Sam

I've been wanting to do that for a while.

Was he insane? And also, what kind of answer was that? My confusion was quickly being replaced with frustration.

Mona

We're friends, Sammy. That's all.

Sam

So you don't love me at all?

Oh, yeah. He was definitely insane. Love? I was barely fourteen, I had no idea what love felt like, and I greatly doubted he knew so much more at fifteen. This could not have been real, it must have all been some elaborate prank, but no matter how many times I glanced over my shoulders, looking for cameras, Ashton Kutcher never revealed himself.

Mona

I cannot believe you.

Sam

You really won't even try this
with me?

My peripherals slowly turned red, as
anger clouded my vision. It seeped out of my
fingertips as I typed.

Mona

You embarrassed me. Do you
have any idea how awkward that
was for me? You just kiss me
and walk away? No, I don't want
to try anything with you,
especially after that stupid stunt
you pulled.

I felt cold. I picked up my pace, never
taking my eyes off the screen as I rounded onto
my street. This message took longer to receive,
and the typing was quick.

Sam

I didn't realize being with me

would be so terrible to you. So I

guess I can go fuck myself,

right?

My eyes rolled so hard, I swear, they could've pulled a full three-sixty in the back of my head. How bold of him to play the victim.

By then, I could see the porch light ahead and I sprinted the last few driveways, up mine, and in through the front door.

"Mona?" Mom inquired from the living room, not too loudly.

"Yeah, it's me," I replied.

"You're home early," she questioned with a tone of concern.

"Just got tired. I'm gonna go to bed," I excused myself quickly without ever having to look at her. She had a talent for recognizing when something was wrong. She always said it was plastered across my face. Well, this face was about to be buried nose deep in some pillow fluff to escape the anxiety this night had brought her, and whatever problems I had at the time, well, I decided that would be future Mona's problem.

*   *   *

I heard a vibration shake my bedside table. I groaned, throwing an arm out to grab it and stop the sound, which at this hour could only be compared to the persistent and annoying chirp of a brood of cicadas.

3am, I noted, as I unlocked the screen to a message from another friend, Jae. Leta had tried to tried to reach out as well, but I'd just told her we'd talk the next day.

Jae
U up, babe?

I snorted at how much the message read like a booty call text. It would undoubtedly be if Jae were not exclusively into men-- lumberjack men, to be particular. I tapped a passive aggressive reply.

Mona

No.

Jae

Well girl, u better get up.

Sammy's havin a ruf night!

Alright, my interest had peaked.

Mona

What happened?

Jae

U know that fan blog he has for

that K-pop band I follow?

Mona

Yeah?

Jae

Peep what he just wrote.

Jae had attached a link to Sam's blog. I'd never bothered to check it out before, I wasn't a huge K-Pop fan, though Sam had mentioned it a few times. A wall of text opened before me, and

I sat up finally. Whatever this was, I certainly wouldn't be able to fall back asleep after reading the novel he had posted. The letters all jumbled together, as there were no paragraph breaks. It read like a giant run-on sentence.

A Personal Rant

It's just not fair how you can do absolutely everything for a person, and they still treat you like garbage. Tonight, I finally made a move on the girl I've been into forever now... let's call her, "Bitch." So Bitch and I have been friends for a long time. I know everything about her: her favorite movies, snacks, food, activities, her shoe size-- I can even tell when she's about to start her period (weird, I know, but *that's* how close we are). We eat lunch together every day, we talk nonstop. We text all night, she'll even text me in the middle of the night, and I'll wake myself up to talk to her. I've *more* than proved my loyalty, I think. So tonight, we were hanging out at a party, and as I was leaving, well... I kissed her! I finally got up the nerve to kiss her, and you know what she said? I was stupid, embarrassing, and awkward. She doesn't love me, and she wasn't even willing to give us a shot. And why not? I'm practically her boyfriend already, so what's the big deal? I do everything for her, and bitch doesn't even appreciate it! Life is cruel and unfair, so I guess I'll just fuck right off and never talk to her again-- we'll see how long it takes for her to come crawling back when she realizes how good I am to her. I hope none of you ever have to feel this way. No good deed goes unpunished, I guess. Stay strong, friends.

My jaw was gaping by the time I reached the end. How could he say any of this about me? How could he make me look so bad, as if our relationship was so one-sided and all I ever did was take and take and take from him? I scrolled down into the comments.

jelliebowler498

What a BITCH. Ditch her for good, she sounds like a terrible person!

5historical6twins7

You're too good for her, fuck that hoe!

cloakedcollarbone42069

This is awful! You totally don't deserve this! Sometimes people just doesn't realize how much something is really worth til it's gone! You're amazing and anyone would be lucky to have you! Don't let this one girl get you down!

xxartisticmile00

GOLD DIGGER ALERT! You deserve better

3weaselsinatrenchcoat

We all about to meet up and hunt this bitch down?
No one messes with our man!

squashbandage64

FUCK BITCH. We're all here for you!!!

They just kept going and going. I didn't even realize his blog was this popular. There were hundreds of comments calling me every name in the book, and crying out in support of Sam. I thought being cornered by his lips was the most humiliating moment of my life, but really, it was nothing compared to this.

Was I really in the wrong? Was this all my fault?

I felt a tear free itself from my eye and trail down my cheek, landing in the mess of red hair laid over my shoulder. It sank between the strands, and all I could do was watch in stunned silence as the situation washed over me.

After a long minute, I backed out of the post, backed out of my conversation with Jae, and tapped on Sam's name in my list, and I finally replied to his last message.

Mona
You know what? Yeah. Go fuck yourself.

CHAPTER ONE

Mona

Rafael smiled and waved at me, heading back the way we came down the hallway. It was so sweet that he wanted to walk me to class, even though we both knew it was a little out of his way, but he insisted, and of course, I'd take any excuse to stare into his gorgeous green eyes for as long as possible.

Those are the kind of eyes I always wanted-- green. My older sister has these really light blue, almost grey eyes. I always thought I wanted that, but there was something so warm about having dark eyes, and the deep green he had was just the perfect shade. He looked over his shoulder to me once more before rounding the corner. I could feel the butterflies rumbling in my stomach a little, but it was time to get back to reality and head into class.

It was the first day of a new semester, which, for me, meant new electives. I always struggled a bit with deciding where my passions lie. If I had actually stuck out "Intro to Art" freshman year, maybe I could be in "Advanced Painting" or "Ceramics 3" by now, but of course I had to jump around from art to theatre to journalism to film and so on. At this point, I was sure I was just committed to learning a little bit about everything than being good at one thing, which is why the second semester of junior year brought me to the door of Mr. Howard's creative writing class.

The door was swung open, and as I entered, Mr. Howard had a stack of syllabuses on a stool to grab and a seating chart projected on the white board.

The room was arranged in two semi-circles with trapezoidal desks interlaced to form an outer and inner curve, all facing a single podium at the front. This was definitely a class designed for presentations.

I scanned the board for my name which was at end of the outer curve, in the front corner of the room opposite the door. I readjusted my shoulder strap on my bag to sit a little more comfortably and headed to my seat, glancing around to see if there was anyone else familiar in the class. It didn't seem that way. This was one unfortunate side effect of taking a new class every semester-- new people, and more often than not, classes filled with freshman and sophomores because they, well, these were introductory classes after all.

I settled into my seat, resting my copy of the syllabus on the desk in front on me and looked at the open chair beside me. I wondered who would sit there, or if whoever my deskmate would be had already dropped the class.

Grabbing a pencil from the front pocket of my bag, I looked back up, that's when I noticed. A thin character, with brown hair curling up and around his ears, and a pair of thin wire framed glasses casting a glare over his eyes. Sam.

I'd done a particularly good job of avoiding him since the kiss two years ago in Leta's basement. I told him, in no uncertain terms, that he absolutely had to delete the post. He said he did, and I couldn't see it anymore, and that was about it for us. I started taking my lunch with another group of friends, we stopped texting all the time and by the time summer came around, we were as good as strangers. That's not to say it wasn't an adjustment. It definitely was. It's hard to lose a friend that way, but it was for the best and I'd been doing well since then. I wondered if he could say the same.

Never Cried Wolf

It wasn't until he excused himself and turned sideways to slide behind my chair that I realized he was going to be my deskmate. I glanced back up at the board, and glimpsed my name, Desdemona M., right next to Tafelski S.

There was a brief moment of silence in the shuffle as Sam took his seat beside me. He set his syllabus down as well, and uttered, "Hi, Mona," just as the bell rang.

Mr. Howard was an insanely tall man, of course, most people were tall compared to me at only five feet tall (maybe add an inch on a good day.) His hair always seemed to skim the top of the projector mounted only a few inches above the whiteboard. He gave the typical "cool teacher on the first day of school" speech about how he hates reading the syllabus and how boring this day is, but he has to do it. I followed along, flipping through the pages of our syllabus packet, and by the time we'd reached the end, there were about fifteen minutes left in class.

"Now," Mr. Howard began, shuffling through some papers at the podium, "We're going to do an ice breaker." The class groaned in response, and Mr. Howard chuckled as he dropped a counted stack of papers at the end of the inner circle, and then dropped another counted stack at me while continuing his direction, "You're going to pair up in twos with the people next to you, and using this questionnaire to get to know each other, you're going to write an acrostic poem about your partner. Acrostics, if you don't know, are something you've probably done in the past."

He clicked his clicker, and the slide adjusted to an example of two acrostic poems, both spelling out his name. "The one on the left,", he began, is probably something you've seen or done in the past. One-word descriptors for each letter."

Honest

Opportunist

Wacky

Artistic

Robust

Dorky

"On the right, however," he continued, "We can see something a bit more complete. You can stretch the lines as long as you need to tell the class what you've learned about your partner."

Happiest

Objectively

When students

Arrive to class

Ready to

Dive into learning.

Mr. Howard seemed proud of his little joke, and I, along with a handful of others, gave him a half-pity, half-serious chuckle. I could tell

I was going to like him, but I just wasn't sure about the Sam of it all.

"Let's get started! You have about twelve minutes, feel free to write in whichever style you feel most confident in, and let me know if you have any questions!" Mr. Howard began a slow stroll around the room, which I watched briefly before turning my head to Sam who had already begun filling in the answers on the questionnaire.

I noticed he seemed to be avoiding eye contact with me. I knew I was doing the same, but also… man this was awkward. Our classmates in the inner circle in front of us were talking and laughing and working diligently. My only other option seemed to be to talk to the wall on the other side of me. That class was going to be really uncomfortable if one of us didn't start talking pretty soon.

I guessed I just had to bite the bullet. It had been years, after all. People change, and really, it had been a while since I'd thought about it. Maybe he was over it too, and we could just move on? Wouldn't that be a lot more gratifying than asking for a change in seat or switching out of the class entirely? Wouldn't that be the mature thing to do?

"You know," I started hesitantly. He stopped writing to focus on my words while I milked the long pause between us. "It's been almost two years."

Another pause stretched out my phrases. It felt almost too long as I waited for him to finally look at me.

"I know I've changed a lot, and…" another, smaller pause, "I'm ready to move on from whatever happened in the past."

Sam's eyes finally met mine. I held his gaze for a long moment, it was like he was analyzing me, perhaps checking that I was sincere?

"I don't see any benefit in holding a grudge, Sam," I said, earnestly. I felt myself holding my breath, waiting for his reply. It came so quickly, I almost missed it. He averted his eyes quickly and gave a single nod.

"Yeah," he said with a small smile, "Let's move on."

I felt a sigh of relief in my gut as the threat of confrontation ebbed away. The olive branch was accepted. Was now a good time to joke around? The clock on the wall read that there were about seven minutes left in class.

"Well, I think we already know a fair bit about each other, so I'm thinking something like this?" I scribbled his name out on the back of the questionnaire.

SupeR
amazing
mind

"I thought about going with "Smart" for the S, but this killed three letters with one stone," I offered a weak chuckle as I attempted to ease a bit more tension.

Sam smiled a little bigger, looking a bit more genuine, and began filling in my name. I watched as he carefully picked his words until the page finally read:

Marvelously
Open.
Newly
Appreciated.

I couldn't help but smile as well.

"Alright class, we have only two minutes left to wrap up. Don't lose these, we'll present them tomorrow to get to know the rest of our classmates."

I felt my cheeks flush as I looked down at the lazy writing in front of me. I made a noise of distaste and confessed, "I'm going to have to rewrite this. Yours is way better." I breathed a self-deprecating laugh.

"Don't worry about it," he answered, "It's the first day, no one's can be that good."

I nodded, "Still, I think I can beef up the vocabulary a little."

Sam shrugged, and the bell rang as I began erasing the three words.

"You know," he started, almost mimicking the way I'd spoke only a few minutes earlier, "If we're going to be friends again, or," he scrambled to think of another way to phrase it, "at least, "cool" again, or whatever…" he trailed off, not certain how to finish.

"You want to hang out sometime?" It was partly a guess, and partly an offer.

"Yes, we should hang out sometime. Or at least get lunch and catch up?"

"I actually just got moved into sixth period lunch if you want to eat together?" I offered.

"Me too! So, lunch tomorrow then? I eat in cafeteria two," He explained as they packed their bags and headed out the open doorway.

"I've been eating in cafe one, but I'll find you in two tomorrow," I said. "Where are you off to now?"

"Math," he explained.

"Ah, gym." I answered the question he didn't ask.

"Then I guess this is where we separate," he noted as we stood outside the door.

"I guess so," I nodded, "But we'll come back together tomorrow." I said with a pleasant tone. Maybe people do change, and things could be better. It felt so good to reconnect with an old friend, and truly start fresh.

CHAPTER TWO

Sam

I don't see any benefit in holding a grudge. It's almost childish how nasally her words repeated in the back of my head. If only she had any idea what she did to me. I watched her long red hair sway back and forth as she headed along the opposite hallway. It swished as it rounded the corner. A devil, she was.

How selfish and two-faced do you have to be? To only be my friend when it's convenient? To throw me out like garbage years ago and waltz right back into my life like nothing ever happened?

I scowled under my breath as I finally turned to head in the direction of my math class, right up the stairs and to the right, but I couldn't stare and loathe all day.

No benefit in holding a grudge? I still couldn't believe it. Talking down to me, and telling me how to feel, like she was such a victim! A victim of what? My time and attention? God forbid!

I couldn't stand her. I hadn't been able to stand her for years. She'd pass me in the hallways, avoiding eye-contact, pretending like she never saw me, and now that it's convenient, we're friends again? She wants to hang out? Get lunch? *Of course, why not!? Why not set myself up to get hurt again? Sounds like fun!*

The snarky giggles played back in my head, echoing everything I wish I had said.

I visualized every other variation I could have written other than that placating crap I gave her.

Misguided

No.

~~Misguided~~ Monstrous

No, no. I had something better.

~~Misguided~~ ~~Monstrous~~ Manipulative

Yes.

Manipulative and
Obstinate,
Naive
Ass

I wandered into class and took my seat in the third row, second seat from the windows. My head couldn't stop pounding with frustration and anger. It was like a migraine that pressed on my head from the outside in instead of the inside out. It kept hitting me, over and over.

Of course it would be nice to be friends again, but how could I ever trust a person who hurt me so badly? Who treats me as expendable?

Dante had come into the classroom and was making his way to the seat next to mine. We weren't close necessarily, but we'd saved each other's asses on some homework questions a few times, so I needed to cool down quickly and not look so shaken up.

I played nice. I have my opportunity. They always say to keep your friends close and enemies closer, right? Maybe this isn't a bad thing.

Maybe this anger will go away, and we *can* move on.

Maybe.

Dante sat down carefully so not to wrinkle his clothes, probably a habit he picked up from JROTC. He always tried to keep his uniform neat and tidy.

"Hey man, sorry I'm late, but did you figure out number eight over the weekend?"

I nodded and pulled my bag up to the desk to start fishing around the compact block of crumbled papers in my bag to find the homework. "Yeah. I did them all, let me just get it out."

Dante went on, "I got held up with my dude trying to talk me into giving his new girl a ride home after school." I never realized eye rolls could be audible, but I could hear it plain as day in his tone.

"Yeah? What's the problem? You don't like her?" I asked absently, still sifting through haphazard stacks in my bag. I found last Thursday's homework, so Friday's had to be nearby.

"Nah, I don't really know her is all, but my guy Rafael is super into her. He doesn't talk about much else right now," Dante confided, pulling his own homework page out of a neatly organized red folder. He was a firm believer in the "red is the color of math" theory. I always said math was blue-- this was a major point of disagreement between us.

"Who is it?" I continued to ask questions, hoping to stall the conversation long enough to come across the right worksheet.

"Mona Murphy?" Dante answered, questioning if I knew her, obviously. Mona was a year younger than us, only a junior this year, and with as big as the school was, I really wasn't imagining it would be someone I knew, let alone the girl I was trying to desperately to get out of my head. What were the odds?

"You good, bro?" Dante asked again, noticing, as I had, that I'd suddenly stopped searching and just stood staring into my bag blankly, dwelling on the thoughts of Mona.

I began flipping through pages again. "No, yeah," I said cooly. "I know her."

"And?" Dante pressed, a wrinkle forming in his dark forehead skin.

"What?" I countered, finally catching a glimpse of the page with Friday's date on it, crinkled into a little according at the bottom of my bag, smashed in between a government textbook and a pencil pouch exclusively housing broken or unusable pencils.

"What do you think of her?" He asked, impatiently.

I shoved my arm down into my bag, feeling a whole lot like Mary Poppins about to pull an entire lamp out of her duffel, and again, stalling.

What exactly was I supposed to say?

I didn't have a whole lot of nice things to say about Mona right now.

My instinct, of course, was to call her out for being the wild bitch she was in front of Dante, my math teacher, God, and everyone.

Was that what I wanted?

What if she found out I was talking badly about her? That was what caused her to stop talking to me in the first place wasn't it? That stupid post I made?

No. She'd been looking for a way out of our friendship for a long time. She just needed a reason to reject me-- it was just a convenience.

But then why would she want to be friends again now? This was all very confusing to me.

I pulled the paper out of my backpack carefully, so not to rip it at the creased edges. I began smoothing it against the end of my desk so it would become legible again.

Dante's dark eyes were pointed directly at my face, evidently trying to read my thoughts. I reached over as the bell rang and rested the worksheet (which at this point could have easily passed for a used tissue) on his desk and pointed out the answer to number eight.

He nodded and scratched the answer down with a freshly sharpened pencil, not totally taking his attention off me.

Our teacher was in the hallway, yelling at the dawdling delinquent kids to get to class already. "Come on, you got one period left!" His yell that sounded half-threatened and half-encouraging.

"What do you know, Sam?" Dante finally asked again.

I still hadn't decided how to respond. I took a deep breath, and in that space, all I could think was, *be honest, you'd want him to be honest with you.*

"She's kind of a…" I racked my brain for any word that wasn't "bitch". "Grandstander," I decided. "If you know what I mean?"

Dante rose an eyebrow. "I don't," he replied.

"Well, she and I actually have a history… of sorts."

The confused expression on Dante's face worsened. *If he says "I thought you were gay," I'll clock him. JROTC or not, I could probably land one good punch in before going down.* He didn't.

"She wasn't my girlfriend or anything," I clarified. Dante's brow lowered slightly. "But we were really close a couple years ago. We'd hang out all the time and get lunch, go to the movies, parties, all that. She'd text me all the time basically, all over me, 24/7."

Dante nodded slowly, taking it all in.

"She likes attention, you know? And I was dumb enough to give it to her. She led me on for almost a whole year. I bought her food, and presents around the holidays, and I was always there for her, but right when things got serious, she flaked. I got friend-zoned bad, and she was all about the next guy giving her attention within a day." Justin. I remembered him clearly. I seemed to conveniently leave out the part about how Mona hadn't shut up about Justin for months, but Dante didn't need all the detail. And besides, it was technically true, she didn't take any time to get over losing me in her life before she was holding hands with him in the hallway, flaunting her new relationship in front of me. She knew exactly what she was doing.

"Damn," Dante grumbled, marking down the last of the problem so he might "show his work" properly. "You don't think she might be doing that to my boy, Raf, do you?" He was clearly distracted with my words.

"Look, I don't know. It's been two years since I really talked to her, but I actually did just get into Creative Writing with her and she straight up asked me to get lunch with her tomorrow. I'm not saying that means anything, but she didn't say anything to me about talking to Rafael or anyone else."

Dante shook his head in shame, or maybe pity for his friend. I could have done the same. I'd only met Rafael a few times, but he didn't deserve what happened to me-- no one did, and if I could stop that from happening again, I'd think that'd be considered a public service.

"Well," Dante started, finally holding the worksheet back out to me, "I mean, they aren't official or anything--"

"Mr. Williams," our teacher, Mr. Saunders, called from his desk, "If you're going to copy answers, you ought to do a better job of hiding it. You'll be a receiving a zero for this assignment." He began to make a note on a page at his desk.

"Wait, Mr. Saunders! Dante wasn't copying, he was just checking his work. Really, he just wanted some clarity on number eight is all!"

Our teacher glanced between both of us, meeting our eyes with his. He held our gazes for long uncomfortable moments before he finally said, "Alright then, I'll let it go this time. In the future though, Mr. Williams, come to me for questions or wait until we review instead of making a show out of returning Mr. Tafelski's work in front of me."

Dante scowled a little at his tone. I glanced at him uncomfortably as he pulled his red, spiral notebook out to take his notes with an air of defiance in his reasonable and polite set of actions as he prepared for class.

I did the same, sliding an (only partially creased) piece of filler paper out of the package in my bag to prepare.

Honestly, it's a good thing I spoke up. I didn't want him to get a zero, that wouldn't have been fair. Really.

I am a good person.

CHAPTER THREE

Mona

"Shit, Raf!" I shouted, glaring at him through the white hatched squares making up the badminton net, "This isn't volleyball, I don't think you can spike a birdie!"

I snatched the little plastic hatted half-ball from the gym floor and snarled as he laughed. "Badminton would be much more fun if you treated it like volleyball! You made me take this class, so now you play by my rules!"

My eyes rolled, playfully. Racquet and Net sports just seemed like the least frustrating gym class, and hopefully wouldn't involve too much sweating either, but Rafael was so much taller than me, and his wingspan so much wider, I suddenly wasn't certain, the image of me, doomed to run back and forth on the courts constantly to keep up with him for the entire semester, felt like my own personal hell. I was never a runner. I run from nothing, and I run to nothing.

Raf was still laughing as a whistle came from behind him. We both looked to our gym teacher, who easily had the most immaculate mustache I'd ever seen on a man, too thick to give pornstar, but not enough beard to pull off lumberjack. "Alright, kids, return your supplies where you got 'em. We'll continue rotations tomorrow. If you finished at Ping Pong you'll go to Pickleball, Pickleball to Tennis and so on. Once everyone's had a chance to feel out the racquets and balls and all that," Raf and I exchanged an immature look and stifled a laugh, "then we'll get started on rules and tournaments for the rest of the semester. Now go get changed!"

"Here," Raf began, grabbing my racquet and the birdie, "I'll return these, you go get changed. I'll meet you outside the locker rooms."

He was such a gentleman. I almost didn't know how to handle myself. We'd met in our mandatory economics class last semester and we just hit it off so well that when the semester ended, we chose our next elective together so that we could continue to see each other. We figured if we both had the same opening in our schedule, we had a better shot of ending up in the same class, and it totally worked out. I still had to get in one more gym credit to graduate. Rafael was just athletic, so this seemed like a fair pick.

I couldn't help but wonder how many of these games had us playing doubles, or if I'd be staring at him across the net the whole time.

It seemed strange to me that he hadn't formally asked me out yet. There is only so much shameless flirting one can do before I'd start to think he wasn't interested, but I couldn't help waiting. I liked to imagine he was planning something big, like asking me to prom, but it was months away at this point, and why wait? I supposed we were different in that way.

I kicked off my sweat-shorts and pulled my black tee over my head. My long red hairs seemed woven into it at this point, but I attempted to free them anyway. I pulled a pair of jeans back on and enjoyed a little time cooling off in the air-conditioned locker room before replacing my sweater.

First lesson of gym class in winter, wear layers. Nothing seemed more painful to me in that moment that covering my sweaty pits with the wool knit I had worn comfortably the rest of the day. If only I'd brought a tank top or an extra t-shirt– just until I cooled down more properly.

I pulled the scrunchie out of my hair and let it fall onto my back before immediately tipping my hair forward and pulling it back into a bun. It was definitely too hot.

I stuffed my gym clothes into my bag and rushed out to meet Rafael, who wasn't quite as sweaty, but he was so handsome he seemed to glisten under the harsh fluorescent lighting. *He* was definitely too hot.

"What's your plan for after school today?" he asked politely, falling in step with me as we headed out to the doors at the front of the gym, waiting for that final bell to formally ring.

"Leta and I were going to meet at her place and hang out. How about you?" I asked, secretly hoping he'd ask to join so I could stare into his hazel-green eyes just a little more today. The netting separating us during class hadn't really treated me well on that front.

"Dante and I are working at the sub shop tonight," he answered.

Booooo, I groaned internally. "Oh, cool," I commented casually.

I wished I would just say things aloud sometimes and admit what I wanted. I would never lie if asked a direct question, but there were still some things I kept to myself. I often wondered if lying by omission really counted as lying, or if it just made these easier, and a little less awkward. Jae was probably the only person who could hear my unfiltered thoughts, if not just read her mind. Now that he's off at State College, I often found myself confused at how often people misunderstood me. It was almost like Jae and I had our own little language with each other, and now I was relearning English.

The bell chirped, interrupting my spiral of introspection, and echoed against the walls of the gym, alerting us our day had now ended.

The halls filled with students anxious to get home as quickly as possible, but Raf and I stayed, knowing our people were coming to find us.

Never Cried Wolf

My back rested against the cement wall. I delighted in the feeling of the cool stones through the wider holes in the knit of my sweater. Raf had off-handedly mentioned this was his favorite color once last semester, and how great it made my ginger locks look. I wondered if he knew the fact that I'd worn this sweater on the first day of our new semester after Winter break was no coincidence. Jae would have known. I couldn't wait to call him after Leta's tonight and update him on the strange turn of events with Sam.

Raf faced me, leaning his body beside mine on the wall. I felt a little knot in my stomach from his being so close. He looked me up and down once, the knot flipped inside my gut. Did he notice the sweater?

"I can't believe you're wearing a sweater fresh out of gym class," he chuckled. I grinned at his playful teasing and gave him a little shove.

Well, at least he noticed.

We looked at each other for a long minute before I heard a voice call out through the doorway, "Raf, let's go." It was Dante, Rafael's closest friend, no nonsense, super practical.

"Hey, Dante!" I called back before Raf had a chance to respond.

I noticed Dante's eyes looked me up and down once, analyzing, just as Raf's had – only, there was something different. His dark eyes betrayed something a bit more... shrewd, and perhaps a bit of disgust? It was as if he was recognizing something he hadn't noticed before. I glanced down at my sweater again, checking for a stain or the classic toilet paper on my shoe trope, but nothing seemed out of the ordinary to me.

"Coming," Raf replied, pushing himself off the wall with his shoulder and exiting through the double doors. I followed, suddenly a bit more self-conscious than I was used to feeling.

"Oh," I noticed another familiar face standing beside Dante in the hallway as he and Rafael patted each other's backs in greeting, "Hey, Sam."

He stood with a blue folder in hand, comically sporting unkempt papers hanging out of every side like an overstuffed drawer in a cartoon. His bag was unzipped in one hand as if he had been attempting to find some crevice in which to stuff the folder.

I presumed he'd been trying a while.

"Hey, Mona!" He replied, smiling rather honestly as he tried once again to insert the thick, bent folder into his bag. "I was just walking and talking with Dante today. Funny running into you twice, eh?"

I nodded, "I'm sure we'll be running into each other a lot more now," I breathed in a laugh. I wondered why he felt the need to explain why he was there. It seemed weird, but then again, this whole reconnection between us felt a little weird. I imagined I'd need a little more time before talking with him felt natural again,

"Is Leta picking you up?" Rafael asked, ready to head out the closest side door with Dante.

I opened my mouth to correct him, but I got cut off by Sam. He must have noticed my hesitation.

"If she's not coming, I can take you home," he announced, rather gallantly. It was a nice offer, but not necessary.

"No, actually. Oscar's taking me home," I answered Rafael first, before turning to Sam. "You remember Oscar, right?"

Sam nodded slowly as he pulled the memories from the back of his mind, "I think so. He and Leta dated, right?"

They had, and they'd ended on a bit of a weird note, not bad necessarily, but certainly… dissonant? Leta, Oscar, and I had always hung around each other because we lived so close by. It was easy to walk to each other's houses before we could drive, and it wasn't all too long before Oscar and Leta were hanging out without me, then they were dating, and then… they just weren't? Leta had felt the distance between her and Oscar forming before they broke up, so she took it pretty well, and they were all still on speaking terms and carpooled from time to time. Something was just undoubtedly different, though I could never put a finger on it.

"Yeah," I responded quickly, as the context circled around in my brain, like a backstory tornado. They never made it to the foreground of her mind when she thought of him anymore, but it certainly always floated over his name, like a ghost whose presence you only feel, but never truly see. "He normally drives me home since we live so close."

My tone felt dismissive, as if I needed to defend myself for still hanging around with Oscar after he and Leta split. I just didn't need scrutiny over the situation from people who didn't really know the details, especially not Sam.

She felt Dante's eyes on her, digging into her skin like a drill. Why did he look so suspicious of me all of a sudden? I know I'm the new girl or whatever, but I thought we were getting along fine, and the sudden appearance of the idea that maybe I wasn't in Dante's good graces didn't sit well with me. What had I done? What was different?

Incidentally, it was Oscar's words that cut through the tension. "Hey, Mona! You ready?" he called, pushing some positive energy in my direction. It felt like a wave of relief soaking me from head to toe.

Thank God for him.

CHAPTER FOUR

Sam

I chose to wait out the regular flood of my classmates rushing about the halls to be the first in their cars and headed home. I wanted to take a walk and relax a little.

It had been quite the day.

Casually, I waved my goodbye to Mona as she and Oscar went out the door and off home. I recognized how weird she was being about riding home with him.

Uncertainty danced around her words as she explained her current plan to get home. I totally understood needed rides home. If I remembered, her sister, Ophelia, didn't get her first car until she was off to college. It made sense that Mrs. Murphy was making her wait too. But Oscar? And her tone?

Something was off about it, but I wasn't going to ask questions.

She and I speaking again was new, surely she just felt awkward accepting my ride.

The slams and bangs of metal doors closing and locking in all directions as people moved about with their lives, absent to the walk I was preparing to take down memory lane.

They say sensations remind you of the past the most-- tastes, smells, sounds, etcetera. I knew that was true. Some days at lunch when served certain food it would remind me of the days Mona and I would coordinate when to buy lunch. Bosco day was everyone's favorite. We got cheese-filled soft breadsticks that oozed and steamed. The cheese was perfectly salted in a nice squishy bread, and we had a little cup of marinara to dip, like a deconstructed cheese pizza, or a giant mozzarella stick made out of sweet bread instead of a crunchy coating. Baked, and not fried, of course.

I stepped into the larger cafeteria and scanned the room. This room was filled with circular tables with no more than eight chairs at each-- the lunch aids made certain of that. I found out old table in the far back corner, closest to the courtyard that was barred from student entry. Legend had it that some time in the early 2000s some student tripped a teacher walking through on lunch duty and immediately booked it outside and shoved a huge tree branch between the door handles so the teacher couldn't get to him. It caused such a huge raucous, no one was ever allowed to use it again.

This time of year, I imagined eating outside would be pointless given the cold, but in the summer months, Mona and I would sit alone at our table and stare outside, hoping one day the principal would decide we wanted to use it again. She never did.

My memory took over as a younger version of Mona, wearing skinny jeans and graphic tees with dorky phrases across the front, dropped one of her two Bosco sticks on the foul cafeteria floor.

I watched from the sidelines.

She groaned dramatically, "Nooooo." I could almost hear her whine through time. "Not on Bosco day." She plopped herself down at the table next to me.

At that time, I still wore wire-frame glasses. I'm so glad I upgraded to thicker rims. Something about the wireframes just made me look so childish. Or perhaps that was simply what fifteen-year-old nerds looked like.

My curly hair sat on top of my head like a nest, completely unstyled.

I wouldn't had considered myself a fashion icon by any means, but I liked to think I had a better concept of dress by this point of my senior year.

Never Cried Wolf

And I wasn't the only one. At this point, Mona had the craziest straight across bangs that never quite seemed to fit her face right. My theory was that her eyebrows were so expressive, they simply kept pushing the bangs out of line. She grew them out by the end of the year. It was a good choice.

"Here, we'll split mine," My voice echoed in the memory. I tore the breadstick in half and we both gawked at the cheese as it strung out nearly my entire wing span.

Mona reached over and ripped at the center of the cheese, wrapping the elongated mass of goodness around the top of her breadstick like a mummy and taking a bite without another word. "I literally love you so much, thank you!" She beamed with her cheeks full of partially chewed bread.

I smiled back at her. "I love you too," I said. I really meant it too. And I thought she meant it. Our platonic relationship with littered with so much love and affection. Really, how would anyone imagine that situation to be platonic?

I turned on my heels and headed back out. I passed the performing arts center and moved into the back hallway, where all the foreign language classes were.

Freshman year, Mona's Spanish class was right before my French class, and my locker happened to be stationed right outside of that Spanish room. She bounded over to me after class with a packet in hand on day, I recalled.

"I got an A!" She twisted the paper back and forth at my eye level so I could, as she would say, "Read it and weep!"

"Guess you're not the only genius between us!" She stuck her tongue out playfully.

"I never said you weren't smart, Mona." I tutted in her general direction, "And gloating is not becoming."

"And gloating is not becoming," she parroted back with an admittedly good British accent. "I know you didn't, doofus. I just don't want you to start thinking you're out of my league because you're an A student and I'm not. How else will I trick you into helping me study if I don't have anything to show for it?" She teased.

Out of her league, she'd said. As if that was possible. She was awkward, but still beautiful in a very classic way. She had big, brown doe eyes, assuming they weren't narrowed at you in jest. Her nose was straight and moderately sized. Her lips were a little fatter in the middle, and she had adorable freckles all over her face, but her stand-out feature had always been her gorgeous, long, red hair. She always kept a brush in her bag so she could detangle. She never dyed it. It was always fluffed and shiny like she was fresh off a blow-out. It made me self-conscious about my tangled curls. I always knew she had the kind of hair women would kill for.

And why would she say "out of your league" if she wasn't talking about a relationship. It only made sense.

I slammed my plum purple locker closed and offered another little smile. "I'll always help you study."

"You should unpack some of your shit in your locker. Your bag is disgustingly full," she'd tell me.

"I'm fine," I'd brush the thought off.

"No, no, no," she exclaimed, shoving her way in front of me and jiggling the lock. "What's the combination? You're unloading some of that garbage."

I opened my mouth to argue, but she turned around and held a finger to my face. "And yes, it's garbage," she said.

The rustling of the plastic combination lock always stuck with me too.

Unfortunately, so did all of the papers from that year. I think I got too stubborn past a point to take anything out. My active resistance to Mona came back to bite me that year in the form of an old yogurt tube that not only expired, but also exploded all over my bag.

Never Cried Wolf

I can still hear her telling me "I told you so," in the back of my brain too.

That locker, number 1084, always held some great memories.

Back down the hallway in the direction of the gym, I spotted where I had just left Mona. Present-day Mona. In her deep blue sweater.

In that same direction was the final stop on my walk down memory lane (slash stalling until the parking lot traffic cleared out). It was the Psychology classroom.

It existed in a little nook past the art rooms and before the second cafeteria. The classrooms back there were so small, they only used them for certain, less-popular electives.

Our teacher had told us it was unusual for the class to be so small. We only had about eleven of us in the little room, twelve including the teacher, Mr. Leonard.

He hated that room so much. The AC scarcely worked, and the heat was no better. A semester long class that started in September and went through January saw all of the worst extremes of weather from hot to cold. It was a running joke how much that classroom bugged him, and he tried to incorporate it into his lessons as much as possible.

"Claustrophobia," he'd say. "For example, the way I feel butted up next to all of you in this classroom." We'd all give him pity laughs, but that wasn't the most notable part of that class.

For me, it was day one, when Mona first walked in. A bright-eyed freshman, with that stunning red hair who couldn't help but be noticed.

My eyes flitted to her upon her entrance almost immediately. There were a few open seats, but the best part of that day was that she picked me.

She sauntered over to the empty desk on my left and asked, "Is this seat taken?"

It wasn't, and I told her so.

"Awesome! Then I have dibs!" She plopped her bag down and smoothly gliding into the seat. It was one of those combination seat and desk situations, which I don't think she immediately realized as she tried to scoot her chair in.

I snorted a little, quietly in an attempt to be polite, but she heard me.

"Ah, they're attached. Of course." I saw a little flush come over her cheeks as she looked at me.

Freshman always got embarrassed a little too easily, I thought. But maybe there was more to that. It started wondering more and more if the blush was not just embarrassment but embarrassing herself in front of me. She wanted to sit next to me. She called dibs on being next to me!

No one had ever done that before-- wanted to be near me or cared what I thought.

"I'm Mona, by the way," she stuck a hand out to shake. I noticed her nailed filed into an elongated oval shape, covered in a holographic glitter polish. Bold, to be sure. And how cute that she wanted to shake hands.

I'd soon learn that was just the way her family was. You always shook hands when you meet someone new, and you always shook well. Firm and with direct eye contact. Maybe that was what made her seem so intimidating out the gate, regardless of how fascinated I was by her.

"Well, technically I'm Desdemona, but I prefer not to be associated with the tragically murdered Shakespeare Desdemona, so would rather be associated with the famous art piece, you know? Mona Lisa." She smiled, satisfied with her little ramblings.

She decided her own identity. I loved her confidence.

"Sam," I said. "Just Sam. No tragedy." She smiled. I think something in our banter connected with her too. I could tell she felt it.

"Well, Sam-No-Tragedy," she started. "Are you a first year?"

"A freshman? No. I'm a sophomore." I recognized she didn't say freshman. Another influence of Professor Murphy. She always said the term "freshman" had a negative connotation. I wasn't buying that at the time, but the closer I got the college, I got it a little more.

"Ooh, wonderful. Then surely, you'll be able to point me to the cafeteria after this? I've got lunch next but I have no idea which cafeteria I should eat in," she said, pulling her schedule out of her bag to read through it again.

"Yeah, I can take you there. I actually have lunch next too. I usually eat in Cafeteria one. It's bigger, so it always seems a bit louder, but the tables are a little more spaced out, which I like." She snagged her schedule back from me as I held it out to her.

"You wouldn't happen to have any room at one of those spread-out tables for an extra, would you?" She wondered aloud with a sheepish tone.

I smiled. She wanted to keep hanging out with me.

She liked me, and I was just over the moon about it.

"Of course," I agreed with a wide smile as the bell rang, signaling the beginning of our first day as friends.

And the rest, as they say, is history.

CHAPTER FIVE

Mona

Oscar's little tan Honda Civic was always parked in the same row. It always sat in the first row, as far from the front door as possible, or in the second, in case he happened to be running behind and the first row had filled up. He was one of those people that believed being in the first row meant you had one of the best spots in the lot, even if it was technically a longer walk than parking a few rows down and still visible from the front door. It was just his way, and there was no use arguing with him about it when they came to school in the mornings. At least, not for me. Leta still liked to complain.

Leta had a Spirit Club meeting after school once a week, and the other four days were band practices, which often meant Oscar and I rode home as a duo.

"First day of a new semester!" I hooted as we pulled the driver and passenger side doors open to plop into our respective seats. "How did it go?"

"Nothing crazy," Oscar replied, absent-mindedly inserting his key fob into the ignition, and starting up his car. It rattled a little, as always, but calmed a bit after coming to life.

I nodded once with an awkward grimace which reminded me a bit too much of the way my mother sighed whenever she asked what I learned at school, and I replied with a simple, "Nothing." Oscar was so bad at talking sometimes, and I just couldn't wait to sit down with Leta later. I even considered texting Jae immediately, but he had later classes now. He was probably busy, I imagined, but that's what texts are for, right? I just had to find my phone.

"Seatbelt," Oscar reminded me as he backed out of his space. I pulled the belt so fast it stalled, and I had to loosen it a bit to finally pull it across my body. Sometimes, I supposed I moved a bit too quickly, but I couldn't help but feel mildly offended every time this happened. It felt like being compared to a car wreck, too forceful.

After hearing the click, I reached my hand down to my coat pocket to grab my cell. It seemed I was sitting right on it. I twisted a bit and tried to raise my ass up off the seat just enough to shove my hand in there, but the seatbelt, as always, loved to make my life difficult. How could something so good also be so terribly frustrating?

The next best option, of course, was to shed the jacket and pull it out from under myself. I started with my free shoulder, shaking my arm loose in an admittedly unflattering fashion.

Oscar snorted to the left of me, and I quickly jerked my head to the side to toss him an accusatory look, "Mind your business," I teased, sticking my tongue out before I continued to gyrate my shoulder back and forth.

He lifted an arm over his head in surrender (keeping one on the wheel, of course), and spoke, "Hey, I won't ever be the one to tell you to stop taking your clothes off,"

I noticed a not-so-subtle sideways grin as he kept his eyes on the road. *What a weird thing to say*, I thought as I shook my arm free, finally, and yanked the other arm out and pulled the coat up onto my lap. I didn't laugh. It was a joke, I knew, but still a weird one. Well, more creepy than weird.

I rescued my phone from the elusive pocket and sent my text.

Mona

Heading home with Oscar now.

Wild first day.

"Doing anything tonight?" I asked aloud, setting my phone back into my lap and readily changing the subject with a cheerful tone.

He looked over at me quickly and did one of those assessing glances. *Why does everyone keep doing that? Was that a weird thing to ask?*

"I actually have to work from 4 to 9. I was going to take a nap beforehand, but I can make a little time if you want?"

For what? I wondered. He had been so subtly weird lately. It was moment like this that allowed the ghost of his strange and sudden end with Leta manifest a little more clearly.

"Well, I'm hanging out with Leta tonight. I have to work the next three days, so we were gonna take today to relax a little. Besides, I have to catch her up on the situation with Raf," I said. That always shut him up, talking about Raf.

I never got why guys were always so weird talking with girls about their love interests. It was like experiencing a rom com in real time whenever my friends were trying to start up a new romance, plus it's always fun to share in their excitement. Outside of Jae (who was often a little too caught up in his own boy drama) the last guy who ever really bothered to listen to me about this kind of stuff was Sam.

That was also before the blog posts.

Buzz. Speak of the devil.

Jae

Take the bus home, babe. u have way 2 many proximity friends.

I took a moment to read that again.

Mona

Proximity friends?

I don't know why I ever thought Jae wouldn't reply to a text, even if he was in class. His fingers were like lightning with how quickly his replies always came, though it was never a total replacement for experiencing his witty retorts in person.

> Jae
> Hes only ur friend because hes around all the time. Worse cuz ur neighbors!!
> Never liked him. Ditch while u can
> Itll make sense when u go 2 college

I felt a little sigh of annoyance escape my nostrils. I knew Jae was excited to get out of this town and have a fresh start at university, but man did I hate how much he bragged about finally being away from here, and away from me.

Was I a proximity friend?

"Do you remember Sam?" I blurted to Oscar. If he was here, and Jae wasn't (*and* so damn happy about it), maybe he'd take an interest.

"Tafelski? Yeah."

"We kind of had a falling out a couple years ago," I started, but never really finished.

"Okay…" Oscar replied, waiting for my continuation.

What should I say? I wondered. *He totally betrayed my trust and I want to be over it to avoid the conflict of it all?* I wasn't mad anymore, at least, I didn't think so.

Maybe my urge to keep the peace was a little stronger than the grudge. Sam and I had passed each other in the halls so many times these last few years and just ignored each other. Was it really a grudge or maybe just a really long fight that we both held out on, being too stubborn to apologize?

Maybe it was a little harsh to cut him off totally. We were such good friends back then, but I guess that's made the betrayal sting so much in the first place.

"What about him?" Oscar interrupted my train of thought.

Right. Oscar.

"So, I guess we reconnected today? And I just don't really know if I'm totally over everything that happened." That was a good way to put it. Do I trust him? *Can* I trust him? I still wasn't sure I really forgave him even.

Oscar shrugged, "I've never had any problems with the guy. He seems nice enough, and we all fuck up now and then, right?"

I didn't reply immediately. I just listened.

"Sides," he started again, "he's graduating soon. Won't be dealin' with him much longer."

This time, I shrugged.

"That's true," I noted, hesitantly.

"And so is Rafael," Oscar added when there was just enough space between our dialogue to tinge the air with awkwardness. It was thick and palpable, and I still wasn't certain how to continue.

"But I'll still be here," he said. I appreciated him saying it, but my relationship with Oscar was so very different from my relationship with Raf, or Sam for that matter.

When Oscar and I spoke, it was so surface level. We never seemed to talk about anything real, and that wasn't an obstacle I saw us hurdling anytime soon. Even at this moment, it felt like he was speaking in generic cliches and not really listening to me. There was something that kept us from being real friends, and I wasn't sure if that wall was mine or his.

"You're right. Thank you for saying that. It means a lot," I offered. What else would I say? He meant well, and that counted for something,

Oscar smiled a smile of accomplishment as he rounded the bend into my driveway.

He slowed to an easy stop right in the center of the driveway, just out of view of my doorway. He normally dropped me off right at the walkway. Again, weird.

"I was just thinking," he said. I felt my stomach knot. No, not my stomach, more like my chest. It felt tight, like an elastic band ready to snap. He looked so casual, but everything about the situation felt wrong, but I wasn't sure exactly why.

"I always pick you up and drop you off and all that, I was just thinking maybe you could *repay* me for the favors?" The question felt slimy as it slithered into my ears and coiled around my brain.

There was a layer to that word, *repay* that I didn't fully grasp. I knew I didn't, but I ignored the air around me and kept speaking to him, like normal.

"Yeah, of course. That makes sense." I replied, unbuckling my seatbelt, and wrapping my coat over my shoulders again, not bothering to put my arms back into the sleeves after all the trouble I went through to get them off.

"Really?" He replied with a look in his eye that read only like a dog salivating over steak.

"Yeah!" I replied, yanking the door handle, and popping the door out so I could step out of the car. I noticed in my peripherals that his face fell the moment I opened the door. I breathed in the cool winter air and suddenly felt a little lighter.

I pulled my wallet out of my bag, resting between my legs on the floor and slid a ten dollar bill out of the center, and held it out to him across the center console.

"For gas," I smiled.

His brow furrowed a moment before he slipped the bill out from between my fingers and said, "Thanks," rather curtly.

I lifted myself out of the car and waved my goodbye with a prompt slam of the car door. Oscar looked at me for an extra-long second before turning to check behind him as he pulled out. I hiked the rest of the way up to the house, and around the walkway to the door.

Mom and dad weren't going to be home for another few hours, and by the time they got into the door, I would be at Leta's. I walked in, dropped my bag and coat on the kitchen table and headed down the hallway, passing my own bedroom and instead opening the door to Ophelia's.

My older sister had moved out last year after graduating college, but she still had a few drawers full of clothes she never packed– namely some extra comfy fuzzy pants perfect for a girl's night with Leta in winter. I was more than likely going to be walking, so I figured this would definitely be the move.

I began to unzip my jeans before stopping a moment to hear Oscar's words replay in my head once more.

I won't ever be the one to tell you to stop taking your clothes off.

I felt a shudder through my spine and looked over to the window, partially to ensure it was closed if I was shaking like this, and maybe also to be sure the curtains were drawn all the way. Of course they were, no one ever came in here but me.

I pulled the jeans off and replaced them with a soft green patterned pair, and headed back toward the kitchen to get to the laundry room where I was absolutely sure my good black sweatpants would be sitting in the dryer. They were a size too big, so I knew they'd fit perfectly over these pajamas. As I shuffled past the table, I heard a vibration come from under my coat. I fished my phone out from under the pile of fabric and unlocked the screen.

Another message from Jae.

Jae

Seriously tho… Run dont walk from him!!

CHAPTER SIX

Sam

Am I a bad person? It certainly didn't feel like it. Honestly, I'd never felt better. This was the ideal mixture of getting all the frustration of the last two years out, but none of the confrontation. I could be perfectly pleasant and cordial with Mona but still seethe under the surface. Well, it wasn't really seething anymore. The steam was ebbing away, I could tell. It was easy to be her friend again, even if I wanted to scoff every time she said something like…

"Oooh, I'm so glad we're talking again!"

or

"Sam, I really missed you!"

Gag. If she really meant that, she would have forgiven me literally years ago, right?

We'd had lunch together all week. We sat at the very end of one of the long tables and looked at each other across our nearly inedible chicken sandwiches from the lunch line, and I imagine we both decided we'd rather bite the bullet and speak to each other than have to eat more than one bite of the foul sandwiches at a time without some time to recover in between.

"Do you remember freshman year, when you bit into one of these sandwiches and immediately got up to complain?" I joked, possibly too soon given the fragility of our newfound speaking terms.

"It was *pink*," She stated, resolutely. "Pink chicken is *raw* chicken, and I wasn't going to eat it." This was one of the many things I'd loved about Mona. She was so gloriously stubborn but so real. You never had to guess what she was thinking, she'd tell you before you got the chance.

I chuckled softly. "And what did the lunch aid say again? That it was--" she nodded with as much passion and conviction as if it happened yesterday, continuing with me in unison.

"Supposed to be like that," we spoke together. So on the same wavelength. We were always like that. Even after all that time.

"I know! What a ridiculous thing to say!" Mona huffed, rolling her warm brown eyes around, then down to look at the sandwich again. She shook her head in disappointment as if the sandwich would somehow recognize that and become a little more palatable.

I realized I was still smiling when I said, "And remember what you did after that?" I was ready to start a full-on belly laugh at the thought.

"Yes," She responded in a tone of exasperation. "I sat down with that disgusting pink sandwich and said, 'Fine, I'm going to eat it, but she's going to be sorry when I get sick!' and I ate the whole thing." She crossed her arms, the knit of her sweater sleeves flashing glimpses of her freckles underneath-- constellations on her skin.

I nodded, smirking a little as I goaded, "But you didn't get sick."

"Whatever," she replied, her lips twisting with almost as much distaste as I had for that lunch.

I really don't know why it was so easy to talk to her still. I should have had a harder time pretending everything was fine.

Perhaps I'm a better actor than I thought.

Then again, perhaps so was Mona.

That Friday, fifth period, as band class was starting, I caught Leta in the music room. I didn't get to see her much during class as we had broken into our different sections to workshop some more difficult parts in our music (well, difficult for the trumpets at least. I had no idea what they were doing half the time, and frankly, neither did they.) I was a percussionist, and Leta played the French horn, so the only time I really had with her was at the end of class as we were cleaning and putting our instruments away.

Leta and I happened to walk into the room at the same time, so I took the opportunity to say hello.

"Hey, Leta," I said at a pretty reserved volume. That way if she ignored me, I could just pretend she never heard it. She and I never really had a big blow-up argument after everything went down with Mona, but we stopped talking all the same. It was like a mutual understanding that things had changed. The major difference was that Leta at least acknowledged me when I was there. She was good at that, making people feel seen. Realistically, she and Mona were polar opposites. Leta was friendly, and sweet, whereas Mona was abrasive and intimidating, and always liked to act shocked when people call her on it.

"Sammy!" Leta shouted, "Hi!" Her smile was ridiculously wide, but then again, that's just the kind of person she was, smiley.

She dropped her bag at her side and came to give me a quick hug.

"Mona told me you two were hanging out again, that's great! How are you!?" She beamed.

Of course Mona had already said something. Why wouldn't she?

"Good! Great even, you know? It's nice to… reconnect." I paused before choosing that word. Was it nice? It felt nice, but I didn't know if it was because I actually wanted to be her friend again or if I felt like this was a "keep your enemies closer" sort of situation. Maybe it felt nice knowing she was starting to trust me again.

Or maybe it was nice to not constantly fear the conflict between us.

"Oh, I know. It feels like I'm meeting and reconnecting with so many people this year, but they're all seniors! It's like we'll only have so many months left, but you really gotta make them count!"

I nodded, somewhat absently, "Yeah," I said.

Rarely did I think about that fact I was leaving, and very soon. I'd received a couple of acceptance letters to a few public universities in the state, but the idea of leaving this place behind scared me, it was all I knew after all.

When friends and family asked if I was excited to go away to college, I immediately said, "No! I'm terrified!"

My older brother, Henry, had stuck around town, and he got a job at a factory downtown. He still hung out with his same old friends and came over to have dinner with us at least once a week. He never "moved on" as my dad said, but I thought he was doing great. He had his own apartment with three roommates that were mostly okay, but still, mom and dad were always pressuring me to go away to college, be a business major, and have the "college experience", whatever that meant.

"But you're going to State College, right? I saw your name up on the acceptance bulletin board," Leta's words popped into my head and propelled my inner spiral like the second on a tandem bike.

I did say I was going to State just so I could get my name up on that board and appease mom (and my advisor who's been pushing me to make a decision.) I hadn't told State I planned to come yet, or anywhere for that matter. For all anyone around here knew, I would be in a State College dorm this fall, but for all I knew, I might drop the ball on a class just so I can prolong my decision and stick around another year without my parents considering me a total failure.

I must have looked like a fish with the way my mouth was hanging open, but Leta, ever the angel, just kept talking through it.

"That's not too far! You could always come back and visit us on the weekends!" She was an empath like that, she knew I didn't really want to talk about it, and she had no idea how much hearing her say that meant to me.

"And that's super nice. I mean, Mona's *all* upset thinking about Rafael going into basic training next year, because he'll be literally states away!"

And she had no idea how badly those one's stung.

It took a lot not to grumble my thanks that she might finally feel the sting of some loss in her life, and not be able to dangle how happy she was in a relationship with someone else.

Realistically, I wasn't really sure I'd even wanted a relationship with her like that in the first place, but that closeness and possessiveness I felt with her must have been love. What other way is there to explain it?

I always sort of figured I'd know what love felt like when it happened. I'd look into some girl's eyes and it would happen in a flash, and even now looking into Leta's beautiful crystal blue eyes her bright smile, her thick blonde ringlets framing her face, and a beautiful personality to match, I still didn't think I'd ever want something more than this kind of relationship with her.

"Yeah, yeah. You know, I don't really know him all too well, but I've got chemistry with him."

"You do?" Leta asked with a flirtatiously raised eyebrow.

Suddenly, I felt a shiver up my spine, and I panicked in recognition of that awful phrasing. Not only was my mouth stuttering, but I think so was my brain... was that possible?

"Uh-- um. No. N-not like that, like, I mean, like class. Science class. Third--uh... period." I managed to vomit up through a series of garbles and groans.

Leta put her hands up in surrender, "Dude, I didn't think you meant it like that! I was just going to ask if he's ever said anything about her. I've gotta snoop at least a little on behalf of my bestie!" She offered an anxious laugh, clearly trying to put a Band-Aid on top of the awkward situation.

The bell rang, which shocked another shiver up my spine. I felt jumpy. My fight or flight response had taken over and I was still taking deep breaths to regain whatever cool I had left.

"Sam, I'm sorry. Are you okay?"

I nodded quickly and repetitively, letting out a deep breath and letting all the jitters go out with it. "It's fine," I said. "Sorry."

"No, no!" She exclaimed. "I'm sorry! I see how what I did could have seemed, I don't know, presumptuous? I get it, it was my bad."

And so she was an angel again.

"It's cool. I'm good."

I don't think Mona ever realized how much I lost after that incident all those years ago. I couldn't even imagine how valuable it would have been to have Leta to lean on in some of the harder moments of my life, like when Henry first moved out, when my little sister crashed my car, or when was getting trolled relentlessly on my blog last year. Honestly, I couldn't even imagine how Leta wound up siding with a snake-like Mona when she'd proven herself to be such a bad friend to me.

Couldn't she hurt Leta in that same way?

Who was to say she hadn't yet?

"Well, I'm gonna go get myself together. Maybe I'll see you after class?" She offered, pleasantly, leaving her regretful tone behind.

"Yeah, you know, we should all hang out soon," I smiled. "Me, you, and Mona."

"Sounds like a blast!"

"Right after school? I can drive."

"Nah, I can't today. I got a jazz band thing, but maybe you and Mona can figure something out? She usually needs a ride home anyway. She'll do anything to avoid the bus but join a club!" She laughed at her own observation.

"Okay, cool. I'll keep you posted," I gave a thumbs-up that immediately felt weird. I put it away quickly, though I don't know if it was quick enough for her not to notice.

"Perfect, see ya!" And so she went with her curly bob bouncing off in the direction of her section.

Mona usually needed a ride after school. I knew that.

I also knew that Mona usually got that ride with Oscar, Leta's *ex*-boyfriend.

Interesting.

Did Leta know that?

I wasn't sure, but either way, I thought it best to keep that little piece of information filed away in my brain.

Tidbits like these always proved to be useful in one way or another.

CHAPTER

SEVEN

Mona

Mom set pancakes out at the kitchen table for me and Leta. A Saturday morning ritual. Leta has been coming over for breakfast in our pajamas on Saturday mornings for years. At this time, more than ever, they were the cornerstone of our relationship. She was so busy with all her extracurriculars, and I gave four or five evenings a week up to a part-time job at the local coffee shop. This was our one constant and favorite part of our week.

"Thanks, Mama Murphy!" Leta cried, already reaching greedily for the syrup while I scooped some butter out of the tub with a knife to slather on my two perfectly golden hotcakes.

Mom may have been an adjunct professor at the local community college, but I secretly thought breakfast food was her calling. Perhaps, in another life, she would have been one of those sassy waitresses in a cute, retro dinner, but no. She decided books were her calling and convinced dad to name her two daughters after Shakespearean women who both died tragically (which was a tragedy in and of itself.) Though I suspect the genuine truth of the matter is that she was a homebody and loved to make things cozy. I supposed making adorable pancake breakfasts with bacon smiles fit that vision. Then her afternoon reading sessions could at least smell like that little dream diner.

"Anything for you, honey! It's rough only having two of us girls around her all the time. Mr. Murphy is getting dangerously close to evening out of testosterone to estrogen ratios in this house," she chuckled at her own bad joke.

I snorted a little too. Dad liked to hole up in the living room and catch up on the news and his TV on the weekends. Family breakfast wasn't his thing, but he always made sure to appear for family dinner, that was his rule.

"I think I'll need to run out and grab some more butter for dinner tonight. I didn't realize we were so low," she added with a quick glance at my plate, glistening with a thin layer of butter atop my two pancake eyes. "I'm going to run out to get some now, and a few other things. Do you girls need anything?" Mom finished with a smile as she slipped her lanyard out of the ugly, chipped bowl I'd made in a sixth-grade art class which now housed junk like keys, extra bandages, and batteries.

"Nah, I think we're good!" I said, clicking the lid pack onto the basically empty butter tub.

"Mona, just throw it away," Mom groaned as she slipped on a coat to head out the door.

"I will!" I replied, replacing the tub in my hand with the bottle of syrup, and began swirling it over my plate.

"Call if you need anything!"

"Yup!" I responded, ushering her out with my passive responses.

Leta and I looked at each other, both waiting for the sound of the door closing before beginning to talk again.

When it finally came, Leta spoke first. "How are things with Jae?"

She knew this was a sensitive topic right now.

"Far as I know, fine. He canceled our call last night because he planned a date with a guy and he forgot about our call, which, I mean, glad he was honest, but not so glad to be forgotten. It just really feels like he's so happy to be away from me."

"It's not that he's happy to be away from you. He's happy to be away from everyone else," Leta sympathized.

"Yeah, yeah, so he says." I sighed, using the edge of my fork to cut off a chunk of syrup-soaked pancake. "It just feels like he's gotten farther and farther away since the beginning of the year. I don't know, I just wish things didn't have to change."

"Change isn't a bad thing, and college is the best time to grow and really become the person you're supposed to be! I know it sucks he's so busy, but you can't totally blame him. We'll be doing that too in a few years. Doesn't that excite you?" She was so optimistic.

"College might be the worst time of my life. I don't know. No one *knows*. I'm doing great right now. I say, if it's not broken, don't fix it. I'm perfectly content with my life as it is." I felt myself getting a bit defensive, but I knew this wouldn't bother Leta. She got me, and she definitely understood my moods.

"Okay, grumpy!" She said, trying to redirect the conversation, "Tell me about something good. Ooh, how's Raf?" Leta's smile widened at the potential gossip.

"Oh! I'm glad you asked! So, he wants to hang out tomorrow, so we're going to lunch on, like, an actual, *formal* date. So I need help picking out an outfit because I think I exhausted all my best options already this week trying to secure the date in the first place," I sheepishly admitted.

"I'm still confused. You two like each other, and you're going on dates... are you exclusive?"

"Yes, I think so, but he doesn't want a label on it," I admitted.

"Red flag," Leta said, her brows knitting.

"No, I know. I just mean he has a lot of responsibilities and all that, like taking care of his little sister, so I guess he doesn't want to give me an unreasonable expectation of being with him or being able to hang out all the time." I tried to explain.

Leta didn't reply immediately, just looked at me with something like a twinge of pity. She had a way of making you say things unfiltered so you could hear how dumb you sounded for yourself.

"Look, I know I sound stupid, but if things are okay, and I'm happy and he's not hurting me, I don't see the harm. At least for now. I can try and talk to him about it tomorrow?" I tried to save myself. Leta's approval meant a lot to me. Although she was like my younger sister, I valued her opinion greatly, and she knew that too.

"Okay, I just don't want you hurt or anything. You deserve a guy who wants to be with you."

"I know, and I appreciate that." She reached over and gave my hand a quick squeeze.

Buzzzzzzzz.

A long vibration came off of Leta's phone. She quickly wiped her hands on her pink plaid pajama pants, letting them soak up the extra bacon grease before, flipping the device face up to assess the notification.

"Whoa," she said with wide eyes, and a faint flush coming over her cheeks.

"What?" I wondered aloud, trying not to lean over to snoop, but definitely looking. I'd be the first to admit I was *very* nosy.

"Have you seen the KWHS Confessions page yet?" Leta asked, still with both hands on her phone.

"No?" I questioned, finally leaning in to check her phone with her.

"It started up a few weeks ago. The band kids are speculating someone just got super bored over winter break," She began to explain without really explaining anything.

I peeked at her screen and saw a Twitter notification.

"I don't want to gossip or whatever, but I set up an alert so I'd know anytime they posted something with 'Leta' in it! Of course, that meant I got alerted when the page called someone a 'tattletale' because it has the letters L, E, T, and A in that order!"

I rolled my eyes and opened up my own phone, tapping my way into Twitter and typing in KWHS Confessions.

I read the description first.

Kettlewood Confessions

@KWHS_Confess

Submit to the link with your honest thoughts about your classmates at Kettlewood High School!

I scrolled down past the pinned tweet with the link to the submission form, and to the latest tweet posted only a minute before.

Kettlewood Confessions

@KWHS_Confess

1 minute ago

"Leta Schneider has the fattest ass! Sit on my face please!!"

My mouth gaped open and my hand flew to cover it.

"Dude," I stifled a laugh, "What is this? Just some platform for people to bitch about each other?"

"Or make a move I guess!" She laughed back at me.

"That's so stupid! How are you even supposed to know who this is?"

"That's the thing, you don't know," Leta said. "It's all anonymous." She whispered as if telling a secret.

I felt my face sour as the reality of that hit me. I scrolled a little further down and started to read some of the confessions.

Kettlewood Confessions

@KWHS_Confess

2 hours ago

"Two more days and I bet I can make Mrs. Fleet cry in class."

Kettlewood Confessions

@KWHS_Confess

3 hours ago

"Calvin T. is weird as fuck. Such a creep!"

Kettlewood Confessions

@KWHS_Confess

6 hours ago

"Nicki keep my name out ur dirty mouth hoe"

"Is this even real? How is this allowed?" I grumbled. I felt the wrinkles deepening on my face, though I physically couldn't stop myself from continuing to scroll in case I saw my name appear.

"It's not super big yet, I think it's bigger among the upperclassman. I just know about it from some of the seniors in my section. I'm sure it would be *way* worse if the freshman got involved," Leta admitted. She was certainly correct about that, but if people kept posting this, it was only a matter of time.

"It's like a train wreck. I can't look away," I noted, shaking my head in disdain. "This might be ruining my pancakes for me."

"I suspect whoever started it posted the first few themselves. One of the tuba players, Greg, is insistent that he can figure out who it is just by finding the common person that knows or has class with the people mentioned in the first ten tweets. I'm fully expecting a murder board in the band room complete with red yarn linking people together on Monday," she laughed.

"This is going to be *so* ugly," I groaned, finally putting my phone face down. "The internet is so lawless, and people can be so mean. I cannot see this ending well."

"Speaking of which," Leta transitioned, putting her phone down as well, "How are things with Sam?"

That segue did have me thinking for a moment… *what if Sam was behind this?* I snapped out of it quickly and thought to answer Leta's question.

"Oh," I said just to fill the space as I began playing with my hair. I still had it in a loose braid draped over my shoulder. I began picking through the copper strands poking out around the elastic as I formulated a response. "I don't know. I feel weird a little still because of, you know, everything," I continued before taking another pause. Leta nodded attentively.

"But honestly, he's been really nice this week, and I guess I kind of missed his friendship. It's nice to not feel so… mad?"

"Yeah, I get that," Leta urged me to continue.

"Honestly," I started, preparing to say something I definitely felt a little guilty about, "I feel like he's kind of filling the Jae void right now. I don't know if I want to hang out with him because I actually want to move past what happened, or if I just want to replace my gay best friend so I can get back to a little normalcy, you know?”

“Well, Sam’s not gay. He’s been very adamant about that,” Leta noted.

I nodded. “Right, right. I guess that’s just kind of what it feels like,” I said before quickly adding, “To me!”

It’s when I said things like this that really made me feel like such a bad person. I did think I was maybe a little too honest and a fair bit blunt, but I could always feel such a difference in the weight on my shoulders when I was completely frank with Leta. I felt lighter-- freer.

Though it was a dangerous game, I knew. Some things were not meant to come out of my (or anyone’s) mouth, and when I was this open, I could always hear my mother shouting, “If you don’t have anything nice to say, then don’t say anything at all!” in a deep echo.

I could feel in my bones how my candor might bite me in the ass if I wasn’t careful, but still, it wouldn't help anything not to be real with Leta.

I had a reputation of being trustworthy, probably because I trusted others a little too much myself, and as I considered that thought, I realized maybe I did trust Sam, but no more or less than anyone else.

"I think I'm starting to trust him again," I decided.

"Well, good! I think this is a good thing for you!" Leta smiled her classic princess smile.

"Me too," I nodded. "He's learned his lesson, I think. I doubt he'd be stupid enough to try some shit like *that* again."

CHAPTER EIGHT

Sam

The week kind of felt like a fever dream, like I wasn't in complete control of my body. Mona and I were friends again, at least, it felt that way. We had lunch together every day, we hung out after school, and when I opened up her contact to ask if she wanted to ride home with me on Friday, I was suddenly confronted with three thoughts.

One, *Have I not deleted any text messages in two years?*

Two, *How do I have any storage space left?*

Three, *What does this say about me?*

Does the presence of storage space correlate to how many friends one has? More friends meant more events, more pictures, memories, and messages all taking up space on my phone, but that stream of consciousness surely was a coping mechanism to avoid having to look back on that message.

Mona

You know what? Yeah. Go fuck yourself.

And after a week of battling the metaphorical angel and devil on my shoulder over the sheer ethics of the situation I'd found myself in, the devil was surely winning.

I was picturing what the rest of the week would look like. I'd be fire and ice-- a big, angry flame burning on the inside, but cool as a cucumber on the outside.

Never Cried Wolf

Really, I should have been an actor, or some sort of military general because the eminent battle between the things I'd think every time Mona opened her freckle-faced piehole and the wavering filter over my own piehole would undoubtedly be intense and powerful.

I needed to find some way to get rid of this feeling, it was uncomfortable and constant, and I began to realize as I got more and more worked up how even now, I still faced the effects of Mona's betrayal. Everyone turned against me. Everyone took her side over mine.

She had friends and people to lean on, and frankly speaking, I didn't.

I spent years floating from acquaintance to acquaintance in classes and making friends through summer jobs that end with the season. There was not a single person I felt comfortable enough to vent to. Maybe Leta could have been that for me, maybe things would have been different if Mona hadn't been so damn vindictive over trying to get my feelings out.

I *could* have yelled at her. I *could* have called her and really yelled at her like I wanted to, but I didn't. I was trying to do the right thing.

Besides, I didn't think she knew how to access my blog. She was never supposed to see that stupid post.

If that experience taught me anything it was that some people online were more supportive than the people I thought were my friends.

It was so easy to get lost in my thoughts when doing menial tasks like shoveling the driveway. The snow this season came rarely, but when it did, it came hard. And of course, it came over breaks and on weekends. Not a single snow day so far, and countless hours in my time off spent shoveling so mom could just come home and go to bed without the stress. I knew the night shift at the hospital was slowly killing her.

I typed the code into the keypad on our front door and used my shoulder to shove the door which fit almost too perfectly in the door frame. It fell open abruptly allowing me inside.

The kitchen looked cluttered with a series of invoices from Dad's landscaping business in barely recognizable piles. I knew Mom would lose her mind if she came home to all this, but I also knew if I tried to clean it up, I'd lose something important. It was probably better if I just left it alone. I elected to clean up just a little by putting the jackets and shoes away neatly in the hall closet, my own included, and I shed my sweatshirt as well, throwing it down the laundry chute. The ends of the sleeves were coated in a thin layer of ice that had melted shortly after entering the house, and I didn't want to deal with the cold wet sleeve. I could always get under some blankets. I grabbed a bag of chips and a Swiss roll from the freezer and chose to eat upstairs in my room to avoid making a mess.

Hannah was in her room, blasting music so loud I could hear almost every lyric between shovels of snow outside. I climbed the stairs, feeling my ear drums pounding against my head from the inside, it was like I was exploding from the inside out.

I mimicked the pounding in my head with my palm against her door, hoping it didn't simply blend in with the natural shake of the door from the base.

Per usual, the volume lowered to a level that no longer shook the pictures in the hallway but was still incredibly audible.

I resigned to believe this was as good as it would get, and I could just pop in my headphones in my room to cancel out the rest.

My door was at the end of the hallway on the right, just next to the bathroom. It was the smallest, but the bathroom access and roof access made it all the better. Snow was frustrating on the roads and all, but the inability to shovel it off the roof so I could sit outside and stare at the sky all wrapped in my duvet and four layers of sweats was almost criminal. Of course, if I lived somewhere warmer in the South, I was certain I'd be complaining about the roof being too hot to sit on and nearly melting off my skin. I supposed the milder climate of the Midwest during the other three seasons made up for the loss of one.

So I supposed I'd sit alone with my thoughts, again, until the roof was clear.

Or browse the internet-- that's what it was for, right?

I hurled myself onto my bed, slipping the earbuds in as planned, and set my laptop on my lap.

As it powered on out of sleep mode (who turns their computers off these days, anyway?) I had several pages open with all the merch I intended to buy. I started to prioritize what I would get first and then last, but it got a little too hard to do, so I closed my laptop and promised to come back to it.

Honestly, I wasn't certain I'd be able to choose today either, so I opened another tab and navigated to my blog. I was certain I had it opened on a few of my forty-plus tabs already, but I couldn't really tell what they were anymore. That was a problem for later as well.

Something had been on my mind since I'd seen that text from Mona again. Was the post really that bad? I clicked through to my account, then settings, then archived posts.

Among closed giveaways and concert announcements with outdated information, I found my personal rant, nestled somewhere a few scrolls down. I began to skim the words.

> Tonight, I finally made a move on the girl I've been into forever now... let's call her, "Bitch."

Okay, well, it may not have been mature, but a little name-calling never hurt anyone for real. I think she's called herself a bitch more times than I ever had. How was this the straw that broke the camel's back? It was the *only* straw.

> I finally got up the nerve to kiss her, and you know what she said?

Never Cried Wolf

I hadn't even scrolled back past the message when she told me to fuck off, but the memory came back so vividly it could have smacked me.

The anger, the hurt, the *unfairness* of it all. How did I earn this treatment? What did I do to deserve to be spoken to this way but be at her beck and call *constantly*? I was basically her boyfriend already! Just like I'd said.

What if it happened again? She hadn't started texting me at all hours of the night just yet, but she might. She was selfish and ungrateful like that-- she never really appreciated me.

Right. Exactly what I'd said once before. I knew Mona, the *real* Mona, probably better than anyone else still. She hadn't changed even a little in the last two years, and here I was, her friend when it was convenient.

Not this time.

I felt a tension in my jaw. I clicked out of the tab and massaged my face with my palm. Everything was tight, my fingers had frozen stiffer than they had been after shoveling the driveway, even in the heat of my bedroom.

It wasn't getting any better, it was arguably getting worse. I needed another distraction-- a better distraction.

I slammed my laptop shut a little too hard. I paused, took a breath, and opened it once more to check for cracks.

There were none. Good. I would have hated to explain that one to Dad.

I gently set the computer back on my nightstand and sighed deeply. I felt the hot air coming off me as my blood boiled beneath the surface. At that moment, nothing sounded more relaxing than cracking open the window and falling backward onto the roof into the fluffy white snow to make snow angels with nothing but my t-shirt on. At least it would cool me off.

Somehow I had enough sense through the rage not to do that, but it still sounded good.

I snatched my Swiss roll from where I'd dropped it on the bed and focused on the satisfying crinkle of the wrap releasing from around it and took a huge bite that filled my cheeks. Again, just something to focus on.

As I began the task of chewing my ginormous chunk of chocolate and frosting, I pulled my phone out of my back pocket and tapped my way to Twitter.

Mindless scrolling. That would help, surely.

Politics. Politics. Other stan accounts for my Queen. Nothing I hadn't seen yet. Subtweets from freshman band kids, subtweets about freshman band kids.

What's this? I wondered as I tapped on a retweet, incidentally, from the same freshman band kid who starred in the previous tweet.

Brianna Rae Quinn

Kettlewood Confessions

@KWHS_Confess
26 minutes ago

"Can we stop sleeping on bandos? Some of y'all desperately need a guy who knows how to tongue something right!"

Kettlewood Confessions? I'd seen other schools and universities make wild pages like this to submit anonymous messages, but I never imagined I'd see one at our high school. I imagined this would end up with a handful of copy-cat accounts, each trying to be better than the last, which was trying to be better than the original before finally, all the confessions were meta complaints about each other. Trends like these only last a few months before they crashed and burned-- it was like a full-time job running a good account on any platform. No one knew that better than I did.

I clicked into the account and started scrolling again, making sure to chuckle at one which commented on Leta. There weren't a ton of followers yet, but my curiosity had peaked (as I'm sure it had for everyone), so I gave the page a follow.

Kettlewood Confessions

@KWHS_Confess

4 hours ago

"everyone at this school is so fucking fake. i'm over it."

Preach. I groaned.

Was that all it took to bring my mind back to Mona? I felt crazy and obsessive, but it was so easy to rationalize. She ruined my life, sabotaged my friendships, and now wanted to act all buddy-buddy again. She was using me again, I could feel it in my burning bones, and this time I wouldn't just sit back and watch her do it.

Within moments, a plan hatched in my brain like the egg of a dragon, bursting from the built-up pressure of a fiery breath. The more time I spent with Mona, the more she'd trust me again. If she left her mouth unfiltered with me, it would be so easy to get real, solid evidence to finally bury her for good.

Little shards of this shimmery cracked eggshell landed haphazardly like a wedge between Mona and everyone else in my brain, ready to sever every bond she had. I just needed to go out and find them.

And to do that, I needed to find more time with her.

I backed my way out of the app and clicked into my messages. Mona's sat at the top from our brief exchange the day before. It was about one thirty now-- we still had some day ahead of us.

Sam

Trying to get out of the house.

Want to go to the mall?

It only took a minute for the response to come.

Mona

Sure!

Perfect.

She would be held accountable for what she'd done to me. I'd be sure of that.

CHAPTER NINE

Mona

The practical, Type A person inside of me knew that the best possible use of the mall time, and the most effective, would be to come in the front center entrance, take a left, go all the way down, come up the escalators, cover the left side of the second floor. Once back at the central point, we would stop for a snack at the food court before wrapping around the right side of the top floor, going down and back out the door we came in. We'd hit everything and not have to walk over the same areas twice.

The only possible flaw in the plan was that the soft pretzel shop was a little kiosk just down to the left, and I had a rule that I could not pass up soft pretzels when the opportunity presented itself. Therefore, I did have a bit of a snack before we got to the food court, and I didn't think I was feeling particularly hungry as we passed the last few stores and the Orange Julius turned from a blur of white and orange into a full-fledged station with defined edges.

"I don't think I want anything crazy after the pretzel," I admitted sheepishly to Sam.

He nodded as if to tell me that was alright and made a suggestion. "Have you tried the new Pho place in the food court?"

"I don't think so?" I replied.

"It's great. The cook makes this incredible broth overnight, and they have fantastic smoothies!"

"Sounds perfect! Lead the way!"

As we rounded the corner into the cramped space loaded with tables, I didn't immediately notice anywhere to sit.

The Pho restaurant was only a few stalls down and had a pleasant-looking guy handing out samples of the Vietnamese spring rolls, cut into thin slices like little sushi pieces. He also had a squeeze bottle of what appeared to be a sweet chili sauce which he squirted on the samples by request.

I excitedly accepted a sample with some chili sauce and popped it into my mouth.

"I know what I'm getting!" I sang with my mouth still slightly too full. I stifled a laugh at how stupid I sounded with my mouth full.

Sam approached the counter and ordered his bowl of Pho and a large smoothie before turning to look at me. "What do you want?" He asked.

"Oh no, Sam, I can pay for myself!" I gestured to the cashier that I wouldn't be ordered just yet.

"It's no big deal. I'm happy to do it," Sam said.

"Really?" I asked.

"Of course!"

I wasn't really comfortable with this. I would have preferred to pay for myself, but things were going good with Sam and I didn't want to make him think I didn't appreciate the offer. I looked behind me to see if there was anyone else in line and if I could turn this into a pay-it-forward thing, but it seemed the Food Court was packed with eaters who had already ordered.

"Well, if you insist," I conceded and asked for my meal. An order of spring rolls and a small bowl of dumpling soup.

The cashier tapped our orders out on her register and informed Sam of the total. He presented his card, and she returned a receipt for his signature. As he signed, the chef packed out orders to hand to us over the bar.

I grabbed the bag and thanked him and began scanning the room for a table.

"Where do we--" Sam began, but I cut him off.

"Ahh! There!" I pointed to a table where a woman was packing her small child into a stroller and strode off with our food in hand to sit at the two-person table, waving to the little girl as her mother rolled her away.

"Yay!" I squealed, untying the bag to unpack our goodies.

I popped the lid off the to-go container housing my spring rolls and smiled at the satisfying tap it made as it bounced against the table.

Sam sat down, peeled the lid off his Pho, and pulled at the plastic around his utensils to get his spoon.

I dipped my roll into the sweet chili sauce and took a huge bit to get through the thick wrap of rice paper around the ends to get to the center. I felt myself smiling again. There really was something about having good food that put me in a fantastic mood.

"Thank you, by the way," I said, swallowing my first bite. "It's nice to actually hang out and eat good food together rather than those foul school lunches," I chortled.

"It's nothing," he said. He didn't quite smile, but the corner of his mouth twitched just before he sipped a spoonful of both between his lips.

"I just think it was a very nice thing to offer. Next one's on me!" I offered.

He glanced up at me from his bowl and said, "Sure." He sounded a little dry. He probably just wanted to eat and not talk so much. We'd been talking since we arrived, and honestly, it was going fairly well. I was sure we'd be chatting away again once we got through our meals.

I finished quickly with my two small orders, and Sam was finishing up his soup while I scrolled through my phone.

Notorious J.A.E.

@jae_moneymoney

43 minutes ago

"Netta is literally the best person I have ever met. I have no idea how I went my entire life and only just got to meet her this year! :')"

I felt a sharp stab of envy in my gut. The well-adjusted part of myself wanted to be thinking *gee, I can't wait to meet Netta! We'll probably get along so great and I'm so glad Jae had friends and is happy.* But more realistically, it just felt like being replaced.

The more I heard Jae talk about his new friends and his new life, the more I think I started to resent him for leaving me behind and forcing me to adjust without him, particularly since he was having such an easier time adjusting to life without me.

"What's wrong?" Sam asked. I must have been making a face. I really needed to be better at controlling my face.

"It's nothing, just Jae bragging about his new college bestie all over the internet while conveniently forgetting about our facetime dates," I sighed.

"So he's doing well then?" Sam inquired.

I made a moderate face of distaste, "Yeah, I just wish I was still a part of his life while he's doing so well."

"I get that. I had a close friend move on without me back when I was an underclassman," he said, sympathizing.

"Yeah? Who?" I genuinely didn't know. I wasn't super up to date on Sam's contacts from the last few years.

Sam made a face and said, "Just a family friend," before sucking the last of his smoothie out of the thick straw.

"Come on," he added, packing his now empty cup back into the bag and tying up the trash, "let's finish our rounds and talk about something else."

I hoped I didn't strike a nerve. I often struggled to know when was the right time to shut up, but it felt pretty clear this time.

We spotted the new set of table scavengers desperately searching for a table in the madness of the Saturday afternoon Food Court. They had slipped into our chairs mere moments after our butts left the seats, but hey, I couldn't blame them.

We began our walk to the right side of the mall. Right at the corner sat one of the nicer dress shops with six mannequins on display, wearing gowns of varying colors and poofiness. I always thought those larger ballgowns would swallow me whole, but man, they always caught my eye.

I felt a little weighed down by my winter coat staring into the windows at all the glitter and rhinestones. They almost defied gravity with how large some of the skirts were, and a beautiful deep electric blue A-line gown with a stiff, structured overskirt flashed peeks of silver at me from underneath. Could I have been drooling? Maybe.

"Thinking about prom already? You still have over a year, Junior." Sam joked.

I laughed and gave him a playful shove. "Shut up, I just like ogling over the shiny stuff," I said, eying the not-too-deep sweetheart neckline supported by thin straps over the shoulders.

"That one?" Sam questioned, pointing to the green, glittery, mermaid gown next to it.

"No, that blue beauty," I answered, pressing my finger to the glass, leaving a slightly sticky fingerprint behind, probably from the rice paper on the spring rolls.

"Blue? Green's a way better color on you," Sam confessed.

"Every redhead looks good in green. Besides, that's Raf's favorite color, and I think I could pull off the rhinestones, don't you?" I said, resisting the urge to trace the twisting pattern of tiny, classy gems all along the bodice and overskirt all over the mirror.

"Who cares about Raf's favorite color? Would you still like it if it wasn't? I mean, especially if he's not making anything official."

This was the first time I had really felt Sam being candid with me again. It felt kind of nice for him to be frank with me like he used to be.

"Yeah, I don't know what's up with that. Things were really great at the beginning of the week, but I feel like something changed. He hasn't really been acting much different, just a gut feeling. A vibe, maybe."

"How do you mean?"

"I don't know," I sighed, finally taking my eyes off the dress. "It's like Monday it felt like we were shoulder to shoulder, and now we're still close, but it sort of feels like he's at... arm's length, I guess? Or like," I looked back at the display, "A window. I can still see him but there's a glare, or a smudge or something between us."

"Poetic. You should put that in your next writing assignment for Howard," Sam teased.

"Don't be jealous, I'm sure you'll think up something just as deep," I laughed and looked once more at the blue dress. "I can always keep it in mind, you know, just in case he does ask me. There's still time."

Sam didn't respond immediately, just let me look a moment longer before we kept walking.

"This is fun I'm glad we did this," I said.

"Me too. It's nice to get out of the house, and I'm glad the roads weren't too bad down here. My street never got plowed." Sam noted, casually.

"You live on a side street, they never plow those," I noted.

"Oh, I know, because I'm always the one out there shoveling my car out of the drifts." It didn't sound like a joke, but I laughed like it was anyway.

"Speaking of, it's so nice to get in a car that's not Oscar's every now and then. I swear I can still smell all the cigars his dad used to smoke in there. It's like embedded into the seats," I joked.

"I'll be real, I think it's super strange he's still hanging around you and Leta if they're not together anymore. I don't know a lot of folks that still even talk to their exes, let alone see them regularly. Has it been weird for them?"

That was a fair question. Sometimes, I wondered the same thing, but it was hard to tell if I was just projecting the weird feelings I had about Oscar, or if something really was weird between them. Leta never mentioned it, so I always assumed it was fine.

"Eh," I began to reply, "They seem fine. I don't think they hang out much alone anymore, I'm usually there too, and Leta's always busy after school which is why it's just us on the way home."

Sam stopped walking and looked at me intently.

"What?" I wondered aloud.

"You tell me, you've got a face again."

I looked back into his eyes. They were blue in a very light, icy way, and with his chestnut brown curls laid just so on top of his head, and in his thick woolen winter coat, he seemed so mature.

I pointed to the bench just up ahead and said, "I can lay down and talk about it if you want, Mr. Psychiatrist," I, again, tried to lighten the conversation.

"Seriously, Mona. What's up?" He pressed. "You can tell me."

I looked over my shoulder as if Oscar could have been standing there at that moment, eavesdropping on her conversation.

I looked back and spoke quickly, "It's just that he's been kind of... forward ... lately.

Like, sometimes it feels like he's making moves on me, but I know he's probably just being funny, but still. I feel weird telling Leta because I don't want to cause drama or upset her or anything."

Sam nodded, "Have you said anything to him about it?"

"No, I just kind of shut it down or change the topic. I think he's getting the hint," I paused to think, "Well, it's not getting any better, but it's not getting any worse." I admitted.

"Okay, well, if anything happens, you know you can talk to me about it." Sam offered, and I smiled in response.

"Thanks," I reached out and squeezed his shoulder. "And this conversation obviously stays between us," I demanded with a wagging finger to show I meant business. I really needed to stop picking up nagging habits from my mother.

"Obviously." He crossed his fingers and smiled back at me, turning to look ahead, our strides just barely out of step with each other.

CHAPTER TEN

Sam

I had no idea why everyone hated Mondays. I loved Mondays. Of course, getting up before the sun was frustrating, but there was something nice about the start of a routine. There were never any surprises, and you knew exactly what to do and when.

I wondered if the woodwind and brass players felt the same as they emptied their spit from the valves on their instruments. Did they find comfort in the mundanity of it? Or was it just gross?

I secretly believed society only hated Mondays because it was the thing to do-- everyone hated them, but I knew better. Monday was new. it was opportunity itself, and I was never one to pass that up.

I loved Mondays *and* everything happens for a reason, and I firmly believed there was a reason I was sitting where I was, knowing what I knew when Leta came to chat. She held her fingers on all the keys and rotated her arm around to release all the trapped saliva from the inside of her horn and prepared to dump it out. She didn't even bat an eyelash at it as a trickle of pure spit came tumbling out of it.

She must have noticed how intently I was watching.

"It's not pretty, but sometimes we just need to get all the gross stuff out to make space for something fresh and new," she chuckled.

Never Cried Wolf

She probably imagined I didn't think much about the process of cleaning out spit given my tenor drums were pretty far from my mouth. I doubt she or any other band members outside of the percussionists would really know how much I drooled on my set, particularly during an intense, focused session of beating.

Her words hit me though. Sometimes we do have to dump the gross and ugly to make room for something new and better. I had seen ugliness this weekend. Mona had no problem letting me pay for her food, as always. She did the check dance to look polite, but I knew she'd want me to pay. She scarcely put up a fight.

I wondered if she ever bothered to do that dance with Rafael or if she just expected that behavior out of him. She never had a problem using people when they were convenient.

It seems wild to me how she totally missed the connection between Jae moving on without her and what she'd done to me. I wondered if she was one of those people who lied to herself so often, she'd convinced herself her lies were true. namely that she was a good person and that she was right in tossing me out of her life like a used tissue.

Which, I mean, Leta could've probably used right about then to clean up her spit. Yeah, I knew it was normal, but it was still a little gross to me. My puddles of drool were never quite so wide.

Leta prepared her horn to put away in her instrument locker, ready to go to her next class alongside me. The lockers alternated in two colors, an awful shade of marigold yellow (which I thought aired a bit too much on the orange side) and a royal blue. As the blue of Leta's locker flashed open before my eyes, I couldn't help but think back to that prom dress Mona had been eyeing. The dress she'd stared at was much more electric, probably more fitting to her spitfire personality.

Spit, gross.

Never Cried Wolf

The whole reason my mind was wandering was to (1) avoid thinking about the puddles of saliva surrounding me at the end of the band period, and (2) wait for that perfect moment to make my move.

I probably wouldn't have hatched this little plan had it not been for what Mona told me on Saturday. She and Mr. Tall, Dark, and Handsome, Rafael, were getting distant. And what had changed during that past week? Well, me.

Of course, she had no idea I'd said anything to Dante about her, but a little part of me liked to imagine that maybe the reason Rafael was keeping his distance was because of my little warning. It was small, maybe insignificant, but it was kind of easy to tell him my genuine thoughts about Mona when he was already unsure. Leta, however, what a different story.

Mona and Leta were best friends. Leta had taken Mona's side in the past, but I often wondered how Leta might have reacted had

Mona done to her what she'd done to me. Could she have forgiven?

I couldn't be sure, and I had to make my next move carefully if I wanted to see everything unfold the way it went in my head.

I wouldn't do anything but tell the truth.

"There you are, my baby!" Leta cooed at her French horn as she snapped the case closed, "Tucked in nice and tight for tomorrow!" She kissed her case as she slid it into the locker and clicked the door closed.

Bingo.

"Careful, Leta. Your boyfriend might get jealous if you keep kissing your horn like that," I smirked with a mix of teasing and little self-satisfaction.

She practically snorted in my face, "Boyfriend? Yeah, I wish. Besides," she patted the locker, producing a crisp aluminum bang, "I wouldn't consider myself particularly *horny*." She slapped her knee dramatically, making sure

I knew the joke was intentionally, horrendously cheesy.

"What?" I feigned surprise. "That's weird. I guess I just kind of figured, you know?"

I was working to be ambiguous without seeming like I was trying to hit on her myself. I hated to sound like every lame lady's man in a sitcom, shamelessly flirting with women in bars with lines that undoubtedly wouldn't work in the real world.

"Why would you 'figure'?" She put the last word in air quotes, her face contorted into a mixture of confusion and interest. "Did someone say something?"

"No!" I started quickly, so I could slide into a coyer tone. "Well, not really. Not about you. I guess I just assumed you *have* to be dating someone."

Her face didn't change. "I *have* to?" Everything was a question. This was going almost exactly as I had practiced it in the mirror. I could see every eyebrow hair, every flicker in my eyes, and even the way my hair moved as I shook my head trying to backtrack on my mistake that was most certainly not a mistake.

"I just meant with whatever Mona and Oscar were doing after school. I figured you had to be dating someone else."

I held my breath as I waited for her response. The interest faded a little to make room for something new etched in her forehead wrinkles. Could it have been a little… hurt?

"Oscar's just taking Mona home. We'd all ride home together if we could." Leta plastered a smile on. It seemed fake. She smiled non-stop, so I knew what they looked like genuine-- this one had an edge.

"Oh," I nodded and averted my eyes not too quickly, so she'd notice and try to follow them. I looked at my hands and began trying to crack my knuckles one at a time, hopefully looking nervous, and giving her a little time to connect the dots.

I knew she would, she was smart like that.

"Who said something?" Leta wondered aloud. "That something is going on? I mean, that's a really crazy rumor."

"I'm sure it's nothing, Leta, I just went to the mall with Mona this weekend and she was talking about her rides home, and, you know…" I trailed off and looked at her as if to urge her to fill in the blank.

"I don't understand," she uttered. Denial. I get that.

"I'm sorry, I didn't mean to upset you," I started.

"No, no. I'm just… confused. What exactly did Mona say?"

My mouth opened then closed again, and I averted my eyes to my thumbs once more. "I--" I stuttered a touch and looked over my shoulder and back to Leta with a hint of desperation in my tone, "I'm sorry, Leta, but Mona said she didn't want me to tell anyone. I really fucked up. I shouldn't have said anything and she's going to be so mad. I'm so so so sorry." I got a little panicking, speaking quickly like I did when I felt little knots of anxiety in my chest and gut. *I was almost believing my own bullshit.*

I kept going, "She said she didn't want you to know, God, I messed up so bad!" I dug my head into my hands and tensed my knuckles.

"Sam, come on, no. Thank you, I… I had no idea. Please, can you tell me? How bad could it be that she doesn't want me to know? Are they like… are they doing stuff? You have to tell me. You didn't do anything wrong. I had a right to know." I couldn't tell if the words were more for my benefit than hers. She sounded like she wanted to console me, but I could feel the desperation and begging like a string through my heart.

The bell rang abruptly, adding a sense of urgency between us, but Leta looked like she barely heard it. She remained seated at the bench, staring at me as she reached her hands to mine. She pulled them away, so my head would come up to look at her.

"You can't tell her I told you," I begged in a low whisper as the band members filed noisily out of the large music room and into the hallway.

"Of course," Leta spoke, nodding with anticipation.

"I don't know any details, but she did say Oscar was making crazy moves on her, and at first she thought it was a joke, and she doesn't want to tell you because it would start a bunch of drama." It was a paraphrase, for sure, and it certainly had a tone shift from the anxious way Mona had confessed her concerns over the weekend. It was clever, I thought.

It reminded me of the game we used to play as kids, Telephone. You'd whisper something into the person to your left's ear and they'd whisper to the person on their left until it got all the way around the circle. By the time the phrase came back around, it was almost nothing like what you said originally. I kept the important parts and maybe filled in some blanks. I made sense of the whispers in the mall, that was all.

Leta nodded, the interest now drained, and replaced with more clear and direct hurt.

"I can't believe it," she mumbled. She looked down at her backpack, resting between her legs. It only took a moment before she was snatching it up and swinging it over her shoulders, clearly ready to catch up with the rest of the school as they moved into sixth period.

"I'm sorry, Leta. I shouldn't have said anything," I said, following her lead by standing but not yet strapping the bag to my back.

"No," she pointed a finger at me, "I'm glad you did. I mean," she sighed, "I get why she wouldn't want to tell me or whatever, but we're best friends, and the fact that she'd keep anything from me is just… bizarre!" Leta's head shook in disbelief, her blonde curls brushing against her jaw which tensed in clear frustration.

I wanted to add a little something to push her further, like a, "You deserve better," or a, "I can't believe she'd do that to you," but I didn't think I needed to drive the point home.

No.

This was perfect.

"You promise you won't say anything, right? I don't want to make things worse."

"I won't say a word, I promise." Leta nodded, consoling me one last time, before checking the clock.

"We should go," she groaned. "We'll talk later though." She called, heading out of the large set of double doors.

I couldn't believe how smoothly that had gone. I couldn't have planned it better, and now with the seeds of betrayal sewn, I thought it might be pertinent to have a chat with Dante before class. Surely, he'd take some interest in Mona's dirty little secret too.

It was a little ridiculous how powerful this moment made me feel. My chest puffed up. I felt ten feet taller, a knight ready to slay the giant, red, freckle-faced dragon.

Brianna Rae Quinn

I wrapped my straps over my shoulders and rode that high right on to sit down at a lunch table with the monster herself.

CHAPTER ELEVEN

Mona

The air felt thick on this Tuesday. It was like looking at a bookshelf and recognizing something was missing, but I couldn't quite tell what. It was nagging at me.

Leta had been quiet all morning. The ride to school felt oddly tense-- it was different. I wasn't used to feeling this way, and I most certainly couldn't discern the cause. I ran a bit behind, but we still made it to school on time.

Oscar always picked me up first in the morning. He sent a text when he left his house as usual. Today, it was a bit earlier than normal.

Oscar
Omw a lil early

That wasn't a problem for me most days, but this morning I tried to put my hair back in a fancy, five-strand braid. I was going for Celtic princess vibes, but unfortunately, I looked a little more like Annie fresh out of the orphanage with a tangled red rope of unbrushed hair down my back. I had to take it out.

I tried to make it work about three more times before I finally gave up and saw Oscar's text. By that point, I was scrambling to find breakfast and my homework from the night before.

Oscar was honking incessantly for probably ten minutes before I finally got out to him, and we pulled up to Leta's probably ten minutes late. Well, at least ten minutes later than she was expecting. She was already waiting and watching out her window for us.

She must have been super frustrated because she looked super flushed when she got into the car. Perhaps it was the windy winter morning, but it seemed to be something more. She sounded *awkward* as she greeted us. I don't think I'd ever described Leta as awkward in my life (let alone quiet.)

The ride was quiet with only Oscar and I chatting back and forth. I could feel Leta staring at us from the back seat, but she never contributed to the discussion. I was trying to tidy up my messy, loose strands of hair, still recovering from the braid disaster when I noticed her in the mirror.

Her brows were furrowed, not in an angry way, but more of a sad way, (possibly at me,) but she looked away so quickly, I couldn't really tell. For the rest of the trip, she kept her eyes trained out the window. It was so bizarre, and then out of nowhere, she dropped a bomb on us.

"I think my mom is going to start driving me to school in the mornings," she said as we closed the car doors and made our way inside.

"What? Why?" I replied, honestly lost for words.

"Just some personal stuff," she replied vaguely.

"Okayyy…" I replied, "Well, I guess I'll see you in study hall."

"Not today. I have to make up a test, but maybe tomorrow." And with that, she hurried away.

I was pretty immediately suspicious of this. I rode to school with Leta every single day. She hadn't missed a day since the start of the new semester a whopping *week* ago. What test could she have missed? And what for?

The math wasn't quite adding up for me. I supposed she'd tell me when she was ready, but it didn't stop the paranoia.

Never Cried Wolf

In Creative Writing, most of the class was dragging their feet, finishing up a pre-test on figurative language.

"There is so much cool stuff we can do this semester, and I want to be able to cut out as many of the boring lessons as I can to make way for big projects!" Mr. Howard had exclaimed as he handed them out.

"Basically, I need you to try really hard for me so we can do the fun stuff. We'll never have time for our cliche poetry contest if I'm still teaching you about hyperboles."

Sam and I breezed through the work. I never found figurative language particularly difficult to grasp, though I may not have been the best at using it.

Sam was just an English nerd, always had been.

And as we sat, watching the rest of the class tap their pencils and chew on erasers, I figured it might have been easier to blend in with the crowd of test-takers by resorting to the old-school method of in-class communication: the note.

I opened my notebook and carefully tore along the perforated edge to make as little noise as possible and began writing.

Wouldn't it be embarrassing if I zoomed through that whole test and still failed?

I folded the sheet in half and slid it about eight inches to my right so it would casually crash into Sam's arm, poking him with the corner of the sheet. I had no idea how he was wearing a t-shirt in the wintertime. The school had heat, but not layering up at least a long sleeve under a coat seemed borderline crazy.

He peeked over at Mr. Howard's desk. He was tapping and clicking away on his keyboard, clearly focused on whatever he was doing. Sam subtly flipped the page open and scanned the words I'd written. He smiled covertly and clicked his pen to reply.

I watched him scribble the words.

You didn't fail. The dude in front of us though?

We looked up at that, made eye contact, and he nodded his head to the large, football-player-sized guy in the inner circle who looked to be reading his test questions intently. Upon closer inspection, he'd fallen asleep with his head in his head. I held back a laugh as my brain briefly wandered to the idea of any tiny movement breaking the delicate balance he had, resulting in him fully flopping onto the desk like a ragdoll.

Sam continued to write.

He's definitely failing.

He slid the sheet back over to me. Mr. Howard still had not looked up from his screen, but I hid my smile and put on my best test-taking face in case he did.

Today's been so weird. Leta said she's ditching the carpool.

Sam's eyebrows raised. His shoulders tensed a bit too. He quickly grabbed the paper, dragged it back to him, and wrote his response.

Did she say why?

Not Really. Just said it was personal.

His shoulders relaxed a little as he nodded in recognition of my words. I continued to write.

Feels like she's avoiding me. Said she had a test during study hall but it's like, the 5th day of the semester. Did she say anything to you?

Weird. She didn't say anything. I can ask if you want?

No. She'll talk when she's ready. The energy with everyone is just so off this week, with everyone.

I sighed at those last few words, and rested my head in my palm, much like our football-player friend in front of us.

Sam snatched the paper back. I could tell we were getting more and more conspicuous, but Mr. Howard hadn't noticed just yet. He probably hadn't even looked up, or he would have woken our friend from his nap.

Did you take to Raf about prom?

I rolled my eyes and groaned my response quietly but pulled the paper back to write anyway.

Too afRaid to Now. He must be psychic oR KNew I was thinKing about it oR something. He just told me out of the blue yesterday that he just "doesN't waNt to go".

Sam held in a smile. His lips pursed a little as he attempted to hide it.

Maybe he just wants you to think

that and he'll surprise you. Don't

give up on it yet.

That was true. it was entirely possible that Rafael would still ask me, but I definitely didn't want to push him and be annoying. Did leaving it alone count as "giving up?" Or maybe I just shouldn't give up hope that he would. I would just have to wait for it to come up organically.

So I'm thinking just leave my

phone open with prom dresses

on it? will that be a clear

enough hint?

Sam snorted maybe a little too loudly. Mr. Howard didn't look up, but the football player stirred a bit. I clapped my hand over my mouth as we both watched him sit up and take in his surroundings as if he was *just* now realizing he was in school (and in the middle of a test). He looked over one shoulder, probably checking to see if anyone noticed he was sleeping.

Sam and I instinctively turned our faces to our finished pre-tests and started flipping through them, still holding in some giggles.

Football guy refocused and began filling in his test again, and Sam reached for our sheet of notes again.

Odds he finishes in the next 7 minutes?

I shrugged and scribbled back.

Slim to None. I feel bad, maybe we should have woken him up lol.

Sam just stared at the words for a moment before he lifted his hand to write, but he put it back, clearly second-guessing whatever he was about to say.

I wondered what was on his mind. he was a bit hard to read at times.

"Alright, class! We've got about five minutes left, so let's start to wrap up!" The voice of Mr. Howard snapped us out of our note-writing. Sam slipped the page off the desk and folded it tightly before stuffing it into his pocket.

Football guy ran his fingers through his hair as he panicked trying to get his work done. I flipped my pre-test through one more time and stared at the clock, counting down the seconds with the red hand, preparing for the bell.

Sam did the same until Mr. Howard spoke again, "Two minutes! If you're done, bring 'em up and set them on the podium!" The projector screen flipped from the slide reading "Figurative Language Pretest" to a slide with a large arrow GIF bouncing up and down, conveniently pointed to where the papers needed to be dropped off.

Mr. Howard was quirky like that.

I started to stand, but Sam stopped me.

"Let me," he said, grabbing my test and scooching behind me, following the arrow to the drop-off zone.

Things had felt so strange in the last few days, I was uncharacteristically grateful for the simple gesture. Not that I wouldn't have been thankful before, but with everyone feeling so distant, it was nice for someone to be pleasant, even in such a small way.

It was nice to be able to count on Sam again. I wasn't sure what the week would have been like without having him to lean on.

CHAPTER TWELVE

Sam

"You know what?" Mona began, almost indignantly. "I don't even care if Raf asks me to Prom. I'm just going to chill out a bit, and if he never asks, I'll just have a girl's night with Leta. We'll need the time to catch up anyway if she's serious about not carpooling anymore."

I nodded along with her. I chose not to dwell on how she was going to plan a little hangout without me and tell me all about it. *Thanks for the invitation.*

"Yeah, because *I'll* be at prom." Okay, that was a bit sarcastic. Perhaps I wanted to linger on the topic for a moment. I never intended to go to prom. I didn't have anyone to go with, and the idea of having prom photos with Mona for the rest of my life actively made me consider leaning over the edge of the lunchroom table and heaving until the contents of my stomach flooded her bag.

Her brown eyes read more sad than the guilt or embarrassment I expected after being called out like that. "Yeah," she said, pausing to swallow, "I know."

She was denser than a pound cake. She should have been so embarrassed.

"Who *are* you taking to prom?" She inquired, folding her arms and staring at me across the table. Her eyes were chestnut brown, not a dark, rich chocolatey color that made one's eyes look deep and expansive. They were shallow, hot, and molten. They reflected a little too much sun when she closed her eyes, blinking the light away.

She twisted a petite, gold Claddagh ring around her pinky. Was she anxious? For what?

I was *not* going to ask her. Is that what she wanted? Was she so desperate?

As if I'd be the second choice for her.

"I'm asking a friend," I said. She opened her mouth to ask who, but I cut her off to continue. "Soon. No spoilers." I held a finger up to her, showing her I wouldn't be saying more.

It was crazy to me how I didn't shake, crack, or break in any way when I lied to her. It was natural and so easy.

I wondered if I played this role as her friend for so long (even if it was so long ago) that my muscle memory just knew how to speak and act with her.

She pinched her thumb and index finger and dragged it across her lips, pantomiming a padlock over her mouth and tossing the "key" over her shoulder.

I wouldn't tell her anyway, given I didn't really have a date in mind.

She'd never been silent on anything in her life, I couldn't imagine any lock and key holding my secrets long. She was the definition of an open book, which is probably what made this so easy.

Mona wore her heart on her sleeve, so I could see the cracks and breaks. There was a time when I would have helped hold her together. I would have scavenged the Earth for every tape and glue to help keep her together, but now I wondered what it might look like to watch the slivers of glass spread. I couldn't wait to watch it snap into shards and watch them rain around me.

This was karma, right? What goes around comes around?

I wanted her to see the consequences of her actions on me. I supposed manifestation is real. It was time for the nice guys to win one for a change.

Never Cried Wolf

Once I'd made my way through lunch and creative writing, I took a deep breath and held it for a few seconds before exhaling and completely relaxing my body. The performance may have been easy, but it was still draining.

I found my negative thoughts dissolving into the background further and further when I spent time around her-- it was nice to not be so inundated with negativity all the time. It was easy to feel like I was drowning in thoughts of Mona twenty-four/seven, but my head was above water now. I was in control, and it felt so nice for once to control *something*.

For once, I knew what came next, and there was so little I had to do. I just tugged on the loose strings around her and let them unravel themselves.

I have no idea how she let things get too messy, really. Even if I never came into the picture, would Rafael have ever decided to take their relationship seriously? Would Leta have just been hurt further down the road?

I'm not the smoking gun. I'm simply the catalyst. I only aimed in the right direction, she's the one who pulled the trigger.

I looked up ahead and noticed Dante's long stride on his way to our shared math class.

I inhaled and exhaled again.

The show was back on.

"Dante! Hey man, what's going on?" I called, quickening my pace to match his. He was easily over six feet tall, having a good half-foot on me. I angled my head up at him as he reached out to dap me. I slapped palms with him as we kept walking, fighting our way through a sea of classmates crowding the halls.

They bobbed and jerked like fish, angling around the slow-moving stingrays, avoiding the sharks lurking in the corridors, and the smaller ones hide behind the teachers, whales, scaring off the bigger fish with the massive weight of their authority. They didn't call groups of fish a "school" for nothing, I guessed.

"Nothing much, man," Dante replied, moving at a steady pace. What kind of fish would he be? Certainly, he wouldn't be. he was more like a squid. He was stoic and elusive but moved with grace and confidence. Oh yes, I liked that for him.

"And yourself?" he continued. That was a good question. I needed something about Mona and Rafael to come up naturally, and I needed it to happen before class. There was a time crunch to set this boat sailing in the right direction.

"Pretty good, pretty good," I nodded. "Just came from Creative writing," I offered as the first thing that came to mind, and suddenly the path appeared before me. I started twisting the wheel. "We were told to write about something that's been on our minds a while, and *I* had the pleasure of proofreading Mona Murphy's."

I never called Mona by her first and last name, except with Dante. There was something about saying a first and last name that was impersonal, and unfamiliar. Like there may have been another Mona, like there is some confusion over her identity.

"Right," Dante nodded, "You know, I saw you having lunch with her the other day," he started. I sensed a twinge of suspicion in his tone. I stepped on the breaks a little, not enough to backtrack, but just enough to… let's say… ease his motion sickness?

I policed my tone a little more, and said, "Yeah, she started sitting with me at the beginning of the semester. I guess she saw me in creative writing and decided to be my friend again." Not untrue. "It wasn't so bad at first, but now it's just getting boring to listen to her talk," I offered a saccharine chuckle.

He raised an eyebrow toward me as he rounded the corner into our classroom, "How so?" He wondered aloud, dropping the strap of his backpack off one shoulder to prepare his slide into his desk chair. I noticed his muscle ripple as he slowly lowered the bag to the ground. With that pensive look and the mid-action pose, I could have sworn I was looking at a Greek statue. I shook those thoughts away to continue.

"It's like I've become a human diary. She's always talking with me about her 'boy problems." I put the last two words in air quotes.

"About Raf?" He asked again, his interest peaked.

I nailed it and stepped on the gas.

"Raf, and others. Namely Oscar Moreno."

"Oscar? What's going on with him?" I liked this little dance. A gossip tango, where he plays coy, not too eager to listen, and I move slowly and deliberately, not too eager to tell. I could feel his arms wrapped around my shoulders as we twisted around the things we wanted to say. It always felt that way.

"Well, she seemed to imply something was going on between them on those car rides home." I shrugged, casually, leaving it intentionally ambiguous, as I did.

Brianna Rae Quinn

The beautiful thing about the human mind is how it fills in the blanks. missing information becomes assumptions, and that was exactly what I needed at this moment.

Full speed ahead.

*   *   *

I dropped little seeds of doubt throughout my days, through every conversation, and I was fascinated to see how they sprouted.

It only took two days before I watched little shoots pop out of Leta's soil. In the silence as we returned our instruments, as a subtle hum of busy classmates surround us, Leta confided in me, as I knew she would.

"You know, Oscar told me and Mona he was coming early to pick us up yesterday, like ten whole minutes early but he still pulled up to my place at the usual time," she said, clearly anxious to start the discussion. I could practically feel myself beginning to salivate. I was so proud of my little seeds for growing so quickly.

"Is that bad?" I asked, dumbly. She couldn't tell Mona without ratting me out. I was the only other person who knew. It was a solid plan, I thought.

"Well, not exactly, but when he pulled in the driveway, Mona's hair was a wreck and she was fixing up her lip gloss and stuff. I don't know."

I had my eye focused on my band room locker as I closed my items inside. I felt a little smile on my lips until I turned to look at Leta to respond. I noticed her lip quiver. I noticed her reddened eyes.

I noticed she was barely keeping it together.

"Oh, Leta, I'm so sorry," I threw my arms around her. She hugged me back, letting out a little sob.

"How could they do that to me? Like I wouldn't notice? He told us both he'd be early. Unless he only meant to text her…" I could feel her mind racing to rationalize the situation.

Of course, I knew the truth. Of course I knew Mona was running late that morning. She told me. It was entirely her fault.

I briefly considered telling Leta this to ease her pain.

I guess until this moment, I hadn't realized this was a possibility. That there were other emotions at stake here aside from Mona's and mine.

I held her another minute before backing off. No tears had escaped her eyes yet, though they looked full and ready to roll.

"Let me get you a tissue," I said.

"No," she replied, pulling her sleeves up past her wrists and using her wrists to dab her watery eyes, "I just need to calm down."

I nodded and watched her steady her breathing. I held her hand as she breathed deeply. The moment was heavy, I knew, but I couldn't help but with that little hint of pride again. Leta trusted me again. I was needed again, and I could prove myself a worthy friend. I was free from the shackles of the past and I could rewrite the narrative. Finally, I was the hero, I would be the Prince Charming and prove everyone who doubted me wrong.

"I know you probably don't want to hear it right now, but I wanted to ask anyway," I started. Leta looked up at me, her eyes now rubbed dry and dabbled with redness, swollen with disappointment. "Do you want to go to prom with me?" I asked.

"Wait, really?" Leta asked in shock. I was a little shocked too when the idea popped into my head, but I did say I wanted my prom date to be a surprise, and what was a more princely thing to do than save the damsel in distress from the dragon once again? (and to help her forget about her dirtbag ex-prince from a kingdom of trash.) Not to mention the added sting of knowing Leta was Mona's prom backup plan. In this way, she was a second choice too, and she did *not* deserve that.

Brianna Rae Quinn

"Yes, I mean, I wanted to ask you because I kind of figured Mona would end up going to Raf eventually and we might all like to go together or something, but now I'm just thinking that maybe we go and have a good time ourselves. You deserve it, you know?"

Leta smiled a soft, sad smile and nodded. "Of course, it sounds like a lot of fun." She squeezed my hand, "Thank you, Sammy."

I beamed. Just as I opened my mouth to insist it was my pleasure, a vibration shook me from my back pocket. Incidentally, it did for half of the band room as everyone pulled their devices out and opened up the same notification.

Kettlewood Confessions

@KWHS_Confess

1 minute ago

"Mona Murphy gives good head. 49/50 dudes agree."

Leta gaped at her phone and looked up at me with her big, blue eyes, looking even bluer against the fading red of her sclera.

Oh, it was just too perfect.

"Who do you think wrote this!?" She exclaimed, her expression overloading with shock.

"I have no idea," I insisted, but, of course, I did.

As I said, I planted seeds everywhere.

CHAPTER THIRTEEN

Mona

"Do you need a ride today?" Oscar asked me as I gathered my papers off my desk. The bell was about to ring, and I was ready to get to lunch and have some social time.

Math is exhausting for me. It felt so rigid and calculated (pun not intended). I just preferred something more fluid and forgiving, I supposed.

"No, Raf and I are going to get milkshakes after school," I replied. I could feel the twist of excitement in my gut. I always felt giddy about alone time with him, because then we could be real with each other *about* each other. It was hard to dissect our relationship with Dante around, and he always had this serious, evaluating look on him-- a laser cutting straight through to my core.

A series of buzzing flooded the room as the phones rested on tables, creating a loud, echoing thrum. I startled and dropped a paper from my hands, and watched as it slid under the bookshelf to my left.

I sighed and set my stack back on my desk, getting to my knees to fish the worksheet out. I noticed a majority of the class pulling out their phones in malicious glee. It had to be another Kettlewood Confession.

Oscar already had his phone out and began tapping his passcode to get into his device, not wanting to miss out on the juicy details either.

"What's this one say?" I asked, sliding my hand under the shelf, and pressing down onto the exposed corner of my sheet to slide it out. I could feel a layer of dust rubbing against my knuckles as the paper came into view.

"Um," his mouth twitched slightly upturned for a moment before settling in a pursed position. I sat up and gave him an inquisitive look, still on my knees, folded, so I was seated on my feet. "It's about you."

I felt a surge of electricity through my back, and I immediately scanned the room. Everyone was looking at me, and if they weren't, they were staring into a screen that reported something on me I still didn't know.

What could anyone have possibly said about me? I remembered the post complimenting Leta's ass, but (1) my ass most certainly could and would quit, and (2) with the way everyone was looking at me, like they were starving and I was a steak, it didn't feel complimentary.

I shifted onto my feet almost immediately and reached for Oscar's phone, imagining it would take too long to get to and open my own.

He kept a grip on it, but let me move it before my eyes so I could scan the page in a panic.

Kettlewood Confessions

@KWHS_Confess

1 minute ago

"Mona Murphy gives good head. 49/50 dudes agree."

My hand clapped over my mouth as my jaw dropped.

"What?!" I yelped in a weak whimper, feeling as though I'd just been smacked. With as quickly as my hand flew to my face, I probably had. The room faded away behind me and I slowly sank into a black void of shock and disgust.

"Who-- I mean… I've never-- ugh!" I shoved the phone back at Oscar as the bell rang. Other students snickered, squishing their way through the doorway to spread back out in the hall and make their way to their classes. I stayed put.

Oscar stayed for only a moment before saying, "I'm really sorry, Mona, but I have to go. I'll see you later," he waved in a half-hearted swing of his wrist and walked so quickly it was basically a run out of the classroom. Suddenly, the black void felt real as I stood alone, surrounded by an empty classroom. Even the teacher had slipped into the hallway, monitoring the crowds from the stairwell while I crumbled into a ball of self-pity.

I heard voices calling back and forth in the hallways, some about me, some not.

It *was* a big school. I'm sure most of the students here didn't know me, but they would now. And worse, this would be all they knew.

I shook my head clear of those thoughts and sighed, checking the clock on the wall. I suddenly wasn't in the mood for social time, but I certainly couldn't shrink.

Never Cried Wolf

If ever there was a time to stand tall and move forward, it would be now. The only thing worse than being talked about is believing it.

*   *   *

"I'm so sorry this happened, Mona," Sam said as I sat with him at lunch.

"It's fine, it's not like you wrote it," I replied, avoiding eye contact. I didn't want to think too much about it.

It was a long lunch having to act calm and collected, but for once, I felt inspired during Creative Writing.

"Describe a feeling in nothing but similes," Mr. Howard had said.

Just one feeling? I couldn't even manage that much. After workshopping a few ideas with Sam, I decided on "uncertainty".

Like feeling for the
Bottom step in the dark
Like leaping off the
High dive and waiting
For the splash
As moldable as
Fresh clay.
Vibrating like the wings of
Hummingbirds
With edges you'll
Never see.

The etching of Sam's pencil sketching letters on his paper filled the space as I finished my writing. Mr. Howard made his way around the class, trying to guess the feelings we were describing.

He stopped and read, his eyes flipping from line to line. His mouth angled as he thought. "Anxiety?" he asked in a low whisper. His voice had a fuzzy quality when he spoke softly. fuzzy in a prickly sort of way. Or perhaps I was just on edge.

"I was going for uncertainty," I whispered back.

He nodded, rereading the lines with this new information in mind.

"What do you think is different about these feelings and feeling anxiety?" His questions never felt like traps, but rather he was genuinely interested in my thinking.

"I guess…" I started to think, "Anxiety is tighter. Like, uncertainty isn't necessarily bad, but it could be. It depends on the situation, and… who you are a little."

He nodded again, slowly, understanding. "Good stuff, Mona."

He rose from his position and squatted beside my table., and scooched along between the inner and outer circles to land himself in front of Sam. I stared down at my words again as I listen to Sam explain to Mr. Howard, "It's about feeling in control. Powerful."

Brianna Rae Quinn

After Creative Writing, Sam gave me a big bear hug before setting me off to class. He apologized one more time and punctuated it with "I hope you have a better day!"

I sure hoped so. At least I had milkshakes with Raf to look forward to. The thought of seeing him alone made me feel a little better. I quickly fought through the halls to the gym locker rooms to change and get to him sooner. I wondered what he'd have to say about the confession if anything.

It just didn't make any sense to me. Frankly, I was still a virgin. I'd never had sex with anyone. I'd never even had a serious boyfriend. I had crushes, and little flings, but nothing ever went any further than the time Jackson Wright tried to stick his tongue down my throat during a game of Spin the Bottle sophomore year. I basically ripped him a new asshole and he never tried anything that stupid again.

Never Cried Wolf

As I swung the door open to walk into the gym, I noticed Raf talking to one of the other guys in class in the far corner of the room. Our gym teacher and some of my more helpful classmates were setting up the nets around the room. Today was tennis, which I was dreading. I didn't know what it was about tennis that was so hard for me, but it's like I lost all sense of speed, strength, and coordination. It was like watching a toddler try to throw a punch.

I walked over to them casually, ready to stand tall and act like everything was perfectly good and chill with me. As I approached, he didn't look up. He kept his eyes trained on the person in front of him, not daring to look at me. The boy, a classmate named Eric, turned to acknowledge me first.

"Hey, Mona, how's it going?" He asked with a malicious grin.

"Fine. And you?" *Don't show them you care,* I reminded myself.

"Good, good," he covered a laugh with a cough. "Are you sure though? You wouldn't say today… *blows*?" He held in broken chuckles.

I looked at Raf. He didn't laugh though. He looked frustrated, annoyed even. *He's so good to me*, I thought.

I rolled my eyes and returned my focus to Eric, "You really believe everything that anonymous account posts?" I questioned with a hand on my hip.

"Why would someone lie about that, Mona?" Raf jumped in. His voice was in a low growl I'd never heard. He normally spoke so warmly, but this felt so cold and sharp. I looked up at him and his eyes were dark and narrow. This was a side of him I never expected. Surely he didn't believe that ridiculous post? We've been talking for weeks.

"I don't know!" I replied, "I've been wondering the same thing all day!"

Eric sensed the tension, and I noticed his feet edge back to give us some space, depending on how big this argument got.

"I'm not stupid," he said. His tone softened to something less frustrated and more disgusted, but he held my gaze. I stared back, keeping my posture straight. I wouldn't back down on this, especially when I knew I was right. The fact that he was even entertaining believing that I had gone down on fifty guys in this school was absurd. The idea that there were fifty boys I'd even look at twice was ridiculous, particularly when they all looked and sounded as stupid as Eric Lowry whose head flipped back and forth as he waited for the next move, unsure if it would be me, or if Raf would continue.

It was me.

"You're really going to believe some *anonymous* forum of posts of strangers over me?" I shot at him.

I missed. He shot back.

Brianna Rae Quinn

"You're going to hang around Sam Tafelski on the weekends and get rides home from Oscar every day and expect me to think nothing is going on? Please. I know you're not paying any gas money. you already said Leta dropped out of your carpool… why is that by the way? Did she finally get sick of listening to you flirt with her ex in front of her?"

His hands stayed solid and unmoving in his pockets, like a statue holding firm.

"And that's only what I know about? You probably had coworkers and family friends, and whoever else that I'd never find out about. All for what? So you could go to prom? That's pathetic."

It was like the barrage of a machine gun. I felt sting after sting after sting in my chest. I lost my confidence. I felt my shoulders slump. I knew I could refute every single claim, but I could hardly imagine where to start. I was jumped with a series of accusations, and with this tweet from out of nowhere-- I was caught ridiculously off-guard.

"I told you I wasn't interested in anyone else."

"Funny way of showing it," His words were final--resolute--and that was when he looked away.

I stared at his eyes, waiting for them to look back so he could see my sincerity as I said, "I've never lied to you. Not once. Why don't you trust me?"

"Why should I? You've fucked over some of your closest friends, why should I expect to be treated differently?" His words were laced with acid, and I felt it burning on my skin.

Or maybe that burning was the feeling of eyes on me.

It was hot, I looked over to Eric, who now stared uncomfortably. I looked back in the direction of my class and saw many of them staring too at the scene we'd just made. Some were polite enough to look away when I turned, and act like they hadn't noticed, others sneered or closed their wide-open mouths.

I turned back, my eyes now anchored to my feet. "So I'll have to find another ride home then." I croaked out something slightly above a whisper. I don't think I'd ever sounded so meek. I never once considered myself a person with doubts. I always stood by my choices but now, I couldn't help but second guess. How did things fall apart like this?

"I would," were Raf's last words to me before he stalked off, with Eric following behind.

I wasn't crying, though I could feel the want welling up inside of me.

I couldn't. I had to make it home first. Not one of these assholes would have the satisfaction.

With my phone in hand, I typed out a swift message to Oscar.

Never Cried Wolf

Mona

Hey. My plans fell through.

Could I ride with you again?

Probably for the rest of the week.

Thankfully, he replied within a minute.

Oscar

No problem! I'll see you soon.

At least *something* worked in my favor today, but even after all the emotions and stress, I still had to play tennis.

Seriously, fuck tennis.

CHAPTER FOURTEEN

Sam

> Mona
>
> He was so upset. I've never
> seen him so upset

I didn't feel bad. As Mona texted me throughout the night, telling me about Rafael's big blow-up at her, I found myself feeling somewhat proud. It could only be likened to unwrapping a Christmas present without tearing a single sheet of paper. The edges were clean.

there were no loose ends, just the perfect fall, exposing the true insides.

> Mona
>
> I didn't even know what to say.
> Everything he said was so out of
> left field. Like I'm some
> pathological liar.

And it did feel like a gift. The universe was finally on my side. Surely our meeting was no coincidence. I saw this reconnection as the opportunity it was. This was a sign that all that had been wronged would be right once again, and it only took two short weeks to watch Mona start to shatter from the inside out.

> Mona
>
> Like I'm the boy who cried
> fucking wolf... I have never cried
> wolf once in my fucking life.

Of course, I played dumb. She said she wouldn't let this get to her. The tweet, the stares, and the whispers. I could see her slowly coming apart. Her once deliberate speech had become hesitant. She seemed to be thinking harder about what she had to say now-- almost like maybe she believed she may have been that liar and manipulator. Like she could see what I'd been seeing.

Mona

I can't breathe. I'm just so
frustrated and I don't know how
to fix this.

Perhaps it is true, she never told outright lies. She never cried wolf in that way-- but she knew the wolf was there, preying on the chickens, and said *nothing*. I was partial to thinking that was considerably worse.

Mona

I don't know what I did to
deserve this.

I did.

Never Cried Wolf

How incredibly vain of her to believe she'd never done anything so wrong. It seemed to me she was fairly honest with everyone excluding herself, and this change I'd set into motion was like a beautiful piece of art-- a little dab of watercolor, branching and bleeding out from a single touch, a ripple from a thrown stone. And I had done it all myself.

The very next day, in Creative Writing again, I studied her features. I watched her brown eyes droop like melting chocolate, her hair tied into a knot at the back of her neck. There were little wisps of hair trailing down her back onto a thick, fleece sweatshirt that looked a little too big for her. Her jeans were not cuffed to fake a tailored look. they were simple, unripped, and blue. There was no French tuck to define her waist. She left her earrings at home, and her necklace was hiding in her chest.

She wouldn't admit it, but she was hiding. Mona didn't look disheveled, but she was blending in. something I had never seen her do.

She could have been anyone today, not the Mona with a distinct sense of style. Mona with beautiful sweaters and jeans with embroidered pockets. She was usually so textured, even her hair always had a crimp, bounce, or curl… but today she looked flat and uninteresting. She blended into the wall.

"Today's assignment," Mr. Howard began, clicking into the next slide on the projector, "will be another comparison poem. However!" He held a finger over his head in a dramatic motion as he readies us for the "twist" of the assignment. "I want to give you some freedom within form today. Four stanzas, four lines each. Free verse is fine, just ensure you add in that comparison. Work with your friends next to you as you see fit. I'm going to come around and conference with a couple of you to build writing goals for the rest of the semester."

I nodded and yanked my spiral notebook out of my backpack. It was so cramped in there. the spiral was a little flatter than it should have been. I forced the cover open and fiddled with it until it laid flat enough to write.

"Write about whatever is on your mind-- how are you feeling today? What happened this morning? Describe your breakfast-- I don't care, but don't just stare! Write *something*, the rest will come," Mr. Howard said, weaving between the outer and inner circles, alternating between pointing at empty papers and searching for some in the stack in his hand.

Mona nodded as well, and slowly etched one letter at a time into his pages. She didn't speak, though.

I looked down at my paper. What was on my mind? Power, of course. I felt strong, decisive, and sure, but not without hard work. I knew what I wanted was coming to me, and all I had to do was be a little patient.

I decided the amplest comparison was a spider, preparing its web for a meal. My ideas come rolling onto the page like a landslide.

I spin gold into
My web
It's never felt
So much like home.

Where dust once
Settled I've
Replaced it with
Glitter and diamonds

I twisted the strands
To hold my weight
And prepare to capture
My prey.

I am the spider
And flies always come.
Now I simply sit
And wait.

The words had crashed on the page within minutes. Each pencil marking and crack between the lines, sharing the truth of myself. I stared down at my writing and smiled. I like the assonance punctuating the last two stanzas. It made me giddy to read and thrilled with my own creativity. It wasn't Shakespeare, to be sure, but I liked writing something about something positive for once. I'd gotten so used to lamenting in my writing, and really exposing my emotions-- this was a different kind of exposure, though still hidden behind the metaphor of the spider.

Mona's chin rested on her hand, smushing her cheek up into her tired eyes. She looped her words around the page, rounding out the second line in a final stanza. Her slow start must have picked up, just like Mr. Howard said.

"What are you writing about?" I asked, innocently.

Mona sighed, "I don't know, I guess. It was the first thing that came to mind."

There was that hesitance again. She'd had no problem explaining her ideas before, no matter how forced or cliché they seemed.

Brianna Rae Quinn

"Can I see?" I inquired with an eyebrow raised.

She shrugged and slid the paper to me. I scanned the partially finished piece with intention.

Desperate. Wriggling wildly.
I crave the sweet flavor
Of freedom on my tongue.
From blame. Or my sins.
Trapped in a silvery web
Of deception and lies,
Enshrouded in clouds of
Darkness again.

He cared for me
Or so he said,
Though now he only
wants me dead.

He's going for the kill,
He'll eat me alive.

Never Cried Wolf

I felt my eyes open marginally wider but caught myself before looking too surprised. Certainly, she wasn't on to me? No, this had to be about someone else. Some*thing* else.

"I'm not done yet," She offered as if to justify her writing, staring directly at her pencil as she rolled it between her fingers. Her head was still supported by her wrist, and her eyes still sagging. Was she avoiding eye contact because she knew something, or because she was dissolving into the taste of her own medicine?

"It's good," I said. How are you ending it?"

She did not answer, only pulled the paper back, and wrote in her last two lines. She'd obviously been considering them as I read.

I quickly read the final two lines.

I'm stuck in the weaving.
I am the fly.

I couldn't help it. I laughed. It was a quick snort, but a laugh nonetheless. I surprised myself as it came out.

She gave a half-hearted, fake laugh back. "That bad, huh?"

I shook my head over and over, "No, no. You don't get it," I pushed my notebook over to her and pointed to my line, "I am the spider."

Her eyes opened wide, and for a moment she started to look like herself again, "No way," she gave a genuine chuckle. Her smile was tame but real.

She wouldn't be joking with me if she meant me. It must be about Rafael. He must have been her spider. Or, at least the spider she meant.

She still didn't suspect me. She didn't suspect a thing. As far as she knew, this was just a rough week. Had I said anything yet? I needed to speak.

"Howard's going to think we planned it," I offered.

"Planned what!?" Mr. Howard slipped around the edge of the inner circle and plopped his elbows down in front of u, leading up to two hands supporting his head on loose fists. He looked like a schoolgirl waiting for the juiciest piece of gossip.

"Look," I flipped out papers toward him and pointed to our coinciding lines. "We wrote about spiders and fly, we both even mentioned the web."

"That's too funny, and such a coincidence." Mona shook her head in disbelief.

Coincidence? I wasn't so sure.

If the poem truly revealed where her mind was at in this moment, then she'd let it slip that she already felt ensnared in the web, but I wasn't going in for the kill just yet.

Just like that spider, I was still waiting. I wasn't sure what for, but if the universe was on my side (as I'd felt it had been) I just knew it would be something big.

CHAPTER FIFTEEN

Mona

I wouldn't say I've ever felt "light" or like I floated through life, but there was something so heavy about the world around me this week. My hands felt colder, I felt shorter, and all I wanted was to curl up into the heat of my own body and lay there for hours. I was lazy and lethargic, and even as the days crawled along, and the next big confession came out, I still considered any attention negative.

Never Cried Wolf

They say all press is good press, but I found that hard to believe, particularly given that I much liked my little group of friends, and it was rare that I would venture out of my comfort zone, let alone with strangers. Now every stranger read to me like an enemy. Even with a look, my fight-or-flight response kicked in. I was desperately avoiding drawing any attention to myself, and worst of all, eye contact. It was like I could read their thoughts.

That's the girl that blew 50 dudes.

She's the one who gives great head.

Does she perform as well on girls?

I bet she'd suck me off too.

It was gag-worthy-- so much so, I often did gag.

And all of this was made worse when Leta seemed to be avoiding me. No one knew her better than me. I knew she was busy, but this week felt different. The air had weight, and it was pushing me down and down and down.

Brianna Rae Quinn

When Saturday came around, she never showed up for breakfast. I ate my crispy bacon alone in my room while I sent a text.

Mona
Where are you?

Leta

Can't make it today. Something came up.

Mona
Are you okay?

Leta

Yup. Nbd.

She was being short. Curt even, and I still had no idea why. I told myself if Leta needed space, I'd give it to her. Surely she'd come tell me when she was ready. She was my best friend after all-- but that didn't exactly make everything better.

I just wanted to get through the weekend and start again Monday, but the new day didn't seem to erase everything that had happened.

Never Cried Wolf

I considered talking to mom but decided against it. There was a good chance it would turn into a discussion about safe sex. It would if they believed any of the tweets, and I couldn't bear the thought of discovering they didn't believe me either. No one seemed to but Sam.

All I wanted to do was cry and scream until all these feelings went away. I tried to Facetime Jae, but he was busy too… surprise, surprise.

Mona

Please answer. It's important.

Jae

babe, im so sry but im in class 6-9. rain check 2 tmrw

Of course I wanted to be understanding of that fact, but he never seemed to have any problem texting or taking calls in class before. And when tomorrow came, he never called. I could have tried again, but I wanted him to remember. Me, our friendship, my text, literally anything. I would have even accepted a response out of sheer curiosity or for the sake of his desperate need for gossip.

He never followed up.

So, it seems he's avoiding me too.

Monday was dark and gloomy, even as the sun rose that morning, it felt like nighttime. But even in night, there was the light of the moon and stars. This was just blacks and murky grays.

As I exited the gym's locker room and headed to the door to wait for the final bell, I avoided eye contact with Rafael. I avoided eye contact with everyone. I'd never been so desperate for a schedule change in my life, but it appeared I only had seven days from the beginning of the semester to request a change. How absolutely perfect for me that the tweet came out on day eight.

It was like living in some terrible sit-com episode in which things progressively got worse and worse, even when I thought there was no possible way for that to happen. like some underpaid network writing intern was throwing every idea he had at the wall to see what would stick-- and it all stuck. Everything around me felt too perfectly arranged and calculated, a script, followed to the letter. All that was missing was a dramatic scene of me staring out the window into the rain-- but this was winter. There was no rain, only snow. If I were crazy enough to believe my life was actually being controlled by some omniscient narrator, and this was all a part of some wild plan to set up my character development for the final season, I might have cursed out loud. but no, this was real. Sometimes things fall apart, right?

I found myself tapping my foot as I leaned against the wall, waiting, and when the bell finally rang, echoing off the walls and hammering into my ears. I took off down the hall to Oscar's classroom at the far end of the building. I'd have to walk back of course, but I would rather make the trip twice than sit and wait any more than I had to.

My schoolmates passed me in hoards, shouting at each other and clamoring for the front door. I weaved in and out of bodies all moving in the opposite direction until I spotted Oscar in the crowd, I pulled a quick one-eighty and fell into step beside him.

"Sup?" He asked, scrolling through Twitter on his phone. I only looked long enough to notice but didn't eye any of the tweets. I was (shockingly) feeling a bit removed from Twitter at the time.

"Nothing, just ready to go home."

"You working tonight?" Oscar asked, shoving his phone into his pocket.

"Yes, but I'm going in an hour later than usual. They have inventory coming in tonight, so they're letting me come an hour late as long as I stay an hour late to help," I explained.

"So you have a little extra time today?" His eyebrows rose at me.

I nodded, "Yeah-- do you need to stop somewhere before we go home?"

"No, no. Just wondering."

We broke through the doors of the school and wandered out into the parking lot. The snow had lightly dusted the sidewalks, leaving behind a clean path where the students filed out of the building and then dispersed out to their cars. I followed in the path to avoid sinking my feet into that half-inch of snow. I liked seeing sections of it untouched. I usually loved the way the snow glittered in the sun as you passed, but the dreary weather made the snow look dull and drab.

We plopped ourselves into Oscar's car silently. The engine started and we began our trip to my house.

I considered using my extra time to try and call Jae again, but I eventually decided perhaps it was better if I took a quick nap since I wouldn't be back until past ten o'clock. My phone lay in my lap as I watched the snow fall through the car window as we drove silently.

I don't know how long I'd been doing it before I realized what I was doing. I didn't want to be that cliche woman looking out the window. Yes, it was snow, but at the moment, it felt too close for comfort.

"You okay?" Oscar asked. How strange. He never asked. He had also cleverly avoided talking about anything real with me in the days since the tweet came out. His lips were tight, and he only made small talk. That's what I'd come to expect from him and our friendship. Polite conversation, even if he tried to turn it into something weird on occasion.

"Mona?" He asked.

I had gotten lost in my thoughts.

"Yeah, sorry. I'm good. Just thinking," I answered quickly.

"Of course," Oscar nodded, keeping his eyes ahead, peering through the windshield wiper as it scraped the melting snowflakes away from his view.

A beat passed before he spoke again. "I've kind of been the thinking too," he said.

"Yeah?" I wondered aloud. The space around me felt slightly heavier. The air felt hot and hard to breathe as my gut tensed like it sometimes did around him.

It was a different flip of the stomach from the ones I felt when I looked at Raf. When I saw Rafael with his deep, caramel skin, gorgeous green eyes, and bright white smile, my stomach to a full front flip, landing upright and at attention.

In these moments, with Oscar, it felt more like a half-flip, where my stomach stayed upside down and pressed into my bladder. It was uncomfortable-- it *hurt*.

"It's just that I'm only taking you home now, and it's obviously a bit out of my way. I mean, we completely pass my place to get to yours."

I narrowed my eyes, and I felt my brows knitting together. "You told me you didn't mind," I recalled.

"I know," He stopped me before I ventured too far into my statement, "But especially with this weather and how expensive gas is getting…" Was gas getting more expensive? I hadn't really noticed. "I was just thinking maybe you could, you know, pay me."

I looked away from him briefly and pulled up an image of my bank account in my head last I'd checked it. His house was less than a mile from mine. How much gas money could he really have been expecting? A dollar a day? Two? One per trip?

"Okay, do you want me to give you, like, five bucks a week or something?" I looked back at him. His eyes left the road for a moment and he scanned me up and down before facing forward again.

I felt a shutter along my body with his gaze. The fight or flight was back, it was that same feeling I'd had all week. It was his eyes.

"Not exactly, I mean, I feel kind of weird taking money from you, but I still feel like maybe you owe me a little something for all the trouble, you know?"

My breathing shallowed. My gut was pressing into me, telling me something was off, but my brain seemed to ignore all of that.

Oscar was my friend.

Oscar was Leta's ex.

Oscar would never say what I think he's saying. what I could not force my brain to articulate.

"I don't know what you could mean," I said, pointedly. Never taking my eyes off him. Suddenly, I found myself desperate for him to look at me, to see my face, and laugh when he realized I didn't find this funny.

He didn't look.

We rolled into my neighborhood. I recognized the house on the corner with the Christmas decorations still up that drove me crazy every time I passed it. At this moment, it felt trivial.

"What if you gave me a little kiss?" He asked.

His words felt slimy as they caressed my ear. I felt the peach fuzz at the back of my neck stand up.

"I don't think so, Oscar," I said in as serious a tone as I could muster.

"Come on, Mona. You *owe* me. I've been driving you all year and never asked for anything," frustration slipped between his words, nailing into me.

"You offered," I countered, but he cut me off, filling the small space with more tension.

"I *offered* when I was dating Leta. We just never reevaluated the arrangement."

I waited for a second before responding. "It's exactly because of Leta that I can't. You're her ex, and she'd be so so *so* upset." My argument felt more like begging than I liked. I wanted him to drop this and forget about it.

"Just one kiss, Mona. She doesn't have to know," Oscar spoke like a hissing snake. I couldn't believe what I was hearing. it was unreal.

Gripping the door with white knuckles, we pulled into my driveway. Although Oscar pulled up to the point where the big red door to my home lay out of my sightline, I knew it was so close. I was prepared to push my way out of the car and run, but when I pulled on the handle as the car came to a stop, the door did not open.

"What the fuck?" I growled back at him as I tried to open the door.

"*One,*" he emphasized.

I swallowed and felt my throat fall into the pit of my stomach. I felt pinpricks behind my eyes because… this wasn't happening. It couldn't be.

The denial was overflowing in me as I racked my brain desperately for some rational explanation for this situation. I knew Oscar pushed the boundaries of our friendship sometimes, but this was beyond what I'd ever expected, brazen and appalling

What could have changed? Unless *he* believed that tweet too. Could he? He was there by my side when I saw it. He saw how upset it made me… or was he just thinking about making this move the whole time? Was he plotting this? Did he double-check to make sure his doors were locked?

Should I have checked that they weren't? Was this me? Did I do this to myself? Should I have cried and fallen apart so he knew how vulnerable this ordeal had made me? Or would that have only made it worse? Was this happening now because I *was* vulnerable. Because Rafael had ended things, and now he didn't have to worry. Did he think I was rebounding?

That's when I realized he was leaning it, closing the gap with a puckered, slightly open mouth. He looked like a fish. His dark, black hair covered his forehead, reddened by the cold. His eyes closed. His hands and fingers reached for me like a greedy animal.

I squeezed my eyes shut and waited for it to be over. I was never attracted to Oscar, and even less so since he dated Leta. He was skinny, and short, with thick hair and dark eyes, and lighter skin which made his naturally dark hair stand out. But he was, by all accounts, average. There was nothing remarkable about him, in his looks, or his personality, and absolutely nothing worth jeopardizing my relationship with Leta over.

Maybe I should have told her he was being weird. Maybe--

My thoughts stopped swirling and focused only on the wet set of lips now pressed against mine. My shoulders tensed, and my lips stayed pinched shut. Just one moment and it would be over.

But it wasn't.

I suddenly felt his tongue, wrestling its way into my mouth. I reached up to his chest to push him back, but he had wrapped his arm around me to pull me close with his right arm, grabbed my hand with the left, and began to guide it toward his lap.

My eyes ripped open as I inhaled a deep gasp of shock. He took the opportunity to force his tongue behind my teeth and begin licking the insides of my mouth like a miner seeking gold. I could have thrown up right into his open mouth. I wished I would have.

He placed his hand between his legs. I felt something hard-- erect, and that's when the panic truly hit.

With adrenaline pumping through my veins, I twisted his arm loose from around me and used both hands to push him back, retracting them into myself almost immediately. I felt myself cradling inward, my knees moving up and into my chest, one hand covering my mouth, and one yanking on the door handle desperately.

I pushed and pushed on the door over and over waiting for a different result, I didn't register Oscar had a reaction at all until I heard him utter the words, "Mona, come on…"

That's when I felt the steaming tears hitting my fingers. My hand stayed cupped around my mouth, muffling a tiny sob I felt escape my lips as I tried again and again to open the door.

"Oscar, let me the fuck out right now."

"I'm sorry," he said. It felt like an instinct though, like it was the polite thing to do, not like he meant it.

"It won't happen again," he said pressing the unlock button to let me out. I practically fell against the door and out into my snow-covered driveway. The cool flakes on my face felt like freedom.

I still hadn't responded, when he said, "I'll talk to you tomorrow."

At that, I grabbed my bag out of the passenger seat floor, not bothering to take the time to get it over my shoulder before slamming the door and sprinting my way into my door.

It took five tries to finally get into the lock to make my way inside. it was hard to see past the blurring burn of tears in my eyes.

And once I was inside with the door closed and locked behind me, there was only one thought going through my head.

I have got to talk to Sam.

CHAPTER SIXTEEN

Sam

Ping.

The noise pricked my ear as my phone vibrated in my back pocket letting me know I had a message.

I pulled up to my spot in the driveway. The house vibrated with the sounds of Hannah's music blasting through the walls and windows.

I didn't turn the car off immediately, so I could feel the heat from the car blasting on me as

I shimmied my phone out of my pocket to check the ping.

It was Mona, with probably the most cryptic message I'd ever seen.

Mona
I can't believe it.

My stomach dropped. I wondered again if she knew what I had done. Had Leta said something? Did she hear from Raf about what I'd told Dante? Did she suspect at all, or was this something else entirely?

I chose to play innocent as long as I could. Not dumb, but innocent.

Sam
What do you mean? What's wrong?

I stared at the screen anxiously waiting for her reply. I noticed three dots bubbling at the bottom of my screen, bouncing to let me know she was responding. How long would it be? Was this a paragraph? A rant to read another two years from now how desperately she wanted me to go fuck myself? Another nasty comment look back on when--

Oh. She'd responded already. Short and sweet. She must and been typing and deleting a lot. All the message said was,

Mona
Oscar.

My eyes narrowed.

Sam
What about him?

I looked up and took in my surroundings. A windy day, but no snow. The sidewalk snow had mostly melted, likely leaving behind some black ice. I never went to find out, but always assumed. The sky was covered in fluffy white clouds. It was really a lovely day, despite the winter chill. My car's interior had warmed up with the heater. I could see the hot steam of my exhaust like a breath in the cold air, clouding around outside-- adding the shroud of mystery to the situation that felt a bit more appropriate.

I really should have gone inside instead of sitting in the car, staring at my phone for minutes on end, waiting for her response. My curiosity gripped me. I found myself counting the repeating bounce of the speech bubble until a new message finally took its place.

Forty-six.

Mona

You can't tell Leta.

Couldn't I? My eyebrows popped. The potential of this situation had suddenly doubled. I already had Leta questioning her relationship with Mona, avoiding her like the plague. Perhaps this might be the final nail in the coffin.

What have you done, Mona? I found myself wondering. Of course, I couldn't phrase my response like that. So, instead, I typed…

Sam

Did something happen between

you 2 on your way home?

I thought I already knew the answer, but the devil was in the details. I needed to know everything. My brain immediately flooded with questions that I should or shouldn't ask-- many of them the same, only rephrased in a slightly less accusatory way.

The continuation of my revenge hinged only on the idea that everyone trusted me. So I resigned to being cordial, non-judgmental, and above all-- naive.

Again, it's not playing *dumb*, it's *innocent*. That's the narrative I had to spin. the plot I would write.

Mona

Can you come over so I can talk
about this? I don't want to type it
all out, and I have less than an
hour before work. I'm a total
mess, Sam. It took me 10
minutes just to calm down
enough to text you.

I thought about it for an honest moment, but no. Whatever she was about to say, I wanted it in writing. Dad always said stuff like that when he complained about coworkers. "Can I get that in writing?"

Having something in writing makes it permanent. Only speaking words out loud means they could be lost in the wind, and float away, out of your grasp. Written words made statements permanent and most importantly, reproducible.

Sam

I'm sorry, I'm chauffeuring
Hannah around today… Can you
tell me the gist? Like… two
sentences or less?

That ought to do it. No details. No buts or caveats. I wanted this text in its most ambiguous form. She typed, then deleted. Then typed. Then deleted. She was fumbling over her words, deciding what was the most important to say. I wanted to be answered. I needed them like air. I felt myself holding my breath and my impatience effervesced into a second message, adding pressure, and hopefully, prompting some oversimplification.

Sam

I'm about to get in the car again.

It came fast. Frantic. It was exactly what I was hoping for.

235

Mona

Oscar kissed me. Car rides
home = sexual favors.

This was it. The smoking gun. I had
exactly what I needed to help Leta see Mona the
way I saw her. Sneaky, underhanded, secret-
keeping, messing-around-with-her-best-friend's-
ex type. The rejecting type.

My breathing was slow and methodical. I
knew my next move with Leta, but what was
there to say to Mona now?

The series of messages that came next
was fast. The wait time was non-existent and we
bounced messages back and forth so I could fully
understand what had happened.

Sam

Did you kiss him back?

Mona

He locked the door. He
TRAPPED me.

Sam

I don't understand

Mona

He told me I OWED him. For all
the rides. He said he just wanted
one kiss.

Sam

That's all?

Mona

Well, no. He shoved his tongue
down my throat and tried to get
me to touch him…

Sam

Touch him?

Mona

Like… his dick.

The last message gave me pause. I hated
Mona, but if she was telling the truth, that's a
really fucked up thing to do.

I felt a switch flip in my head. Suddenly,
I didn't want ambiguity. I needed details. I
wanted to know everything.

Sam

Mona, that's super fucked.

Mona

I know. I'm crying. I can't stop.

But I didn't pause long. I started reading into these messages like I was goddamn Sherlock Holmes. Where were the holes? Where were the lies? Why would she lie?

Was she… not lying?

Could I believe that Oscar was capable of this behavior?

Sam

Did he, like… do anything to you?

I wasn't sure how specific I wanted to be. Could he have hurt her? Assaulted her? Worse? Did that happen to people I knew? It seemed like I was so removed from things like that-- like this tiny midwestern town on a lake where people took their kids fishing, and left their doors unlocked had anyone capable of such evil. It was almost unbelievable.

Mona

I got away. Just started crying
and I think I freaked him out
enough to let me go. He
unlocked the door and I just ran.
It was so rapey, and I just can't
relax.

That was it? I wanted to ask.

He kissed her, had a little tongue, and the door was locked. Who was to say that wasn't a coincidence? Women like men who take initiative I thought. Hell, *I* had kissed her. Does that mean she thought I was "rapey"? A rapist? Me?

At that moment, I felt a flood of red on my face. My blood was boiling at the thought that two years ago, Mona would have been texting Leta about how I was "rapey".

This bitch was willing to ruin my life and now wants to ruin Oscar's? For *what*?

I noticed the dots bouncing again. I let out an ironic, exasperated laugh.

"What more could you possibly have to say?" I grumbled out loud. I heard a growl at the back of my throat.

Mona

Can you take me home for the
rest of the week?

I was mad. Madder than I had felt with Mona since we reconnected. It was like opening the wounds all over again. I felt the seams ripping away from the inside, letting the rage bubble right under the surface of my eyes, my nails, and my lips.

At least now, it all made sense! Oscar asked for some sort of payment for the rides home. She didn't want to give it, and now she's coming up with some shitty revenge plot of her own? Coming up with some horrible, miserable excuse so I might take pity on her and go out of *my* way to take her home?

Never Cried Wolf

Was this the plan all along? Once again, she wanted something from me. Once again, she ruined someone… or at least tried to.

I typed my response carefully, and measuredly. I wanted to be sure that the fire I felt did not show. Seething, but methodically, I reread my message, and tapped "send."

Sam
Of course. G2g. Talk soon.

I threw my phone on the passenger seat and stared ahead at the closed garage door of my house, which still vibrated violently to the incessant boom of Hannah's amplifier. Suddenly, the sensation didn't seem so bad.

Suffering the pressure of the sound waves pushing back against the anger that was trying so desperately to wrestle out of me seemed ideal. I needed something to keep the monster in his cage-- to mellow me out. I grabbed my bag and phone and quickly twisted the ignition off to head inside and, quite literally, face the music.

I started this plot to avenge myself. I began my journey for selfish reasons, I could admit that. But now, something more was at risk. Leta, Oscar, Rafael. I knew what I had to do. I had to save them.

They did not have to be a part of her game.

I wouldn't be either.

Not anymore.

CHAPTER SEVENTEEN

Mona

Oscar was silent. He didn't send any texts or try to call. For some reason, this was simultaneously exactly what I wanted, and totally infuriating. I wanted a genuine apology or an explanation. I wanted to understand better what had happened. But at the same time, the very thought of speaking to him made my eyes burn again.

I had tried and failed to keep myself together the night before, at work. A coworker tapped my shoulder while I was steaming milk for a latte and I could have sworn I jumped out of my own skin. She apologized profusely. I told her I was fine, but she could tell from the involuntary shakes in my hand as I poured the milk into the mug that I was decidedly not.

In the last week, I had felt more watched than ever, like I was prey being stalked. From the tweet from Kettlewood Confessions to this strange, isolating energy surrounding me, I knew something was wrong, but I had no idea where to begin looking. It took all of my willpower to pretend things were fine for the rest of the night.

Deep breath in… deep breath out, but the effort of staying calm raked away at my brain. Completing inventory was a surprisingly relaxing activity. It kept my mind off of the incessant, nagging feeling of being beaten in the legs until I fall.

I found myself desperate for comfort more than I'd felt in a while. I always thought it was easy for me to feign confidence. I don't know if I ever considered myself "confident" by definition, but my pride was an image best kept up. I found myself looking into the mirror that Tuesday morning and lacking the motivation to do… anything. What was the point of brushing my hair, covering the zit on my forehead, and even putting in the effort to wear a matching outfit if I knew people were thinking badly of me anyway?

Why was I trying so hard to impress a crowd of strangers in school who have made their minds up about me? If I wore a shapeless sweatshirt and baggy jeans, would they change their minds? Would they see I was not a run-of-the-mill skank, but rather the victim of a nasty rumor? Or would they laugh at how I tried to hide it? Deny it?

Do I even want to be seen as a victim?

It felt like a lifetime that I stared into my own eyes through the mirror. I wasn't sure what I was seeing, but I didn't like it. It was wilted along the edges, but still holding its shape. I just had to cling onto that shred of dignity still holding strong.

My pupils were pin-pricks, making the warm brown of my eyes stand out against the pale whitish yellow of my sallow under-eye skin. I didn't want to see them any more than I had, so I averted my eyes from my reflection and loosely brushed the tangles from my hair, wrapping the long, red tendrils into a low bun, then pulling it out again, favoring the way they covered my face. If I swooped it over into a side part just right, it covered that pimple on my forehead.

I pulled on a thick black turtleneck and considered my options for layering. Usually, I would have selected a blazer. Something vintage, floral, or jacquard. Something with gold fibers that made me twinkle. This time, I was drawn to an oversized sweater vest. Cable knit. Cream.

Was I even thinking in full sentences anymore? It was hard to tell. These trivial decisions were made dull and succinct to make room for the processing of the remaining mess of my life. A quick pair of jeans and some black oxfords later, and I was ready to go.

That's when it came.

Oscar
Still need a ride?

My heart leaped into my throat. I tried to swallow. I *wanted* to swallow and push it back down, but instead, I choked on that fresh lump in my neck. I felt the sobs coming.

I looked down the hall to mom and dad's room. Their door was closed. I could have asked one of them for a ride to school, but then they'd know something was wrong (and the idea of dealing with my mother's pre-coffee morning rage seemed exasperating.)

The time was 7:05am. I still technically had enough time to catch the bus, but I wasn't totally prepared for that particular hellscape.

Which was the lesser of the two evils? I tossed a glance over my shoulder back down to my parents.

The choice was clear. I'd take a familiar evil over the unknown any day of the week.

I slipped down to the master bedroom and slipped the door open. The strip of light miraculously fell on my mother's eye line beside the door.

I saw her squeeze her eyes extra tight before opening one. Her pupil shrunk to a tiny hole, as mine were mere minutes before. People always told me I looked like my mother, but I didn't really get it until this moment when I took a full minute to realize I wasn't back in the bathroom looking at my sad reflection in the mirror.

"What's wrong, baby?" Mom croaked with her freshly awoken voice.

"I need a ride to school,"

"You can't ride with Oscar?" She asked.

I felt a jab of betrayal in my gut, although I knew she had no idea, it still hurt. I never asked her for rides to work. I found myself wishing she would just recognize that and go without question.

In response to her question, I only shook my head, and once again tried to swallow my heart back down my esophagus.

"Okay," she groaned, rolling over onto her elbows. "Make coffee. I'll get pants on."

I nodded, shuffling back down the hallway to pop a K-cup in the Keurig.

That was relatively painless, I found myself thinking. There was almost no whining. Could this have just been a good morning? Or did she immediately know something was wrong?

That must have been it-- why else would she have asked "what's wrong?" so immediately.

As the coffee dripped into the mug, I typed my response to Oscar. I wrote it in the Notes App first so I could copy and paste it into the chat. I didn't want him to know how long it took me to figure out my message, and more so, I didn't want to have to see his name on my screen while I figured it out either.

Brianna Rae Quinn

And as I typed, I found myself more frustrated with *my*self for not asking Sam to take me to school in the morning too. I would have to ask him that day.

Mona

No. Got it.

The only really debatable part of the message was whether or not to say "thanks". I opted not to because frankly, I didn't feel as though he deserved my thanks anymore. Not if I was *paying* for his shitty car rides.

I couldn't even really tell if I was more sad or angry. It changed from minute to minute, depending on which invasive thought plagued me. At this moment, I was mad.

As I capped the steaming travel mug of coffee (overloaded with French vanilla creamer) for mom, she closed her bedroom door, leaving dad soundly snoring inside, and snagged her keys and coat off the rack, immediately ready to go out to the car.

She may have been tired, but she was still as efficient as ever.

We wordlessly made our way out to the car, leaving our footprints in just the barest millimeter of fresh snow on the pathway to her car.

As we settled in, closing the doors on the chills outside, I could tell mom was deeply regretting not telling me to auto-start the car while I was making the coffee, but there was nothing to be done about it just then.

She revved the engine and almost immediately began backing out of the driveway without putting her seatbelt on.

"Mom, belt." I reminded her. She scowled at me slightly, then pulled the belt over her chest before shifting into drive.

I didn't think not having a car would be so frustratingly difficult. Everything usually worked out when your friends and job were within walking distance, and one of those friends always gave you a ride. I guessed I never imagined running into this particular problem.

Mom and I rode in silence for most of the ride. She sipped desperately on her coffee, probably with as much intent to warm up and wake up.

As we pulled up into the row of cars with parents dropping off their children, at the school, mom's voice finally broke the silence.

"Are you okay, Dezzy?"

My ears pricked a little at the phrase. Mom rarely called me Dezzy anymore. It was my preferred nickname in elementary school before switching to a much more mature-sounding Mona in the sixth grade. Beyond that, I thought Mona suited me better. Mona felt big, like the Mona Lisa. She was formal and serious. Dezzy was more childlike and cutesy-- someone who still needed a mom.

Though just then, I wondered if I'd started feeling more like a Dezzy again. Could I feel as I had been feeling and still have the right to be Mona? I sure didn't feel like a Mona.

Or was I back somewhere in the middle, where I could choose? Was I Desdemona again? Undecided on my fate? My identity?

"You look upset, and something seems off." Mom continued when I didn't answer.

When had I become so quiet? When did I start thinking so much before I spoke?

"It's fine, it's just been a long few days." That was mostly the truth. I could live with that explanation.

I only hoped mom would accept it. She didn't have long to question me before I popped the car door open to hop out and thanked her for getting up early for me.

"Anything you need, sweetie. I'm always here."

It was those words that let me know she didn't believe me. I couldn't blame her. I barely believed myself. How could I when no one else did?

*　　　*　　　*

Before asking Sam to travel halfway across town to pick me up for school in the morning, I considered one more course of action: Leta.

We usually shared third-period study hall together, and though she'd been working on some projects in the days prior, I finally caught her at a table in the back of the study hall room.

"Leta!" I cried, thrilled to finally see my friend after nearly a week apart. "I didn't realize you were here. I was sitting at our usual table."

I slipped into the seat beside her at a small two-person table against the windows. I never wanted to sit here in the winter because of how cold the air felt.

"Just trying to get some work done," she replied, not looking up from the Chromebook on which she was typing furiously.

I nodded slowly. Why had my heart leaped back into my throat?

'Well, I can leave you to it, I just wanted to know if maybe I could join in on your carpool to school in the mornings? It's weird not seeing you." I chose to leave out any details about Oscar. besides, I certainly didn't want her to think this was more about my disdain for Oscar than my love for her.

She shook her head, "Can't."

She did not elaborate. She still did not look at me. Clearly, this was not a negotiable situation.

"Okay. I get it." My swallows strained again. Was I about to cry? Was I that desperate? I waited a moment, steadying my voice, before saying, "So I don't think I'm going Prom at all. Shit kind of hit the fan with Raf, and--" she cut me off.

"Mona, I'm working." Her words were razor-sharp. I hadn't heard her like this in a long time-- if ever.

"No, I know. I'm just trying to say I miss you, and if you're going to be so busy, maybe we can just set some time aside sometime… like, prom night… to have a girl's night, just the two of us? I know it's far off, but…" This time I trailed off naturally.

"I'm already going to Prom," Leta said after a moment of silence. Her blonde curls were so rigid and unmoving. Their bounce was missing, Leta's winsome tone now felt stark and pained.

All I could think to ask was, "With who?"

"Sam."

My mouth shut as I considered her words. Sam did say he planned to ask someone. Why hadn't he mentioned it was Leta? Why hadn't Leta mentioned it?

The silence was so loud. she had stopped typing but still hadn't looked up.

"Are you upset?" I finally asked, feeling my words slipping through the invisible barrier between us like light through blinds. Only pieces reached the other side for Leta to recognize.

"I have *work* to do, Mona. I told you. I'll call you when I'm ready to talk or whatever."

She cleaned needed time and space, for what, I wasn't sure. I always ran straight *to* Leta when I was upset, but maybe she was different. Maybe whatever happened was different, and she just needed to be alone.

It wasn't often Leta was negative. She had bad days, of course, but even when they came, she never dwelled on the bad. She was an optimist at heart. What could have made that change in her?

Then again, could this have all been in *my* head?

Maybe this was just bad timing, and I was looking for another bad thing to add to the absolute trainwreck that had been the last few days.

If this was rock bottom, there was nowhere else to go but up.

I just needed to wait this out, just like everything else.

"Sure. I'll see you around then," I got up, pushed my chair in, and began my short walk across the room, back to the table I'd come from. My books and papers still strewn about the table, waiting.

And all I heard in parting from Leta was a simple "mm."

CHAPTER EIGHTEEN

Sam

I ripped through my bag trying to find whatever remnants of my math homework from the day before were stuffed in any available crevice. I could have sworn I'd seen it in between my history textbook and a folder for science, but, to be fair, there were about seven other rumpled sheets of paper in that same spot, and when I pulled it out, it wound up being a worksheet from the first quarter.

Brianna Rae Quinn

My mom always told me I was one of the messiest children she'd ever had to deal with. I resented her comment every time she made it. I could clean this trainwreck up any time I wanted-- it was keeping it clean that was the issue. Whenever I got around to cleaning out my backpack (usually at about that time of the year), it took forever. It was exhausting and undoubtedly ended in papercuts that I didn't care to receive.

Every stressor in my life came down to one thing. Time. I didn't have the time or the energy to deal with it properly. If I had the time to take my folder out of my bag and gently insert my work into one pocket and gently put it back, I would-- just like I would take the time to clean out my bag if I had the time just then, but I couldn't take that time because I *had* to finish my math homework before study hall was over.

My priorities were relatively well in check.

Never Cried Wolf

"Finally!" I grumbled, maybe a bit too loudly as I managed to get my fingers pinched around the right page in my collection of old classwork and slipped it out onto the table.

I glanced up to make sure no one looked in my direction. No. It was almost as if everyone was too focused on their own work to care about me struggling with my dumpster fire of a book bag.

It was at that moment I noticed, just a few tables down from me in the crowded study hall room, sat Oscar.

I don't think I'd ever realized we'd shared a study hall together. Perhaps it was new with the change in the semester only a few weeks prior, but I couldn't recall seeing him in this room with me before.

I caught myself staring, contemplating Mona's story. I'd found myself wondering a lot since our brief text conversation the night before. I tried to imagine it, Oscar's hands holding Mona by the waist, wrapping around her neck, gripping her tight.

Is that how it might have happened?

His mouth pressed against hers, a tongue breaking through parted lips to explore the insides…

So wet.

Hot.

Breathing into me. Breathing back. Did he pant and murmur words I'll never be certain of, so caught up in the moment?

Could he have slipped one of those hands into my back pocket and squeezed and caressed so I could feel him pressed up against me? Could I have--

Wait… *I*?

Mona.

I meant Mona, of course.

This had happened to Mona, not me? Why was I suddenly the star of this little fantasy?

I supposed my empathy got away from me. I was trying so desperately to understand

Mona's feelings, I must have dived a little too deep into her shoes and found myself there, wrapped in Oscar's reasonably muscular arms and feeling the slip of his puffed lips over my own, swollen from the pressure and the passion of our kiss.

Her kiss.

Oh boy.

Thunk. I'd hoped the noise and vibration of my bag dropping to the ground beside me might shake me out of my visions.

I scooched my chair up under the desk further to hide my legs and turned my head to my math homework.

I groaned. The mental shift from where my mind had just been to math was like a first attempt at a backflip-- far too complicated without any practice or training. Nearly impossible.

If anything, that moment was the wake-up call I needed-- I absolutely had to stop sympathizing with Mona. This was far too uncomfortable, and it made this sticky and complicated. I didn't care for this feeling or explaining it.

Okay, Find the axis of symmetry and vertex of the following parabola: $y=x2-3x-5$. I read the directions once. Twice. Then a third time. Was I just not paying attention? Where else was my mind settling?

I knew, of course, but again, priorities. Did I have the time to entertain these thoughts I had of Oscar? No, absolutely not-- then why wouldn't they go away?

I looked over my shoulder again to the table where he sat.

I could go over and talk to him, but it sure felt risky. I wasn't certain how to stir the pot with this new information without totally crumbling the trust I'd built up with Mona. Was I ever far enough in my little plan to sacrifice it?

I tapped my pencil on the table. *Tap tap tap tap tap.*

Fuck it.

Never Cried Wolf

I pushed my chair away from the table and stood confidently, loosely, and nonchalantly headed a few tables down to where Oscar was typing a text into his phone just under the table so the study hall monitor couldn't see.

"Hey," I said, dropping myself into the chair across from him.

He looked up with confusion rippling over his features. He really was not that handsome, judging solely on his face, but he was probably passable to some women… or men, or whoever.

"Hey." He replied, locking his phone from under the table, and slipping it under his leg to sit on it. He didn't seem particularly friendly and actually looked quite suspicious.

He must have known I was friends with Mona. I wondered in that moment, (as he looked at me with the same expression one would make after smelling a fart) if he assumed I was there to call him out over what happened with Mona the night before.

Perhaps he thought Mona had told me everything, which, of course, she had-- but what he didn't know was how badly I wasn't buying her little cry for attention.

I could feel his gaze etching into my face as he scrutinized my intentions. I kept my face neutral, waiting to see if he'd break and speak first, or if I'd have to.

"What do you want?" He asked.

"Umm…" I grimaced and looked around for anything to possibly distract me long enough to formulate a plan.

Do I even need one? I wondered. Everything else had already gone so well. did I even need to think? Had I already positioned Mona's reputation on the line and all I needed was a push for everyone to watch her crash and burn with me?

More importantly-- was Oscar the type to defend her if I told him what she told me?

No. Probably not.

"I talked to Mona last night, and I just thought it was really fucked up what she was saying, and I thought you deserved to know."

I don't remember thinking of those words before I said them-- they came out fairly quickly.

I watched with morbid satisfaction as his eyes brown eyes darkened from suspicion to primal fury, with the faintest hint of a snarl over his lips. I felt a pang of curiosity about what they might feel on mine once more before taking a breath to maintain my composure.

"What did she say exactly?" Oscar inquired in a low grumble. His fingers laced together into a ball on the table, looking equal part apex predator and driven by a business translation. He wanted my information-- would he be willing to trade it for silence?

"I don't want her to know I said anything. I'm not trying to cause problems," I offered. It was definitely a fib. How could anyone do what I was doing and insist they weren't trying to cause problems? Yet, in a more realistic sense, I was definitely trying to keep some trust-- perhaps the killing blow was yet to come? Why stop here when there was the possibility to go higher-- the pro-revenge to end all pro-revenge.

"She's not even talking to me right now, so I think it's safe to say I won't tell her you said anything." He resigned to say with a sigh to relax himself a bit and appear slightly less feral.

He was mad. I could tell, and I hoped that was a good thing for me.

Time to take the plunge.

"She said you tried to rape her."

Oscar's eyes widened in disbelief. The same disbelief I had imagined.

"Rape?" he clarified. I nodded in response.

"*She*," he started, "Let me kiss her! Just sat right there and let it happen! No fight, no argument! She only got freaked out because of Leta! I bet she's just trying to save face, so she doesn't feel like a terrible friend for making out with me, or whatever. And she wants to cry *rape* because she made a bad choice? She didn't *have* to kiss me." He was babbling a bit, I could tell.

And as he spoke, I felt validated. I knew it. I knew Oscar wouldn't have forced Mona to do anything. I knew there must have been more than she was saying, and she must have just been telling me this wild story so that if and when Leta ever found out, she could deny it and say she was forced into it.

"*Asking* for a kiss isn't *rape*," He continued. "Women always love the spontaneous shit, and they cry rape when they regret it later." He threw his hands out in a motion, shoving the ridiculousness of it all off of him.

He slumped back into his chair with his arms crossed, and a scowl across his face. I glanced around the other tables. I noticed some eyes flicking our way, but no heads. It seems some people heard. Let's hope their present discretion didn't translate so much. Nothing seemed more delicious to me than having this little morsel spread about.

This was serious shit Mona was talking about, and making light of it for some ridiculous pride is unacceptable. She needed to own her mistakes, and take some accountability, just like everyone else.

"I'm really sorry. Like I said, I thought you deserved to know," I offered.

"I'm glad you did. I'm so done with that fucking whore. She better keep her nose down and stay away from me. I'm not holding back next time she opens her mouth." He was explosive, and it felt good to see.

"I get that," I affirmed.

I looked over my shoulder to my worksheet, still sitting unfinished at my table. "You know, I got some homework to finish, so I'll just leave you now." I attempted to excuse myself, but he stopped me.

"Nah, man. Bring it over here. You don't have to sit alone," he offered in a much more relaxed tone. How could this nice guy have ever done something so egregious as an attempted assault on a woman? It didn't make any sense.

He welcomed me to his study hall table. We talked about whatever, shooting the breeze, and lamenting about calculus on the whole until the bell rang. He bid each other farewell and promised to catch up again the next day, where we'd meet at this same table again.

I'd made a friend.

All things considered, Oscar was perfectly pleasant, and Mona had tried to ruin him to protect her own dignity and reputation. A reputation that had frankly been fouled long before.

In Creative Writing that day, as I listened to her wonder, "Is Leta upset with me? Why doesn't Rafael believe me? Why would Oscar do such a thing?" I played so flawlessly dumbfounded at how all of this could be happening. I watched the beams crack and bend all around her.

Soon enough, that bridge would have been fully burnt.

And every time I walked away from these little interactions. I wondered again if all this really made things better. Was all this effort going to make me feel good? And so far, yes.

I was like a composer, listening to my song-- crashing cymbals in the percussion line, and letting the sound reverb until they cracked again.

I was the omniscient narrator, orchestrating her demise-- and it was so damn empowering to finally be the one in the driver's seat.

"You can still take me home tonight, right?" Mona's words broke the spell allowing me to revel in my fortitude.

"Of course!" I replied. "I'd never let you down."

CHAPTER NINETEEN

Mona

Kettlewood Confessions

@KWHS_Confess

12 minutes ago

"Everyone in this school is fake as fuck. Can't wait for college."

I stared at the words as I walked through the halls. It was Wednesday, and Tuesday had just felt so exhaustingly long. These words resonated with me in a way I couldn't quite describe. I could feel that frustration in my bones, radiating out of me. Every move I made and every word I spoke was dripping with this level of cynicism. The worst part about it was how badly I was craving positive energy. Yet, I just couldn't muster up the motivation to fight off my foul moods. Life had been so sucked out of me, and I wondered how much of that had to do with being without Leta.

She was still acting strangely. I spent so much free time trying to catalog all the reasons why she might be avoiding me. It had been a week, and nothing was looking up.

I was at a desperate loss for an action plan. This sitting-and-waiting nonsense just wasn't working out for me. My body was unsteady, and my sleep was nonexistent. I found myself going to Sam with more and more, unloading my feelings until I could have sworn he was tired of hearing it, but he always listened and never complained.

Never Cried Wolf

"I feel bad," I'd said to him at lunch the day before. "I feel like all I'm doing is complaining, and I'm doing all the talking all the time. How are *you*?" I tried to turn it around. Maybe I would feel better if I could focus on something other than the present state of misery I found myself swallowed in-- the belly of the whale I could not escape.

Things were darker. Dank and uninviting. I was paranoid that something was out to get me, whether it be the universe or something more concrete, I couldn't be sure.

"Don't worry about it," Sam answered. "I don't mind listening to you talk." His response was so genuine. I had no idea why anyone would want to listen to me wallow in self-pity for hours on end, but Sam always did, and he never complained.

At that time, it was becoming clearer and clearer to me that he was my closest friend. We'd gotten over the hump of an awkward reconnection. We'd rebuilt the bridge I thought he'd burnt all those years ago, and we were able to pick up where we left off.

He came back into my life at just the right time-- I needed him now more than ever, and his willingness to be my go-to person and confidant for nothing in return was nothing short of Christ-like behavior. Not that I imagined relationships were transactional in any way, but more reciprocal. I always surrounded myself with people who would do the same for me that I'd done to them-- partners and teams to get through the hard stuff together. I hadn't at the opportunity to prove my respect and gratitude to Sam just yet. I wanted to be a friend to him in the same way he was to me, but it felt so stupid to be blindly wishing for something terrible to happen to him so *I* could help him through it. For all he spoke, things were going fairly well for him.

"No complaints," and "I'm having a surprisingly good day," were accompanied by layers of ambiguity and no details were common. I remembered him having much more to say in years past. I wondered if that's what it was like to be content, or complacent. Things were going exactly as he'd hoped-- what was there to discuss?

Jae had sent me a message the night before around two. After restlessly tossing about my bed for several hours, I was relieved that when I checked my phone this time, there would be something new there to see.

Jae

thinking about u!

I almost leaped out of my bed to reply. My fingers frantically, desperately tapping at the screen, hoping I would be able to finally speak to him after weeks of near silence. A little shred of hope ripped open inside of me, and I felt some light pour in again.

Mona

I'm actually awake right now.

Can I call you?

I don't know why I expected any other response than the one I got.

Jae

sry bb roommate asleep. soon tho!

My fingers did not even begin to type a response. Instead, I laid back down, pulling my duvet up to my neck and wrapping it tightly around my body. I stared at my phone, resting at the edge of my nightstand, letting the wet corners of my eyes drain out and soak into my pillowcase. I wasn't quite to the point of sobbing, but I could tell I was damn close to a full breakdown.

I couldn't have been greedy. That message brought enough light in to at least get me through this day- over the hump and into the weekend. I had *something*, however small.

Of course, just then, walking into the hardest part of my day, it felt like that shred of light was getting sewn up tight. My feet carried me, unwillingly, to math class when I would sit in the same room as Oscar and avoid even looking in his direction for as long as possible. Yesterday, he had done the same to her, electing to avoid the awkwardness.

My shoulders dropped in a display of calm, but so tight, if someone tried to move me, I'd be a statue, like an elastic band, ready to snap.

I suppose there was one more blessing in this ginormous shitstorm that was my daily life as of late-- my math teacher didn't have assigned seating. I walked into the classroom, took one of the desks toward the back that were always available, and kept my head down until the final bell rang, allowing the period to begin.

"Alright, class," the teacher's voice filled the room over the sounds of zippers and crumpling paper while the class prepared for the lesson.

"Last Friday, we started our project by selecting a research article and reading all the literature and methodology. Today is part two. Get back with your partners from Friday and we're going to plot the data from these articles into the bell curve."

Partners. I looked up at the board, immediately reminded of this project from Friday. *Oscar* was my partner. *Fuck, fuck fuck, fuckity fuck. What do I do? What do I say? Do I say anything? FUCK.*

Anyone could see the panic on my face. My eyes felt wide. I was blinking more frequently to combat how dry they were being exposed to so much more air. I took a deep breath in through my nose blew it back out through my mouth. This was it. I had to do or say something that minute.

Talk to the teacher. Say you don't want to work with Oscar anymore.

No. Don't. Then you'll have to explain why. What would you even say?

Whatever voice was talking to me in my head was not mine, or maybe it was. It was me talking, but outside of my head, yelling at my body to do something… *anything.*

Try talking to Oscar first.

No. I don't want to.

Well, tough shit! If you won't tell the teacher, then you have to talk to him anyway.

Maybe he won't say anything about it?

Maybe.

Could I do this? Could I pretend it didn't happen?

I guess I had to.

I stood up abruptly while my classmates were seating themselves comfortably with their partners-- laughing and joking like nothing was wrong. Like the world was not crumbling beneath my feet.

Every step felt shakier as I moved to my old desk, on the far left of the classroom, right next to Oscar's.

I sat down, wordlessly. I didn't even look.

"You have some fucking balls on you if you think we're still working together," Oscar's familiar voice lashed my ears.

I shot a shocked glance up at him. He'd never spoken to me like that... he'd never looked at me like that. His nostrils flared like a dragon's, ready to breathe steam and fire. The lines between his brows were thick, firm, and unmoving, and his thin mouth stretched into a tight line.

"Excuse me?" I felt the burn of anger at the back of my mouth, ready to spew pure vitriol at him. Like *I'd* made some fatal error by approaching *him*? What the hell was he on about?

"You heard me. I don't work with two-faced skanks," he hissed at me.

"Two-faced? Are you *kidding*?" These were the only words I could muster as my brain grasped at straws, trying to rationalize how my rejecting him made a skank? Not to mention two-faced? Did he somehow think I was *leading him on*? That was a fucking laugh.

"Are *you*?" He slammed his hands on the desk, garnering some jumps and shocked stares from the two groups nearest us. He stood up and pointed a finger at me, not two inches from my eyes. "You are a lying *bitch*, and I ain't messing around with your shit anymore. Watch your *fucking* mouth with me you desperate. *Disgusting.* Whore.*" He didn't yell. He didn't have to yell. His words were pointed, and direct- - arrows to the face. They hit me between the eyes, or at least, they must have given the intense stinging I felt behind them.

I was going to cry.

The teacher was clear on the other side of the room, working with a pair in the back, completely oblivious to the venom Oscar was spitting, but that didn't stop others from noticing, looking, and worst of all, hearing. I rose from my seat, abandoned my bag and all my papers, and walking at a pace too brisk to be inconspicuous, dashed out the door.

Brianna Rae Quinn

I heard my teacher's voice, calling from behind me, sounding soft as I put more distance between myself and the barrage of stares, "Desdemona, where are you going?"

I had rounded the corner before hearing Oscar finish his response, "I need a new part--". I knew what he said. He would be the one to explain, while I was leaving pools of saltwater on the bathroom tile. No one would be able to tell, as it blended with drops from the leaking sink and students shaking their hands dry.

I trapped myself in the further stall and finally broke into my sobs. The elastic had snapped, my breakdown was here, and all I could think about was how sad and pathetic I must look. I lost. I let everyone else beat me down. They won. They'd stolen my pride and all I had left of who I was even just a few weeks earlier. That entire class watched me become something unrecognizable, even to myself.

My sobs came in broken gasps. I choked on my own breathing as I groaned out every frustration I'd been folding neatly at the back of my mind. All the folds had sprung open at once. Oscar's words were just too much to fit.

And was this cry even helping? They still floated around in my mind, taking up space. They didn't fall out with my tears. they stayed. They mocked. they--

"Desdemona Murphy, please come down to the office." The staticky, old PA system screeched through the bathroom speakers. I knew what had happened.

The teacher had called the office, likely saying I'd skipped.

I found myself suddenly hoping this was a suspendable offense, and I could just leave.

Couldn't I just leave? I recalled the day, Wednesday. Mom wasn't due to teach her classes at the university until two, and it was only eleven.

I sniffed and yanked out my phone.

Mona

I need to leave. Can you come get me?

That wasn't good enough. I sent an addendum.

Mona

Please?

Thank God for Candy Crush, because she responded within a minute.

Mama

On my way. Be there in 7.

I took another shaky breath. I felt burdened with all the ugly wails I still had trapped in my chest, but there would be time to let it out at home for today. Maybe even tomorrow.

When would I feel right again?

I ran my fingers through my hair, draped in my eyes, and pushed my way out of the stall and into the hallway.

Being strong was stupid. I'd earned at least a day of being plagued by insecurity and hiding from the world in the stack of blankets

resting on my bed.

287

CHAPTER TWENTY

Sam

Lunch was quiet. Well, I supposed it was actually quite loud, per usual. Wednesdays were particularly strange in the cafeteria. Some junior years ago started this wild tradition and called it "Water Fountain Wednesdays." Every time he got up from the table to use the water fountain, his tablemates would clap for him., probably for staying hydrated, no one really knew, (and the story changed depending on who you asked), but it soon moved to clapping for anyone who used the water fountain, and the tradition stuck.

Arguably, Wednesdays were the loudest as people cheered every time someone sipped from the fountain, but frankly, this time of the year most people just avoided the water fountain in the cafeteria (or simply went to another fountain) to avoid causing a ruckus. It seemed the novelty had worn off, but never completely.

There were about three good cheers throughout the period, which made it a particularly loud lunch, but it still felt quiet and a little lonely for me, specifically.

I didn't think I would miss Mona's presence as much as I did. it sort of made me realize how ingrained in my daily activities my time with her had been-- enough that I noticed when she was gone more emotionally.

I don't think I was sad, exactly, but I was certainly missing the thrill of waiting for something new and exciting to come of my little scheme.

Brianna Rae Quinn

I had seen her that morning. we'd waved at each other as we passed in the hallway between first and second. She seemed perfectly normal to me-- at least, as normal as she had been for the last few days.

I arched my back so I could slip my phone out of my back pocket and tap out a text to Mona.

Sam

Where are you?

I looked around to be certain I hadn't just missed her waiting in the lunch line or over by the restrooms. Nothing. She had to be somewhere, surely, and she wasn't the type to skip. I knew she skipped a couple of times, but she always did it by talking to her counselor about various stressors, or college, or whatever. That way she could have a pass to back her up when she came into class late. I never considered her to be a genius, but she was savvy in more ways than one. That's the mark of a manipulator, I always thought. Bending the truth to see what she wanted to see, like how she *never* skipped, but she was definitely skipping. She just covered her tracks really well.

Then again, why would she skip *lunch?* I remembered she'd been called down to the office during fifth period-- maybe she'd gone home? But surely, she'd tell me.

I looked around again, after a few minutes and some bites of my sandwich, and still never saw her approaching me with her lunch in hand and a bad excuse.

I decided to text her again.

Sam

Lunch is very boring without you

here.

I wasn't sure what to do. The period was halfway through my bagged lunch had been reduced to nothing more than a collection of plastic and crumbs, and I'd done nothing but wonder and worry about Mona.

It felt gross to be thinking about her and worrying-- like I was betraying myself and my own feelings about her. How could I simultaneously miss her and hate her as much as I did? Surely this wasn't all about watching her fall apart in her misery. I guess I didn't realize how nice it was just to listen to someone talk and feel important to them in their lives.

I wondered if maybe this was the push I needed to start hanging out with friends after school again. Maybe I could take Leta home and just talk about whatever was on her mind. I'd even found myself talking more with Oscar, and he seemed like a genuinely cool guy with a lot of interesting hobbies. He played ultimate frisbee on the weekends in the rec center. He had even told me I should join him sometime.

I wanted to! I missed feeling like a part of a friend group. I'd grown so used to minding my own business and keeping to myself that these little connections I had were a source of life for me. I was thrilled to be in school again and see everyone.

And apparently, that included Mona. How strange.

Sam

Mooooooonnnaaaa.

I groaned. There was so much time left in the period, and I actually was *anxious* to talk to someone. I needed conversation and human contact. It was a new feeling for me. What did I use to do when I ate lunch alone?

Right. Homework. I knew the answer to that. I let myself look busy so others wouldn't approach me-- now I rushed to finish my work during study hall so I could focus on socializing during lunch. What was there to do now?

My foot tapped against the tile, waiting unashamedly for Mona to respond to my text. I locked and unlocked my phone, staring at the shockingly one-sided conversation. My phone blinked on and off while I blinked at it, waiting for something new to appear when my eyelids lifted again.

Fine. If she wouldn't message me back, then I'd have to figure it out myself.

I clicked out of our conversation and tapped into my contact. A new contact was added, fresh at the top. Oscar. I knew he had a class with Mona earlier in the day. I wasn't sure when, but I could probably ask him if he'd seen her or if she'd shown up to class.

My finger hovered over his name for a moment too long as I debated on whether or not it was weird to text him. Would he be confused by the message? Or weirded out?

It was these little moments of hesitation that made me wonder how anyone managed to get anything done. Certainly other people had to be this worried about the way others perceived them too, but really, I should have been used to being the weird guy-- I always was a bit of an outsider-- but now I felt a little bolder, and within the quick second, I felt the newer version of myself taking over and start typing a message.

Couldn't think too much about it, or I might have stopped.

Sam

Did you see Mona in class?
She's not at lunch but I thought
she was here this morning.

I watched the message after it sent for about thirty seconds, and in that time, I noticed the little check part pop up at the bottom of the screen. He read the message, and then came the speech bubble of dots. *Pop*. The next message came. it was a bit thrilling actually.

Oscar

Yeah. She tried to talk to me last
period. I told her off and she ran
out.

My eyebrow raised slightly. I replied quickly.

Sam

She left school, you think?

Oscar

No clue. Teacher called her in
for skipping tho. Why?

I found myself nodding as I processed the new information. So did she get sent home, or was she still in trouble in the office? It'd almost been over an hour. I doubted she was still sitting in the principal's office.

Sam

Gotcha. Just wondering. You
didn't let her know I told you,
right?

Oscar

Nope. Just called her a whore
and she cried, lol.

That last one came as the bell rang, but before I got up, I decided to add one more thought to our thread of messages.

Never Cried Wolf

I imagined that might earn me some points in Oscar's world given how frustrated I knew he was with her. I scooped up an armful of garbage to dump in the trash can on my way to Creative Writing where I would continue to be alone, and that was fine.

As I filed into the classroom behind a snake of students coming from the cafeteria, I let a wave of calm come over me. Things were fine. Oscar didn't say anything, and Mona was finally beginning to feel a fraction of the way I felt all those years ago. This was *exactly* what I wanted, and yet something still ached in my bones. It was a weird, slimy sensation I couldn't shake about her sudden disappearance from the building. She probably just hadn't relaxed from their altercation. She would text me sooner or later. I knew that for sure.

And the bell rang again. Time really flew whenever I was stuck in my own head.

Mr. Howard stood up at his podium at the front of the classroom and pointed to the board behind him.

"Perspective," he said, "We all got it."

A small chuckle came from the class as he continued.

"Today, you're writing two poems. I'm cutting the line limit down. You're only required to do ten instead of sixteen for both. I want to see two perspectives on one situation-- bonus points if you throw in a rhyming couplet. I'm feeling feisty today!" He announced.

One person at the back of the class snorted before shouting, "Nothing gets me feistier than a good rhyming couplet."

"That's what I'm saying! Now write!"

Did I dare?

Was there ever a better day to let loose and finally write about my little game with Mona? When she wasn't here?

Never Cried Wolf

She'd never see it, and it seemed tempting to finally get some of my honest thoughts down on paper.

I found myself instantly inspired to write a simple ten lines, using quite a few rhyming couplets for my bonus points.

I scrawled.

It took years to find the moment when
I could make things right again

So I could make you feel the way I felt
So you might play the cards you dealt

You hung a curtain so you could hide
I pulled them promptly to the side

I slashed the holes so all would see
The nasty beast you'd surely be

You let out a deep, piercing wail.

For now, we saw you through the veil.

I usually found rhyming poetry a bit stiff and uninspired-- perhaps it's different for the writer. I was impressed with how quickly the words came. I only erased a few lines before I found it passable.

Now for the other side of things. I had to ask myself, what *was* Mona thinking?

Of course, I didn't know. I could only guess. Truly, how naive did I believe her to be? Could she understand that this is all deserved, or was she so deranged she truly thought this series of bad luck was nothing more than a coincidence?

I started to write again.

Never Cried Wolf

As I wrapped up my words, I noticed Mr. Howard making his way to me. It was time for our conference.

"No Mona today?' he asked, crouching her tall body behind the desk so he could get down to my level.

"Guess not. She hasn't said anything to me," I answered nonchalantly.

"Alright, well let's see what we've got!" He collected my page and scanned through the first poem.

"Great couplets, Sam! I love the second stanza specifically. The repetition is great, plus this whole image of the man behind the curtain is really clear. Very Wizard of Oz," Mr. Howard said, moving his eyes to the next poem.

I noticed his eyes squint and his head cock to one side. He seemed confused. *What's confusing?* I wondered. I thought this was a fairly straightforward set of poems.

"So, it looks like you wrote from the same perspective again in this second one," Mr. Howard finally provided his feedback, giving me an idea of the cause for the confusion.

"What do you mean?" I asked. "I explained, through her perspective, she was oblivious to what happened around her." I pointed to the top half of the poem.

"Right, and that's a great start, but you should probably focus more on what she *does* see instead of what she doesn't. People don't notice the things they don't notice, right?" he asked in response.

"Or even,' he continued, "Just try writing using the first person. Make *her* the *I* in your piece and see how it changes. I'll come back in a moment." He got out of his crouch and snaked around to the next student.

I listened to Mona complain about something almost every day. How could I not understand her perspective? That's *all* I ever heard.

Maybe I just wasn't clear?

So, I scrubbed my page clear of the words and tried to start again.

CHAPTER TWENTY-ONE

Mona

"Do you want to talk about it?" Mom asked me. I opened the car door and entered wordlessly. Doubtless, she could tell my eyes were red and puffy, but, ever the sensitive mother, she wanted to wait for me to speak when I was ready. However, ever the nosy mother, her curiosity only outlasted the sensitivity by about seven minutes of silent driving in the car.

"No," I responded promptly. Mom settled into the silence for another twenty seconds before I continued. "I don't want to go to school tomorrow," I admitted.

Her eyes flicked over at me and back to the road. She had long dark hair, just like my sister, Ophelia. I was always told I looked just like my dad. Well, my dad's sister. Despite Ophelia and Mom looking so much alike, I was always closer to Mom than she was. I, of course, love my sister and my dad, but Mom and I always just seemed to get each other implicitly. She never seemed to question me, particularly when I got out of sorts, like this.

"Okay, baby," she replied. "And you're sure you don't want to talk about it?" She tried again.

"Not now," I noted, finalizing my decision by looking out the window and away from her.

"I understand. Take as much time as you need. I'll call you out tomorrow, even for a couple days if you need it. You've barely missed any school this year, I think we can give you a few mental health days." Mom was obviously trying to goad me into continuing the conversation, but I wasn't in the mood.

That really only seemed to make me feel worse. I felt guilty and ungrateful. I didn't even say thank you. I only tightened my lips and continued my gaze out at the trees passing by as we made the last turn onto our street.

The quiet stayed with us until she parked, and I left the car and went to my room, taking my silence with me.

*   *   *

My pillowcase sat cold against my cheek. It had been a game, back and forth since I'd gotten home. I would cry for a solid ten or fifteen minutes hysterically, take a few deep breaths until I stopped. The wet fabric would cool down and remind me how sad I was. There was a split between my unsad, disassociated self, and the self that was a complete, inconsolable wreck and

I processed my entire life blowing up in the last week.

I'd been dragged through the coals with a baseless rumor posted on an anonymous Twitter page. I lost my boyfriend. my best friend wouldn't talk to me. a close friend took advantage of me, and no matter what I tried, it seemed like my other best friend had slowly forgotten my existence over the last few months.

The only person who even seemed to notice I'd gone was the teacher who thought I skipped and Sam.

Sam

Where are you?
Lunch is very boring without you
here.
Moooooonnnaaaa.

All energy had left my body. I saw the messages coming in as they flashed in front of my eyes as they came in, but I couldn't bring myself to respond.

Brianna Rae Quinn

Every conversation I'd had with Sam in the last few weeks had felt like my dumping every negative feeling I had on him. He must have felt overloaded by now. He didn't deserve to have to listen to me continuing to moan and grieve, no matter how badly it hurt right now. It would go away. It had to.

I didn't know if there was something like a God or any divine entity that could hear me out in the universe, but I found myself begging for some normalcy. I wanted to go back in time and be happy with my people again. Not person, people. I wanted Leta to give me one of the fantastic hugs she was so well-known for. I wanted Raf's ambiguous flirty texts, aching to make me smile like he used to. For a moment, I even wondered if I wanted Oscar's company. But I didn't want him as he was just then. I wanted him the way he was before. Quiet and casual, but always there.

I wanted Jae to complain about this tiny town and every person in it. I wanted to see his eyes roll into the back of his head and watch him anxiously run his fingers through his dark hair as he debated which emoji would be perfect for his latest fling from some school downtown, where he always said the "gays were better." I never had the slightest idea what that could have meant, but I took him at his word.

I wanted to be alone, but I wanted everything back.

I wondered over and over again how I ended up in this situation. I tried to calculate the last time I'd cried so openly and shamelessly. I could count the number of times I had on one hand-- but every day now felt the same. Like attempting to climb out of a six-foot grave. Every time I sunk my fingers into the earth, it crumbled away and left me stranded at the bottom, soaked to my ankles in mud and rot.

I blinked and another tear escaped my eyes, creating a singular warm spot in the chilled puddle against my cheek. I felt another wail crawling up out of my gut, but I tried to keep it back. I could tell I was hurling myself into weeks of coughing fits with how scratched my throat felt from my unfiltered whimpering.

I pulled on one strand of hair, focusing on my breathing to stop the tears again. I noticed my nail moving against the ripples of my hair. The edges were jagged, ripped down to just stubs. I'd chewed most of them clean off, and the only remaining pieces were those pieces I knew would bleed if I kept biting. This was probably the first time I'd attempted to control myself. I had to start thinking practically. I couldn't let mom and or dad see (or more likely, hear) me like this when they got home. They would immediately try to solve my problems as if I hadn't, and then I would just get frustrated. Mom and Dad always say, "We were kids once too," but I sincerely doubt they ever had the entire school receive an automatic update on their pagers about how great mom was at sucking dick.

Gag. Alright. It was time to think about something else.

I reached out to my phone, dragging it closer to me over the sage green silk sheets I'd just gotten for Christmas. The slide of my arm over the soft fibers was the most comforting thing I'd felt all day. I ran my pinky back and forth to latch onto that comfort as I unlocked my screen and started scrolling, still avoiding the messages from Sam.

It was on my mind, so I couldn't help but check.

Kettlewood Confessions

@KWHS_Confess

1 hour ago

"Ella Huron, smartest girl in school, cheated on her math exam. Guess we know how she got her scholarships now!"

I didn't know Ella. She must have been a senior if she had scholarships. I wondered if this tweet was ruining her day the same way the tweet about me had ruined mine. Was she currently arguing with a counselor or friend over *her* lies, or was it just me?

Or worse, was she trying to prove she wasn't lying like I had?

Did no one believe her? Was she anxiously trying to get out of the building so she could go home and cry? Was she already home, laying on her bed and crying with me on the other side of town? My disdain for the account grew a little more at the thought, but I kept scrolling.

Kettlewood Confessions

@KWHS_Confess

43 minutes ago

"Stairwell probably isn't a good place to get bent over. the walls are glass… just sayin"

I felt my head shake, and I kept scrolling through the newest additions.

Kettlewood Confessions

@KWHS_Confess

25 minutes ago

"Where are all the gays in this school? I'm tryna have plans this weekend.)"

I took note of the handful of likes on the post. I imagined this was an easier way to figure out who was fair game at a school of over a thousand students.

Kettlewood Confessions

@KWHS_Confess

2 minutes ago

"Alana, you are the absolute best friend anyone could ask for. Even if we don't see each other a lot anymore, I know i can always count on you!"

My heart skipped a beat. I ached for that feeling right now-- having someone I could always count on.

Perhaps it was the tweets that pushed me to take the next step, or maybe I'd been looking for an excuse to do it all afternoon, but that was the moment I picked up my phone to call Jae.

I should have still been in school. He knew that, but I wondered if he'd be so interested in my early call that he'd take it out of sheer curiosity, and answer on the second or third ring.

I was right.

"Heyyyyyyy! How's my favorite girl?" His long, drawn-out "hey" flung me back into the past, and the lilt of his voice struck me right in the chest where I felt a black cloud around me. I felt a little lighter, and of course, I felt the tears spilling again.

I didn't even answer, just shaky breaths as my sage pillow case darkened with wet stains, seemingly like a marshland with strands of red hair like small beams of sunlight breaking through the dense treetops.

'Babe, are you okay?" Jae's voice echoed into my ear again.

The question bounced between both eardrums. My brain wanted to process it, but all it could do was send more messages to my eyes and I can only guess read, "Cry," or "Cry more".

When the first gasp of a sob broke past my lips, I heard Jae's tone darken.

"Mona, what's wrong? Can you talk? What happened?" He was worried, and as much as I hated to be the cause of the worry, I was secretly thankful for it. It was like he cared again. He could *hear* me again, even though I hadn't really said anything.

"Everything's..." I got out between trembling breaths, but I needed another few moments to get out, "Wrong."

"Okay," Jae said, listening carefully. "How can I help?" He asked.

A few more gasps vibrated out of me as I attempted to steady my breathing. I sat up and looked out the window at some falling snow as I prepared to speak again.

"I want you to come back," I said promptly, and continued, cutting him off before he insisted he couldn't. "I know you can't," I explained. My breathing just a bit more even, "That's just what I want."

"What happened, Mona?" Jae repeated. A hint of sadness, or maybe pity, at the fringe of his words.

"Just," I wondered how to explain it briefly, "Stupid rumors," I said.

"Babe, you can't let rumors get to you--"

"I *know*, Jae, but they *did*, okay? I *know* I'm supposed to be bigger than that but no one *believes me*," my chest shook as the truth tumbled out of my mouth so quickly, the sobs were able to latch on and ride out with them.

This was exactly what I was worried about Mom or Dad saying: lame, cliche platitudes with unactionable advice that helped no one, but the advisor feel like they'd done *something*. They didn't. If it were just that simple, wouldn't I have done it already?

Jae was silent.

"No one believes me," I repeated, breaking down once again into a full-on bawling fit.

I could tell Jae was waiting for me to calm down. Jae never liked to talk about things when he was sad, especially when it felt like it was unfixable. I told him I was the distractor, and we'd have Distraction Days. We would go out and have fun and forget the bullshit for as long as possible, or stay in and watch the old, animated Barbie movies to the point we started calling "Code Barbie", no-context needed. He always wanted the silver lining. I liked to be that silver lining. Now, I needed him to be that for me.

"Can you please come home soon?" I could hear how much my question sounded like inconsolable begging, but I was past caring. "Code Barbie."

I hoped using those words would be like a mallet to the head, and he'd be swayed by nostalgia at least to come home. It took a few seconds before he finally answered, "Mona, I can't come home this weekend. I have an event I need to go to for class points."

I felt my lip quiver. He responded to be as if he saw it, saying, "Please, don't be upset. Saturday afternoon we can do a Skype call and watch Barbie, though? You're choice. I'll buy it to stream, and we can screen share, and we can both make popcorn and it'll be great."

I nodded again, knowing full well he couldn't see it. I hoped he just knew like he always seemed to. My lips were curved into a wavering frown, guarding the lament against leaving me again.

"I know this is, like, the last possible thing you want to hear. but I am literally walking into class this minute and I *have* to go. You know I'd skip it if I could!" He called. He sounded genuine, but I was not at all certain he'd skip it if he could.

"Text me if you need anything, okay?"

I finally got my words back enough to say, "Okay."

"Okay, bye babe. Please feel better!"

"Mhm," I hummed back, "Bye."

"I love you!" Jae called as I reached for the "end call" button.

"You too," I mumbled back before closing the call.

The screen stared at me, reflecting the seven-minute call I'd had with my friend. I couldn't help but wonder what I needed to do to get eight, or even ten? Was I worth that time to him anymore?

I couldn't think anymore, the tears were coming up, rolling off my cheeks, roaring like fire, and burning my eyes.

My phone landed on my nightstand with a fat *thunk* after I tossed it mindlessly, and I cried again until I finally fell asleep.

CHAPTER TWENTY-TWO

Sam

"She's been out since Wednesday, and she hasn't said a word to me," I said to Leta. "Look." I showed her the messages from Thursday morning on.

Sam
6:32am
Hey, just checking in. Are you good? Do you need a ride today?

Never Cried Wolf

11:21am

It's lunchtime. Wondering how
you're doing.

11:26am

Are you sick?

12:02pm

Mr. Howard had us write daisy-
chain poems today. It sucked.

12:14pm

Class is lame without someone
to talk to

2:07pm.

You must be glad to not be
driving home in this snow rn.

5:33pm

Eating tacos for dinner. I'll bring
you extra for lunch if it'll get you
back to school.

10:56pm

Miss you, Mona. Hope you feel
better tomorrow.

6:10am

Morning sunshine!!!

7:09am

Guess not.

"Oscar said he called her out in class for acting like a whore, and she just dropped off the face of the Earth," I explained. Her lips angled into a passive thought. I wondered if her newfound disdain for Mona would leave her apathetic, or if she still might feel some worry or concern.

"I still can't believe all that," she replied, shaking her head.

But you do, I half thought, and half manifested.

I didn't necessarily think I was worried. I called it a bit of morbid curiosity. Mona's life had become so intertwined with mine then that I couldn't help feeling as though something was missing on Thursday and Friday throughout the days. For all I knew, she had already transferred to another school, and I had no idea how my flawlessly executed revenge pie came out of the oven. I wondered if that was what I really wanted or if I would be satisfied with making her miserable until she graduated. Even then, I wouldn't be able to see the fruits of that labor. I only had a few more months before I graduated. Was five months of misery enough? Did that make us even. after two years of being a hermit with friends almost exclusively living on the internet with the computer screen separating us forever? Had I healed enough to accept if that was all the retribution I witnessed?

Until then, I hadn't considered any of this. When would this little game end? How long would I be playing both sides before I'd decided enough was enough and it became overkill? I knew I'd been sending nothing but negative energy in Mona's direction for weeks, but I wasn't a cruel person. I resolved to find my way out of this two-faced persona I'd taken on the last few weeks at the next possible opportunity. I was cruising down the highway, patiently waiting for the exit.

In a beautiful twist of fate and serendipity, I saw it just on the horizon.

"I mean, I hope she's okay," Leta began again. "But I really think I need to stop thinking about her and everything. I really just want to focus on the people who do care about me right now, you know?"

"Of course," I answered with a series of sharp nods. "Maybe we should do something this weekend. Let's just hang out and decompress a little."

Let's nails were freshly painted ice blue. They rippled through her curls as she pulled on her hair in an anxious gesture. I watched individual clumps stretch and then spring back up into her perfect ringlets. It was lovely how they always fell back into their patterns where they were comfortable. It takes weeks to get those perfect patterns- habits.

"We should invite Oscar. It couldn't have been easy to call Mona on her behavior, and I really appreciate that he had enough respect for me to tell her to hop off. It sucks it was so public, but honestly, I'm glad he said it because I don't think I could have," Leta confessed.

The little lies were so natural at this point, it almost didn't feel like lying. When everyone around you finally sees things your way, it was easy to ignore the little details that painted Mona in a better light. I quite liked the image of her in my brain then as a renaissance witch being tossed into a river with rocks tied to her ankles by an angry mob of townspeople. Her red hair was always the focal point, and her brown eyes were almost black against her wide, fearful pupils. Her cheekbones peaked under sunken skin, weighed down with the guilt she recognized in her new reality. It was almost hauntingly beautiful how precise it looked, yet aged and delicate.

"Sure. That sounds nice! Maybe we could play the new indoor mini-golf course or something?"

"Yes!" Leta squealed, "Oh yes! I've been dying to find someone to do that with me! It's all glow-in-the-dark, you know?"

"Really!?" I exclaimed back at her. I knew, but I wasn't going to spoil her excitement.

She smiled and looked down at her shoes briefly. I could tell she was debating on whether or not to say her next words. She spoke in a strangely forced-casual tone. "You know what there's actually this guy in my chem class I think you could really hit it off with," she paused, "If you don't mind me inviting someone else?" She offered.

I raised an inquisitive brow, "A *guy* I'd hit it off with?" My response was automatic. Defensive, I knew, but this happened all the damn time. Another subtle, but glaringly obvious attempt to ask me if I was gay without asking if I was gay.

I could tell Leta recognized her fuck-up pretty immediately.

"Nevermind!" She waved her palms in front of her, slicing through the tension she'd let slip between us.

Never Cried Wolf

Beeeeeeeeeeeeeep. The monotone class bell rang, saving her the uncomfortable back-pedaling I knew would come, and letting us know we could head to our next classes.

I insisted we were all okay as we shuffled behind the clog in the doorway, but I knew her little Freudian slip would fester in the back of my mind for the rest of the day, especially as I prepared myself for another lunch alone. Instead of dwelling, I resolved to preoccupy myself with a few texts to Oscar.

"I'll talk to Oscar next period," I quickly babbled to Leta as we started to break apart in the hall, "and I might have another friend who will want to come, too."

"Game on. and you can bring whoever! Can't wait!" She called, waving behind her back to me as she headed off to her English class.

I immediately thought of inviting Dante, and then Rafael as a natural addition. Wouldn't it be lovely to have everyone who had been stabbed in the back by Mona Murphy in one place to commiserate? Like a little group therapy session-- a little trauma bonding never hurt anyone, and I was simply dying to finally feel at peace after the hail storm of frustration and disgust which had been raging in me for the last two years.

I wondered if this could be my out. The grand reveal of my plot so Mona would recognize I fucked her over just like she did to me, and every other person in our potential little golf group.

That image in my mind was almost as clear as the Mona mob renaissance painting, only this one was lush and floral. It was framed in gold and featured real gold leaf in the sun. It shined and sang like a fanfare of trumpets-- the sweet, final moment of dramatic irony revealed. I would be like Ashton Kutcher on Punk'd, and Mona's old friends would be my studio audience. Fans, really. Thanking me for the laughs, and applause echoing forever in a chorus.

I sent the message on the way to the lunch room, and sat at my end of the table, alone, as I had been for the last few days, but I hardly noticed.

Things were different. I had changed. I'd felt a freedom I didn't have before. Finally, I felt seen and heard as the people around me began to understand everything I'd been saying for years. I deserved this feeling of rising out of rock bottom and taking my place on top of the world.

Well, perhaps not on top, but really anything was "on top of the world" compared to where I had been. Even a few rungs up the ladder made this difference.

I supposed it was true what they say. Sadness is necessary to know true happiness. If I had always been happy, the thrill of the win wouldn't have been anywhere near so exciting.

Buzz.

Oscar

I'm free Saturday afternoon.

Sam

Awesome. Will send details later.

I took my time eating lunch and turned my attention to my phone completely. I scrolled through some related blog posts. No new content to reblog or interesting news stories to share. My posts had been stale for the last week. Typically, that would have bored me to tears. thankfully I had some other forms of entertainment.

Part of me noticed I wasn't checking the blog as often anymore. Still once or twice per day, but even just last month, I was completely *living* online. Change never smelled so good, of course, it probably helped that it was cheese fry day for the lunch buyers. I supposed change never smelled so much like cheese fries.

Never Cried Wolf

Was I acting giddy? Chipper, maybe? Was there a pep in my step and hordes of other cliches lining up to describe my emotions at that very moment? How else was there to explain when things were going so wonderfully and utterly *right*? Especially when I knew it.

There was still a fair bit of time left in the period, at least ten minutes. I rounded up my paper bag and sandwich bags to toss into the trash can and made my way over to the bathroom. I didn't particularly like using the school toilets, but sometimes it just had to be done.

I pushed open the door and walked in toward a urinal, but stopped when I noticed a familiar face, leaning against the wall with a classroom pass hung around his neck on a blue lanyard.

His green eyes focused on his phone, while the rest of his handsome face sat relaxed, looking like an effortless American Eagle model in the harsh fluorescent lights against the white cement block backdrop. I knew it couldn't be when I noticed the JROTC green t-shirt tucked into baggy pants and belted tightly around the waist. That was the only that that meant it had to be Rafael and not some ridiculously handsome male model.

"Hey," I said before I'd even fully realized what I was doing.

"Oh," he looked up from his phone, evidently not realizing he was no longer alone. "Hey." He tucked his device into his pocket and waved. His smile was crooked. Thank God he had *some* flaw. The rest of us mortals struggled enough to keep up. "Just heading back to class," he explained, unnecessarily, as he headed over to the door I just entered.

I nodded and started to take a step when his voice stopped me.

"Actually," he began, "I kind of wanted to talk to you."

I felt my stomach drop a little. "Me?" I wondered.

"Yeah. I know you were talking to Dante about Mona weeks ago," he said.

I didn't think it was possible, but my stomach managed to sink lower. Good thing I was in the bathroom already, because I felt just about ready to completely shit my pants. Did he know something? Was he going to yell?

I couldn't help but look at his exposed arms. He was muscled. Not as beefy as Dante, to be sure, but I sure would not like to be on the other end of a fist from that arm.

Even if he knew something, would he want to fight me? Or shout?

Would that be better?

I swallowed hard.

"Did you know she was messing around?" He asked.

I felt my stomach rise back up a hair. "No," I answered promptly. "Well, I mean, maybe I kind of assumed when she rode home with Oscar almost every day, but I never asked."

He nodded slowly, considering. "But you know now?"

"Um, yeah. I guess." I remembered the tweet, how it was like getting a growth off my back, or a parasite, or tick. And seeing the tweet go out was like watching it get squashed.

"So why are you still hanging out with her?" He wondered, looking at me, with his toes still poised to head out the door. He didn't want to have this conversation. I knew that. I didn't want it either, but clearly, it was important to him.

I opened my mouth to reply, but he kept going. "You're clearly not a bad guy. I mean, otherwise, you wouldn't have warned me." He stopped a considered, "Well, warned Dante, who warned me. I just don't get it," Rafael admitted. His terrible teeth revealed from a curled lip, just below his perfect nose, wrinkled in disgust.

"I don't know," I confessed. "I'm just so used to having her around, I guess." This seemed true enough. "I don't have many other friends.'

The confession felt natural, sad as it was. And it did have a twinge of truth to it.

Rafael let out a light sigh of understanding. "I get it," he said. After one, uncomfortably long moment, he added "Maybe you can come hang with me and Dante after school sometime."

Bingo. I felt my demeanor shift as I nodded, "You know, actually, Leta Schneider and I were just talking today about wanting to do something this weekend to kind of forget all the drama with Mona this Saturday. Would you want to come?"

Rafael looked up and off to the side as if trying to remember something. I noticed the tiniest shake of his head before he smiled and said, "Yeah, actually. That sounds cool. Let me get you my number.' He moved away from the door and over to me with his phone out of his pocket once more.

The universe was really looking out for me, or perhaps the narrator. Bending the truth shouldn't have been this easy, and every parable I'd ever read had warned me I'd die a horrible death by this point. This was the final nail in the coffin in my battle against Mona Murphy, a final act of revenge. She would understand finally what it was like to see her closest friends choose someone else over her, all because of some manipulated half-truths. Maybe I did cry wolf a *few* times, but I didn't regret it. The difference was, there was actually a wolf to cry about in my story, and this weekend would be my silver bullet.

Never Cried Wolf

CHAPTER Twenty-Three

Mona

"How much do you think Tim Curry got paid to voice this fugly rat?" Jae wondered aloud, shaking his head. His face on the screen was blurry as my computer struggled to play both his video from his front camera and *Barbie in the Nutcracker.*

I didn't care. This was all I wanted. Leta, again, didn't show up for breakfast, and frankly, neither did I. I didn't bother. I could tell mom was growing increasingly concerned as I refused to leave my bedroom. She came knocking once or twice every night to check in on me, but every time I told her I was still sick and I just needed sleep.

Evidently, sleep was not helping. Mom brought me soup at some point. I'd eaten about half of it and just left it until she came to collect the dishes later. I had taken another nap and it was gone when I got up. I'd received nothing but texts from Sam and a couple of random spam notifications. Jae was the only person I was willing to talk to, and if he wasn't available, then again, I just slept and played Family Guy on a loop, occasionally crying when the topics got a little too real for me. I imagined Seth McFarlane would be very upset with that reaction to his work, but realistically, I'm sure he didn't care. It didn't seem as though anyone cared.

My laptop was set up on my nightstand, just close enough so I could reach out and select "Continue Watching" anytime Hulu assumed I'd died. I noticed Hulu gave you a few more episodes before bothering you with a button compared to Netflix, so I seldom ventured away.

Mom hadn't asked any questions, which I was intensely thankful for, and neither did Jae. He knew his role as the distractor, and he wouldn't break the silence until I was ready. I didn't know when I would be. I couldn't even fathom getting out of bed for anything other than a quick trip to the restroom, let alone going back to school and facing Sam, or Leta, seeing Raf in gym class or avoiding Oscar in math. There was a time when I was jumping up and down excited to be able to see my friends throughout the day or even fought for it with my counselor in the case of Raf. Now, it was like a living nightmare that did nothing but cause me pre-anxiety anxiety because I knew I would have anxiety and that made me anxious too. Anticipation of a tight-chested, tense-fingered panic attack was enough to cripple me entirely, which was evidently why I was acting like a bedridden patient with a terminal illness instead of the victim of… I didn't even know what. Life?

"God, I love her dress," Jae said again. I couldn't help but make the tiniest, thinnest smile at the sound of his voice. It was so comforting, in a way that even *Barbie and the Nutcracker* couldn't be. The present craving for nostalgia was much less an inner child's want, but more desire for a fucking Time stone. If Dr. Strange burst in through my window and offered to take me back to Sophomore year and let me stay there reliving the rest of my life in some sort of Groundhog Day-esque hell, I'd go with. I thought it would be better than the way I was, curled in my bed, wallowing in self-pity.

My curtains were shut, but that didn't contribute to my vampire lair energy. My room was so clean, white, and green. The curtains were completely sheer with little embroidered vines and flowers along the bottom. My satin, sage sheets wrapped around me in the limpest, most uncomforting hug. My walls were cream-- some

Benjamin Moore shade a Youtuber recommended that I just had to have, and light wood accents on my bedframe, dresser, and other furniture. It would have looked like a catalog bedroom were it not for the collections of pictures and art prints of different mountains and castles across Europe littering the walls. Grandma had given me one every birthday and Christmas until she died. I'd never say I collected them, but after a while, I grew really fond of them. They reminded me of all the cool places in the world. Travel always appealed to me if I wasn't such a homebody. I found myself really grateful I had these prints instead of tons of pictures of my friends, like most people. All those were on my desk and were very easy to push off the top and right into a drawer to be dealt with another day.

I thought looking at them would only make things worse.

"Are you frozen, love?" Jae asked.

"No," I mumbled back. My face was smushed up against my pillow, distorting my words slightly.

"You haven't moved in a minute. It looks like you're not breathing."

I took a deep breath and stretched my jaw a bit as my body shifted up to show his screen was not, in fact, frozen.

'Look," he started. My eyes glazed slightly. I knew what was coming. "I know Clara hasn't woken up from her dream, yet, but I need to get going to this event. My friend's here to pick me up." He sounded apologetic. It didn't make it better, though.

"He's already there?" I felt a little whine escape my lips.

"Yeah, actually. Want to say hi?" He asked with a smile.

He didn't wait for my response. He waved someone behind the camera over and shifted his computer to the side to make space in the frame for another person.

Brianna Rae Quinn

A pretty, curvy girl with split hair poked her hair into the frame. One side was blonde, and the other was a natural brunette. She had curtain bangs falling away from her face. Her style was so long, I figured the locks had to be extensions. I couldn't tell much else about her other than she clearly wore some dark eyeliner or eyeshadow, only really on the top lid and a very bright pink blush. She was pretty in an edgy sort of way.

And I was immediately jealous.

She waved and said, "Hi, Mona! I've heard so much about you!"

"This is Netta," Jae explained.

My thoughts immediately bounced to saying something along the lines of, "I haven't heard shit about you!" but that would make it sound like I was mad at Netta when I was really more upset with Jae. I wondered if I would have heard more about her if he ever bothered to call. What could he have possibly been saying about me if we rarely spoke anymore? Old anecdotes and good stories? Or maybe he was upset with me too, just like everyone else. And that's why he didn't call.

No. I had to stop spiraling down this black hole of hate. I had to let wins be wins. He was still talking about me. He hadn't forgotten me.

Yet.

"Hi," I waved back lightly with another small smile.

"I'm sorry I have to leave. I love you, babe. Keep your chin up, and make sure Clara gets home to her grandpa's safe for me!"

"Of course," I nodded once in response.

"Thank you!" He blew an obnoxious, squeaky air kiss to me before clicking out of the Skype call, and I stared back at the screen.

I never did see Clara get home safely. I just closed out everything and pulled my phone to my chest, hiding under the covers to find my next distraction.

Kettlewood Confessions

@KWHS_Confess

7 hours ago

"Kati Lowe. What do I have to do for you to go on a date with me? <3."

It's hard not to be bitter and jealous when you're hurting. I liked that I was at least self-aware enough to be able to tell when I was lashing out. It was the only part of my personality that I felt was still intact at this point. I'd hate to know the person I'd become if I lost that-- even if I already couldn't recognize myself in the mirror.

Kettlewood Confessions

@KWHS_Confess

5 hours ago

"Nothing like going through a hard time to remind you who your true friends are."

That one stung.

A veritable shanking by the very account which seemed to set off this shit tornado that now appeared to be my life, and yet I kept coming back to it.

Maybe it was nice to see other people struggling the same way I was. Maybe that made me a horrible person for being grateful that bad things happened to other people as well. Or maybe it made me feel worse because all I saw, heard, and felt at that time were dark clouds and bad vibes. I just needed to get out of this funk. I didn't even care if I felt happy again. I just wanted to feel numb.

I didn't think it could get worse.

Kettlewood Confessions

@KWHS_Confess

1 hour ago

"Mona Murphy is a disgusting liar."

Again? I couldn't understand. Who was doing this to me? Who hated me so much that they'd write such awful things about me and kick me while I was down? Did anyone even know I was down? Oscar did.

It seemed the answer was obvious. The villain of my story had a name. I had someone to blame, and still, nothing felt much better.

I clicked out of Twitter and closed down the app. I started at the little blue and white bird icon on my screen. It all but came to life to spit at me through its silhouetted beaks. I retaliated with a swift uninstall, and a shaky breath.

Somehow, I hadn't burst into tears yet. Evidently, I'd gotten used to the injustice and the unfairness (or I'd run out of tears). It was simple to delete an app. A first step to peace. Unfortunately, I couldn't just delete high school.

I swiped around until I got to Snapchat and opened it up. Something about watching one of those oddly satisfying industrial crusher videos on the Discover page, but before I got there, something else caught my eye.

Leta's story, still fresh at the top of my inbox, featured the face of … Rafael? There was no way. Did Leta even really know Rafael?

Never Cried Wolf

I couldn't help my curiosity. I shot up straighter than had in days and tapped the circle and began watching 2 minutes of photos and videos that shoved me right under that industrial crusher. My insides flattened and spread out in an explosion, like playdough, curling at the ends from the force of the extrusion.

First was a car picture, featuring Leta in the front seat with Oscar. My heart flipped, and my throat dried. Next, a ticket stub for the new indoor mini-golf place at the mall. My tongue started drying too.

Another video of Oscar lining up his shot and failing to get his ball over the hump. A chorus of groans behind the camera let me know Raf was there, and probably some others.

Then Rafael and Dante, posing like a small penguin statue with some horribly painted eyes. It would have been a hilarious picture was the context a bit less depressing.

Lastly, I saw a group picture. Leta held the phone out to capture the whole crew. Just behind her were Raf and Dante, Oscar leaned in from her right, and on the left was Sam.

Sam was there. Sam was with Leta. He was with Oscar and Rafael.

I'd gone away from him for three days, and it seemed like he'd totally given up on me. He moved on, with all the people who hurt me.

Now, he was one of the people who hurt me.

I dropped my phone into my lap, and just stared ahead at the wall.

I wasn't as used to this sadness as I thought. One tear had escaped and found its place back on my silk pillowcase.

CHAPTER TWENTY-FOUR

Sam

I sat on one of the four wooden benches lining the entrance hall of the building on Monday morning. Rafael and Dante laughed at a meme on Rafael's phone while I finished up some math homework which Dante was supposed to be helping me with. That was the whole reason I'd come to school early, was to get this homework done, but I didn't mind.

The frustrated, bitter Sam was long gone and had been replaced with a much more relaxed and chill Sam. Sam didn't even seem to fit me anymore. I wanted to be Sammy, or maybe a Samuel. Sammy was chill. Samuel was cool. Could a person just up and change their name? I wasn't truly certain I was in the cool zone yet, but I was down for a friendlier nickname like Sammy. I watched Dante's arm slap Rafael on the back with a deep laugh. His voice was smooth, like butter. It slipped in one ear and out the other, wrapping my brain in a warm, velvety blanket. I could listen to him talk all day.

His Adam's apple bobbed up and down as he spoke. It mesmerized me, putting me in a trance and distracting me from the homework. I was almost resigned to doing nothing else all day when I heard a voice.

"Hey, look who's here." It was Rafael's words that broke the spell, causing me to turn my head to the front door. Among the mass of students entering the frosted glass doors, I noticed a familiar brown, plaid peacoat between the puffer jackets and matted furs no one knew how to launder correctly.

Mona was evidently trying very hard to blend in with the people around her. Her cream knit scarf was wrapped around her hair to cover her ears, but I could recognize her long red locks anywhere. It was hard to blend in with hair like that. And even when she tried to fly under the radar, she stuck out like a sore thumb. Her sense of style was so recognizable-- or at least it was to me, and evidently to Rafael as well.

It wasn't hard to see why he would be interested. She walked with so much confidence, she looked about five inches taller than she actually was. However, after the last month of intervening in her life, she actually appeared about 2 inches shorter, which is shocking when considering she was only about five feet tall. I couldn't totally tell from the distance, but it looked like she'd skipped her makeup. Her under eyes looked dark and puffed. If she did have anything on, it was doing an awful job of covering her up. She didn't just look tired, she looked sick. Her lips were pale. Her entire face was almost bloodless and colorless.

She took small steps angling her body around the other bodies to get inside quickly and silently. She was alone, and she was small.

"Finally back after skipping for…what, three days?" Dante asked, looking over at me, the resident Mona expert.

Her eyes were trained at her feet. There was a chance she wouldn't notice any of us if she kept on walking with her head down.

I was encouraging everyone to take so many pictures at mini golf this weekend and post them wherever. Snapchat, Instagram, Twitter, I mentioned it all at some point. I wasn't certain which posts Mona had seen if any. I was suddenly struck with the realization that even though Mona and I had reconnected almost a month prior, she hadn't added me on many socials again. I was completely in the dark regarding what she may or may not know as only Leta and Rafael's stories would have been visible to her, assuming she'd blocked Oscar, and I knew she and Dante weren't exactly close.

Suddenly, in this moment, I wasn't sure I wanted her to see me with Rafael or Dante. I felt my instincts flipping me into "Mona Mode" where I was still her friend and cared about her, but I was supposed to have given up on that. I basically solidified myself as untrustworthy to her when I went out with her former friends and ex-boyfriend this weekend without her. Why was I still hoping for her approval?

Why was I just the tiniest bit worried that she would be upset with me?

Wasn't that exactly what I was going for?

It was then that I noticed Mona was taking the scarf off her head, she leaned back to tip the scarf off her hair, her eyes rising for just a moment.

And she noticed me. Her chin made the slightest double take as she tried not to look directly into my face. She recognized me sitting with her ex-boyfriend, and his best friend and all three of us were staring at her, of course.

My eyes flicked to Rafael who sneered and looked away almost immediately. Dante continued to stare her down in a way that almost felt scary. His eyes were nearly identical to my dad's. It reminded me of how disappointed he looked when my brother said he wasn't going to college. It was a look a never wanted to be on the receiving end of.

Mona's lips never changed or twitched, only her eyes which shifted immediately away from our gazes, and back to her black, pointed loafers, keeping her moving forward.

I briefly considered running after her. I still hadn't heard from her since that Wednesday when she left. It had been almost five days with no contact. It actually made me wonder if she suspected something before now, but I was fairly confident that wasn't the case. I'd been on the other end of her wrath before, and she would have ripped me to shreds. She'd done it before.

Instead of leaving the boys, I responded to Dante's question. "Yeah. Maybe mom wouldn't let her stay home again?" I offered the explanation.

"At this point, she might as well transfer," Rafael hissed bitterly. "I can't stand cheaters." He stated with a hint of finality in the topic.

I opened my mouth but closed it back up. I wanted to shout back at him about how he and Mona were never actually together because *he* kept stringing her along. How *he* never made the commitment to *her,* and *she* didn't really owe him anything.

The last thing I wanted to do was defend Mona, so why was that all I wanted to say?

Why did I want to catch up to her and let her cry and be vulnerable with me?

Why did I text her all week and hope constantly that she'd respond to let me know she was okay?

I was the one that did this to her, and for some reason, just then, I wasn't proud of it.

Something in Mona's dark brown eyes read so cold and cynical when I was so used to her warmth. She wasn't a light to me, but she was comfortable. I knew her, and she knew me, (at least, she thought she did.) Mona was my access to this world and these friends, and something about her looking so horrible and depressed tugged at my heartstrings in a way that made me ache to speak with her.

But I shouldn't have. I *couldn't* have. I did this. This is exactly what I wanted, and my damn empathetic side decided now was the time to feel a little guilt.

Obviously, this was a good sign. Bad people didn't feel guilt for hurting others. Of course it sucks that I had to fib a little and spill secrets Mona had told me in confidence, but it was all for the greater good. Every fantastic superhero in the movies had to make hard decisions. it only made sense that I would have to make some tough choices too.

Life had never been black and white, and this was the exact definition of a moral grey area. I absolutely would let a train run over one person if it meant saving five, and wasn't that what I'd done? This was a real-life train dilemma, and I had no qualms about making my choice. Of course, I could have walked away, but I still believe that doing nothing is a choice as well, and only cowards choose that option.

I was not a coward.

*　　*　　*

Around lunchtime, when I went to the cafeteria with my bagged lunch in hand, I settled myself into my usual seat and scanned the room for Mona. To no one's surprise, she appeared to be missing again.

Oscar had sent a picture from his math class, where he was sitting behind Mona. He flipped a fat middle finger in her direction, the focus of the camera on wrinkles where his knuckles bent, framed in a soft blur of Mona's ginger mane.

Oscar

**Now I have to look at this bitch
all period. fml**

Sam

Ouch. Good luck

That was only the period before. I knew Mona was still here, it was only a matter of where.

I had only taken a few bites of my carrots and ranch when I heard the chair in front of me screech as it was pulled from under the table, and a petite frame entered my peripheral.

I looked up, and Mona was looking at the table, obviously avoiding eye contact.

'Hey!" I said to her in a tone of surprise.

Hey." She replied, melancholy flooding her lips.

She had a lunch tray from the line, housing only a cup of fruit, which looked like peach sliced and cherries, and a milk carton.

"Not hungry?" I asked, attempting to keep the conversation light. I was at a loss for what to say.

"No, but I have to eat something."

A lump formed in my throat. Why was that the most depressing thing I'd ever heard a person say? I only nodded.

"I tried talking to Leta," she said out of nowhere. "She's clearly avoiding me, but I finally got her to agree to talk to me during study hall this week."

I wasn't sure why she was telling me this. Did she not see the posts from this weekend after all?

"Oh," I answered, punctuating my interjection with a loud snap into a carrot.

"I want to apologize… for whatever I did. I obviously hurt her. I just don't know how."

The lump solidified and I almost choked. "Are you sure she'll tell you?" I couldn't decide if this was a good or a bad development just yet. On one hand, Mona's ignorance of the realities of why her friends were dropping like flies around her was making it very easy to avoid being caught. On the other, how would Mona ever learn from her actions if no one ever told her what she'd done wrong?

But she was a manipulator. What if she managed to weasel her way out of her social exile? Was she even in the right mindset to try?

"No. Honestly, I don't even care. If she wants to take the time to just yell at me, I'll let her. I just can't stand this… uncertainty. It's like I'm feeling my way around in the dark right now, all the time."

I nodded again.

In the space between us, I recognized an invisible wall that hadn't always been there. She had more she wanted to say, but she was holding me.

"Sam," she started, still not looking up at me.

"Yeah?" I asked, watching the bridge of her nose, waiting for her head to rise so I could scan her face for any hint about what was to come.

When she looked up, her eyes were red, and her irises a molten, golden brown, glossed over in the beginnings of some tears. I watched her nostrils widening as she took a deep breath in through her nose.

"Never mind," she murmured. "I'm going to go ask for some missing work. Maybe I can sit in the guidance office and finish it. I'll see you later."

Her words came quickly, each syllable blending into the next as she escaped the conversation with me. She slipped out of her chair, and took the two steps to the trash can, dropping her entire tray, complete with her unopened cup of fruit and milk, inside of it. Then, she took off in a brisk walk in the direction of the main office, her red hair swishing behind her as she whisked around the corner.

I did not see her later.

CHAPTER TWENTY-FIVE

Mona

That morning, Mom sat next to me on my bed and asked earnestly, as she had each morning since our silent car ride if I was up to leaving the house that day.

That day was different because I said yes.

It didn't really matter anymore. The technicalities and morals were minor compared to what I experienced in the last few days.

For almost a week, I'd been sitting at home, calling in sick to work, and refusing to get up for food or school. As far as anyone knew I was encased in a bubble with horrible contagious pneumonia that made it nearly impossible for me to speak, let alone stand.

That's the kind of illness that keeps you wrapped up in bed for days at a time. Instead, I had no motivation. It's hard to do anything when it feels like everyone will hate you, regardless of what you do, no matter how hard you try, or how much they liked you before.

However, that's the perfect situation, isn't it? I must have had at least enough energy to find the last wisp of a silver lining in my life. The phrase kept repeating itself in a loop at the back of my head. *everyone hates me. Everyone hates me. EVERY one hates me. Everyone hates ME.*

Any possible rise or fall in inflection, any emphasis or dip in tone, I'd heard it taunting me for days. And at first, I imagined this meant I should stay away from everyone. Why would I put myself in a situation where I could possibly be hated more?

But that was just the thing. Was it even possible to hate me more? And if Sam or Leta, for instance, suddenly hated me. Would it matter how *much* they hated me? Would that change the ways things were? No.

I wasn't committed to confronting Sam with the reason he'd gone out with the group of people I once considered *my* people. It was a stupid question. For all I knew, he was trying to invite me, or spend time with me, but I ignored his messages. That could have been my fault. He stopped sending me anything on Saturday, and the Sunday after was exceptionally dark and gloomy, even with the sun reflecting off the patches of melting snow in the yard. It felt like I'd been plopped into a simulation with how artificial the sun felt-- like it was trying to break into my body and lighten me up and lessen the weight on my muscles and bones.

Perhaps it worked a little. The only thing that hit me hard, like a frying pan to the back of the head, was Sam. How he seemed perfectly content with being around Oscar *knowing* what he'd done to me (or tried to do). I'd thought about it so much, and every time I considered telling my mom or *someone* about it, I froze. I imagined them telling me there was nothing to do. He didn't *actually* hurt me. He didn't *force* me to kiss him, *I* let him. *I* didn't stop that. Naturally, he tried to get more, but he couldn't *make* me do anything. I thought of my aunt telling me that boys do stupid things when they like you. They make mistakes. Boys will be boys, after all, and they have needs. She reminded me of this almost constantly when I was seven, and any time this absolute trash-bag of a kid in my elementary school pulled on my hair or forced me into a hug, she'd say, "That's because he likes you. That's how boys show it." And "What's so hard about giving him a chance? You might turn out to like him." that's what happened with her and Uncle Frank, after all!

So I'd stop myself from saying a word and go back to feeling gross and betrayed again.

I go back to wanting a shower, but not wanting to get up, and feeling sick, but not having enough food in my stomach to throw it up.

That was the thing with adults. they always try to turn the little things into "teaching moments." I repeat a funny joke, and it turns into a lecture about bullying. I wasn't paying attention and did something wrong? I have to listen to the same set of directions again. I forget something once, and it snowballs into an interview on my ability to take of myself in the real world. Did someone treat me badly? What did *I* do to antagonize them? Did I *deserve* it?

I knew mom always had the best of intentions, but most of the time, I didn't want to hear the same old over and over. I just wanted someone to hold my hand and tell me it would be okay. So I just chose to stay silent until I was ready to go back to school.

That's what friends are supposed to be for. To talk, bitch, and moan about all the little things I'm too afraid to tell the adults about.

Friends understand the nuances of the social climate that parents just don't.

But like I said: none of my "friends" could possibly hate me more, right?

So why not ask a friend? Why *not* ask Leta to talk? The best-case scenario was that I got my friend back, cleared up whatever wild misunderstanding had occurred, and I'd be able to get all this off my chest. In the worst-case scenario, she… what? Actively avoids me and never wants to talk to me again? *SURPRISE.* I was already there.

It was decided. I was going to talk to her. If she'd listen, would tell her everything that had gone on in the last couple of weeks. I would ask for forgiveness if I missed something in my present state. frankly, I felt I'd been going through a lot. Did I forget an event? It wasn't her birthday. I didn't miss her parents' annual anniversary party. I knew that, but my mind might have been less than reliable while I had been so preoccupied with all the little things and stressors which caused me to lose focus. Would she see that as an excuse? Maybe.

Maybe this wasn't even the problem. Maybe I did something so heinous I blocked it out of my memory?

Regardless, I would be apologizing for it (whatever *it* was) that day. As soon as I got to study hall, I'd track her down at the table by the window and figure out what happened.

I spotted her across the room and immediately pointed my feet in her direction. I slipped into the chair across from her and dropped my bag to the floor in one swift motion, scarcely giving her time to recognize I'd appeared.

"I'm sorry," I said with the entirety of the breath I'd held as I made my way to her.

She just looked at me with a knit in her brow. I wasn't sure if I'd ever seen that little line before, at least not directed at me the way it was now. Her mouth never made a move to open, she just stared at me, evidently waiting for me to say more. So I did.

"I don't know what I did to hurt you, but you have to know I never meant to. We haven't spoken in weeks, and you seem super upset, and it's killing me not to know why." All the words were rushed and scrambled on the way out, but I thought the point was still there, so I paused to let her say her piece.

"You don't know?" Leta asked her voice far more even and calm than mine, with a light sprinkling of hurt on top.

"I--" I started. She cut me off.

"Mona, I know everything that happened with you and Oscar."

I felt my jaw drop slightly. I almost didn't know how to react. Had Oscar told her what he was going to do? Did she know and let him try that disgusting shit on me? Is *that* why she left the carpool?

"You know?" I felt my heart crush under the weight of the moment. Is she upset because I didn't tell her?

"Yes, and I can't believe you didn't just tell me about it." She shook her head and looked back down at the homework in front of her. It looked like chemistry.

"I *wanted* to, it just seemed too hard," I confessed. "And complicated."

"I was your best friend," she replied pointedly, still not looking up.

Was?

"I didn't believe it at first. I couldn't imagine you sneaking around like that and trying to hide your little… I don't know… afternoon delights from me."

I breathed an uncomfortable laugh through my nose at the phrasing, which proved to be the wrong move.

"Don't laugh. I was so worried you two were just laughing about all this mess behind my back because I didn't know."

That one set me off. "Why would I think any of this is *funny,* Leta?"

She just stared at me.

"Why would it be funny that your ex-boyfriend practically forced me to do shit with him?" I looked away, almost trying to spot the cameras for whatever prank show I was suddenly featured on. "And you're mad at *me* for all that?"

"Go away, Mona." She snarled in disgust and pulled her pencil up to her paper again.

My lips tensed and I took a shaky breath in and out. I couldn't just walk away after the progress I'd made. I had to relax again.

"Why are we fighting like this? Why are we mad at each other when this is *Oscar's* fault? *He's* the one getting in between us."

"Don't do that!" She finally raised her voice. "Don't try to put the blame on other people! *You* fucked up, Mona. *You.* And now you're shoving the blame off on someone else because *you* got caught."

Never Cried Wolf

The silence of the immediate space around us was palpable. It clung to the air and suffocated me slowly.

"I don't think you *actually* know what happened with Oscar," I ventured to say.

"I don't care." She replied.

It was cold and callous. Something only said by someone who was really, truly hurting. And I'd caused that hurt.

I nodded once and looked over. A few tables held some students, trying to look like they weren't paying attention, some even turned their heads away so they wouldn't be caught staring. Others absolutely couldn't have cared less, but the eyes of those who did burned into my skin like hot knives, slicing my last shreds of motivation to dust.

Turned out, it could be worse.

I shuffled away just as quickly as I came in, navigating to a table only a few rows down from Leta, behind her so our backs would be to one another. I attempted to pull out my missing work. I still had a poem to write from Howard's class. I thought was the only assignment I even had a fraction of a shot of completing given my mental state.

I scribbled and scratched out words over and over until the bell rang, alerting me that it was time to head to history class.

I groaned in frustration, staring at the words that managed to survive on the lines of the ruled sheet before me.

They said to smile
They said, "Be Nice."
They said, "Be gentle
when asked your advice."

"Be thankful and
truthful, be there
when in need, and
You will succeed."
I wish that were so.

But smiles and kindness
are rarely enough
when love and friendship
are built on trust.

Who would risk their life
To reach for the fruit swinging
At the end of the branch.
When she hasn't proven

How sweet she really is?

I ripped it in half and crumbled the sheet into a small ball. Maybe the metaphor would have made sense if Leta didn't know me, but she did. We'd been friends for years, and she still lost her trust in me. She'd given up on me because she trusted *Oscar* more than me. I had clearly made myself untrustworthy by keeping secrets from her. One mistake, and it was over.

So, I guess I was wrong.
It could be, and was, so much worse.

CHAPTER TWENTY-SIX

Sam

I scrolled through the various recommended posts on my blog feed. Nothing struck me as noticeably interesting. I snapped a pretzel in half between my teeth and chewed slowly, taking my time to make sure my food lasted the majority of the lunch period. Turns out you don't really need thirty minutes to eat lunch if you don't have someone to talk to. I knew that fairly well back during the first semester, but I must have forgotten in the time since beginning to eat with Mona.

Eating lunch alone was always the norm. I'd sit in the corner and chat online with some virtual friends I had never and probably would never meet in person, and I was reasonably okay with that. There was even one follower who talked to me almost every day. He said his name was Axel, but I always assumed that was a fake name. I didn't care.

Axel was *cool* and was always up to interesting things. He played in a band and wrote fantastic songs. The songs were always in this unique reggae-rock style with a casual groove to them.

He was actually part of the reason I'd gotten interested in taking the creative writing class in my last semester of high school. I even told him so.

Sam

Your lyrics are so great. I love
reading them. They always stick
with me.

Axel

I appreciate that! :)

Sam

I actually think I'm going to take
a creative writing class next
semester. I'm literally so inspired
by your writing.

Axel

Well, maybe someday when we
meet for real I can find some
new way to inspire you.)

That message made my stomach do a full front flip. I thought about that winky face for days. I never asked what he meant. The mystery was so enticing, I wouldn't dare. Not to mention, the idea of meeting him made me nervous in such thrilling ways.

I could imagine our first hug, the touch of our chests to one another, and how warm and inviting it must be, to finally be with someone for real for the first time. Well, physically *with* each other, not like *with* him with him.

Realistically, I'd be stupid to not think Axel was attractive, but obviously, I'm not gay, so I knew these little fantasies were strictly platonic.

In my mind, his arms were always a safe space, and I just wasn't all that used to feeling safe and welcome until recently, when our messages had grown slightly more infrequent.

Until Mona.

And something about starting lunch without Mona felt different. It made my mind restless. I wasn't sure if she would come late or come at all. I never knew if I should expect her to be acting normally, or if she'd be falling apart.

I supposed at this point, falling apart was normal for her. I'd watched the world help me beat her down and down until she took up so little space, it was easy to forget she was there. Of course, I never forgot she was there, but I noticed basking in her misery wasn't quite as sweet as it was at the start of all this. It seemed the novelty of the situation had worn off. I had what I wanted, but I just couldn't stop. It was like being a double agent. I felt so important to both sides, like a missing link in a chain, connected to reality. Leta and Raf and Oscar got to see Mona for the succubus she was, and Mona got to see the consequences of her own actions.

Yet, I just couldn't stop myself from wanting to comfort her when she was down or tell her it would all be okay, even if I knew it wouldn't. Even though *I* was the reason it wouldn't.

In a way, it was like overkill. But perhaps, my subconscious was treating this whole experience like a zombie movie. *Always* double tap the enemy. Don't just assume they're down after one whack over the head with a fire extinguisher. That's when they take the chance to come up behind you and bite your shoulder, effectively getting you killed by the rest of the team.

No.

I was smarter than that. I knew to play both sides as long as possible, even if it felt a little icky while doing it. That was going to ensure my own safety in this new world order for as long as possible, and ensure Mona stayed down.

A tap came on my shoulder, and I jolted a bit in fear, twisting around in my stool to see who had touched me.

It was a distressed Mona, her hand still angled at my shoulder. She didn't appear even slightly taken aback by my jump.

"Oh, Mona," I exhaled in relief. "You scared me," I confessed with a small, uncomfortable laugh.

Her eyes were so warm, they looked like brown storm clouds swirling around her wide pupils. Despite the disheveled vibe she'd been giving off, her eyes stayed as alive as ever.

Perhaps that should have worried me more.

She crossed her arms in front of her chest. She wore a loose, apricot-colored mock-neck sweater with some little ruffles on the shoulders, like tiny little fins. They were the most interesting part of her otherwise plain outfit. I remembered her telling me once she loved neutrals because they made her hair the focal point of every outfit, and she loved her hair so much.

I wondered if that were true as it lay stuck under her arms and slightly tucked into one armpit as she spoke. "Why did you hang out with Oscar last weekend?"

I paused, processing the affront to my loyalty to her, however warranted it may have been.

This gave her more opportunities to speak.

"And Leta. *And* Raf? What exactly were you trying to do? You never hung out with them before."

This was it. This was exactly what I was afraid of, and suddenly, all the power and control over the situation I'd felt left my body. I was shriveling into a worm, attempting desperately to wriggle free from the situation.

"I don't know," I answered automatically. What a bonehead response.

"No?" Mona asked. I couldn't tell if she was more hurt or angry. If my head had been a bit clearer at this point, I'm sure I would have been able to tell, but my head was too busy spiraling into the worst-case scenarios that could incur past this moment.

Would she hit me? Would she scream and cause a scene? I didn't necessarily want all that attention.

"I mean, Leta invited me, and I said yes. And Leta invited Oscar and I invited Dante, who invited Raf." I mean, at least, I wanted to invite

Dante who would have invited Raf. Did it matter who I invited first if they both would have come? I'm sure it did to Mona at that moment, but I certainly wasn't going to be giving her any ammunition. "Dante and I are in pre-calc together. We do homework and stuff sometimes, I was just trying to be nice."

Her next question came straight out of left field, and quickly like it had been planned.

"Did you all talk about me?"

I felt my jaw opening and closing as my head bobbed around looking for answers in the air that were obviously not there. I was at a loss. I didn't know what to say that wouldn't incriminate me too.

"Not me," I said. "Some of the others did though."

"And you didn't say anything? Not even in my defense?" Her arms dropped in disbelief. I could have sworn I saw her shoulders droop. At this point, I imagined she was more sad than frustrated. Great news! She probably wasn't going to hit me.

"Of course I did!" And that was true. "Oscar asked us all if we wanted to go and toilet-paper your house on the way home and I said not to because that's childish!" This did actually happen. It was a mixture of not wanting to get in trouble, and not wanting to spend my money on toilet paper for a lame prank. I'd already gotten my revenge, if Oscar wanted to get his revenge, it would be on *his* dime. But again, I wasn't going to say all that.

"Wow," Mona nodded sarcastically, almost laughing. "That's it? Because it's childish? There's no other reason you could think of for why they should vandalize my mother's home? Gee, Sam. *Thank* you. You're such a fucking hero." Now she was angry, for sure.

She hadn't spoken to me like this in years. I was suddenly transported back in time, to years past when she was so upset with me after that stupid party all because I wanted to take our relationship to the next level. And even with the hint of familiarity of the moment, I knew it was different. Mona was speaking to me, directly. She wasn't sending some shitty message to me telling me to fuck off at four in the morning. This time, it was the middle of the afternoon, in the middle of the cafeteria, and I could see her face. This time, I wasn't angry with her.

I was fucking terrified.

"What else did they say about me?"

That's when it clicked. I wanted to deflect and say she should ask Leta, but she said she was already planning to. So I asked, "Did you talk to Leta? Is that where all this is coming from?"

"Yes, and she's pissed. She thinks I was interested in Oscar or something. I just…" She stopped her sentence, gave up, and almost as if those were the magic words, the sad took over again. Her arms came back up to her chest, protecting her heart, as I watched her crumble again.

"He must have told her something. He must have gotten to her first and made some shit up."

That's when I stood. I put a hand on her back and guided her to sit down. I watched the swirls of amber in her eyes well up as she tried not to cry.

I hadn't seen her cry yet, and it really did set off an ache in my heart somewhere. I realized just then, it doesn't matter who's producing the tears-- watching someone at one of their most vulnerable moments can really get to you.

Mona dabbed her eyes, leaving dark, wet spots on her sleeve. She sniffed once and shook her head, refusing to let the tears flood her lashes.

"You're all I have left, Sammy. You can't leave me too." She said.

A bona fide twist of the knife. And it shouldn't have been. I shouldn't be feeling bad for her. I shouldn't be feeling this empathy. All of my pain was supposed to just go into her. *I* was supposed to be free of this.

Two years prior, Mona had ditched me for every one of these people. She chose friendships with Leta and Oscar, (and maybe not Rafael, but certainly some other boyfriend that wasn't me), and left me to rot. Now everyone was leaving her to rot and I was "all she had left".

A near-perfect karmic cycle had made its rotation back to her.

And I still felt like shit.

"Let's do something after school. Just me and you."

"I have to work," Mona said.

"Well, this weekend then. I missed you all last week and we have to catch up." I offered my most sincere smile. "I want you to know I'm still here for you."

She nodded and leaned in to give me a hug. I wrapped my arms back around her and she left her head leaning on my shoulder for an extra second longer than normal before she made the laborious move to support her own weight again.

It looked like it took a toll on her, and all her energy was in her neck, keeping her chin up.

The hug was warm, probably because I felt cold as a result of my conscience's sudden appearance.

Apparently spending all of your time for several weeks pretending someone is your friend makes some part of you think you're actually friends. That's the only way I could explain it.

I'd have to find a way out another day.

CHAPTER TWENTY-SEVEN

Mona

On Friday, Mr. Howard told us we were to write prose. Specifically focusing on the things we want the most. He said, "Reach down deep into your heart and reveal an unexpected desire. Show me what it looks like! Prose has no gimmick! They're just words, so make them count, and make them meaningful."

Never Cried Wolf

He advised us to brain-dump first, and I did. I sketched out little words for things that were on my mind.

gRief   fRieNdship

  loss   eNcouRagemeNt

I remembered the Intro to Psychology class I'd taken sophomore year and the stages of grief. I remembered the bargaining stage and the feeling of wanting to negotiate and argue things back to the way they were. What was I willing to do? What was I willing to give up to get what I really wanted? I really wanted my life back.

  baRgaiN   wish

beg   God?   time

  debt   actioN

I wanted to go back in time. And if I couldn't do that, what did I need to do to earn the people I'd lost back into my life? Could I repay my debt to them with action? Show not tell?

If I appealed to some higher power or the universe and asked for assistance, or prayed for these things, what if the power answered? What if I didn't like the answer? What if He tells me to move on and leave this behind me? What if my best friend becomes a thing of the past?

There were some things I didn't want to leave behind?

What if I said I'd do anything? Be anything?

doll   puppet   toy?

pulling strings   control

marionette

Would I even be myself anymore?

Would it even matter?

I was ready to write, and it came fairly naturally. I wrote it like a letter and signed it.

Never Cried Wolf

I've fallen to my knees, but I'm begging to be picked up again by whoever may be listening. Winds, spirits, I'm screaming to the clouds to God, and through the crust of the Earth to the Fates far below to let me stand once again. I cannot walk without a stutter or shake. I cannot even step without a falter. My knees are weak and unsteady.

Paint my eyelids with dark liner, and add whites to the corners of my eyes. Make me over with red paint to

Rouge my lips and cheeks. Give me life again so I can feel like somebody.

I don't need pity or autonomy. I need to stand. Weave a line through my spine to raise my chin back up. I want to tangle with the masses and blend in with them again.

Wrap the strings around my wrists and tighten them til I bleed, and lace them into perfect bows. Make it so I cannot slip through the loops and back to the soil again. Polish my arms, legs, and joints so I can shine once more.

Tell me what to do, move me just so. Make each motion part of your plan so I can finally rise.

Tell me who I must appear to be so I might be accepted once again.

Tell me where I must go to have the happiness I held before.

Do not condemn me to dwell among the insects and fallen leaves where I may decompose, and rot away to nothing.

Pull me left, then pull me right. Let the strings hold me upright.

At least a limp marionette won't feel so lonely.

And maybe in time, I can go alone.

But for now, sweet universe, and clouds, and stars, and moon. Tell me what to do to appear alive.

Please answer.

Please.

Sincerely, me.

Never Cried Wolf

I doubted I'd ever been too vulnerable in any piece of writing. I second-guessed every word as I etched it into my notebook paper, leaving dents in the page with the intensity with which I pressed.

The impressions pushed into the pages behind the original, I knew, but I was feeling a little too hard to care.

Sam carelessly swiped his pencil across the lined pages. I noticed he'd started writing in pen at the top and scratched so many words out before switching. I supposed writing was a lot like math in that way. Mr. Howard warned us at the beginning of the semester we might prefer pencils, but some of us were stubborn or otherwise stuck in our habits.

I certainly was. One couldn't get this upset over a change without being a creature engrossed in their own routines, and the last few weeks had been anything but.

Mr. Howard noticed my pencil had stopped moving, I assumed, which immediately had him weaving through his two half-circles to get to me.

He spun the notebook around to face him and he began to read, line by line. He always tried to read with a smile to start. I wondered if it was to intimidate us less or if he was actually that excited to read our works.

I couldn't imagine this angsty teenage drama garbage I'd just smushed into the paper was up his alley.

That seemed clear as his smile slowly faded and his eyebrows raised.

I considered for a moment that he might be preparing to call the school psychiatrist to pull me out of class to talk about my feelings, but he didn't. Instead, he said, "Mona, this is fantastic. You've grown so much since you first started writing here. I can tell you really let yourself go in this one. Would you mind sharing this with the class?"

My eyes flicked over to Sam, who had overheard Mr. Howard and now looked at me expectantly. He shrugged as a form of encouragement. A subtle "why not?"

I could think of a couple reasons why not, namely I couldn't fathom crying in class again. This stuff hurt to think about, and it was possible that reading it out loud might crack my facade in half.

On the other hand, I seemed to get through writing it just fine.

Perhaps reading it aloud wouldn't be so bad, and this was hands down the most positive response I'd gotten on any of my poetry from Mr. Howard. Maybe this would be good for me.

"Okay," I spoke. The words came out soft and cracked a little. My uncertainty was evident, but Mr. Howard seemed not to notice.

"Class, I'm going to have Mona read her piece out loud. I'd like for you to listen for the running metaphor and see how you can really picture what's happening," he said, absent-mindedly returning my notebook to me so I could head over to his podium, where the students usually read their works to the class.

The class was small, we only had about fifteen people in the room, less if someone was absent. I imagined there were about twelve today, but I was too busy looking down at my words to count. I'd done tons of speeches and presentations in classes before. I always considered myself fairly good at talking, but this was different.

Or maybe I was different.

It just didn't feel the same.

I took a deep breath in tandem with the silencing of the class and spoke, "I've fallen to my knees," I stopped at the comma and took another breath before finishing the line, "But I'm begging to be picked up again by whoever may be listening."

And over the next two minutes, as I read through my words, it was real. On paper, it seemed like a metaphor, but saying it out loud made me genuinely feel as though I was begging.

I begged the class in front of me, and the whole world, to let me feel like a person again and not a crumbled sheet of paper tossed into a trash bin.

I doubt half of the class even listened, but I heard the quakes in my breath and the voice of a beaten-down soldier slamming my brain against the walls of my skull sending messages to my eyes to cry.

As I uttered my final pleas, the class faltered for a moment of awkward silence before a handful offered simple applause as was customary. The two douchey kids in the back left of the semi-circle always snapped. That was their prerogative, but it always read a little more pretentious than they thought.

"Thank you, Mona," Mr. Howard said. He'd come up behind me but I hadn't realized. He motioned for me to go back to my seat. I could tell he was being gentle.

I looked over at my desk where Sam sat staring at me with a set of wide puppy-dog eyes.

The pity on him hit me like boiling steam. It was hot and uninviting.

"Can I use the restroom, please?" I asked.

"Yes, take as long as you need," Mr. Howard said with a solemn nod.

This was the worst. I couldn't take the sad looks I recognized on every face around me. I knew I shouldn't have read aloud. I should have just insisted it wasn't done.

With my notebook in hand, I shuffled my way out of the room and down the hall.

How was this the best I'd written all year?

How could that be?

What was so bad about everything else?

I'd learned a lot about authors struggling with depression, alcoholism, and drug issues in some cases because it did something to their writing.

For the first time, I wrote about something that caused me pain, and it's the finest thing I'd shown my teacher, and I'd "grown." Why did it seem so much like I had to be sad to write well? Was it that much more relatable, or do people like Mr. Howard and the rest of the class just revel in how things aren't so bad for them, and I'm just a reminder to be grateful?

That was bullshit.

All of this was bullshit.

This was the one thing that had gone right all week, and it still felt like a smack in the face.

My face was hot, and my eyes stung. I must have been crying, but when I pushed into the bathroom door, my cheeks were completely dry according to the mirror on the other side of the entrance.

I simply stared at myself, wondering how I could have thought I was crying. The sensation was so similar.

There was only one explanation. I was out of tears to cry, and that was probably for the best.

CHAPTER TWENTY-EIGHT

Sam

I simply tracked Mona as she scurried across the front of the room and broke out into the hallway. Her walk probably would have looked casual to anyone really looking, but I could tell she was anxious. I knew she was upset.

Fuck, *I* was upset. Something that had been stirring inside me finally broke loose and all I wanted to do was find Mona and talk this out with her. I really, truly felt guilty.

Never Cried Wolf

Up to this point, I'd felt somewhat removed from the situation. I had this perfect image in my head of what her misery would look like. It was that picturesque oil painting with dark shadows and tons of color, almost baroque. Mona was frozen in time with a single tear coming down one cheek as she sat alone. It was hauntingly beautiful, the way I always imagined it.

But the reality was so much different. It wasn't a momentary sadness. It was constant. It didn't end. It was the movement of the tears down her cheeks, the rise and fall of her shoulders in a sob, the sounds, the heaving against, and every little moment that looked so beautifully posed in my head that made it so much uglier and nastier when it was happening in real-time.

I was at a loss for what to do. Listening to her words, and her voice losing a battle not to break. I could tell she was holding back. My gut told me she had gone somewhere to cry. And wasn't it my job as her only friend left to go after her and make this better?

I rose my hand but shoved it back down again.

How was I supposed to make it better? Wasn't I the one who made it worse?

Wasn't this all my fault? And how was I supposed to make it better for her without making it worse for me?

This quest for revenge had turned into something very physical. Everything seemed a whole lot like throwing a punch. I wanted to make her hurt, and in the process, I bruised my own hand.

I felt the throbbing all over my body, and all I could think was, "Was what she did really all that bad?"

Could I really rationalize this guilt away?

Every little technicality and explanation felt small. Too small to be real or realistic. I was mad, I knew that was true, but now that I saw her knocked on the ground after the punch, it was all so petty. It was childish. I'd thrown a tantrum and destroyed the candy aisle of the grocery store in the process. There wasn't any sweet reward as I'd intended.

Just a gross, swirling evil in my gut.

I *saw* what I'd done, and it really had a way of reframing everything to make me feel like a complete ass.

Mr. Howard crouched at the edge of my desk. "You need something?"

Turns out I didn't put my hand down as quickly as I'd thought.

"No. Well…" I trailed off into silence. I felt my words start and falter over and over as Mr. Howard patiently watched and waited for me to respond.

"Do you want to go check on Mona?" He attempted to fill in the blank for me.

"I'm not sure," I confessed. "I'm afraid," I said without thinking.

"The heaviest things feel lighter when you share the load. Share your fear, and she'll share hers and maybe you'll both feel a little better."

I didn't expect that to hit as hard as it did. It struck me in such a way that I immediately stood up with a plan of following Mona. Perhaps it was the newfound vulnerability I was experiencing, but those words brushed up into an open wound that never healed.

I was still hurting from Mona, and now Mona was hurting from me. Maybe just being upfront would solve our problems.

Maybe we could *genuinely* be friends again instead of circumventing any true friendship I found with her.

If I didn't want to be her friend on some level, surely I would have dumped her when I had the chance. It wasn't just about avoiding confrontation. I *liked* having friends, and people to talk to.

These last few weeks had been wonderful, always feeling like I had something to do or someone to talk to, even when it wasn't important in the slightest… was getting back at Mona worth losing that connection?

Clearly my subconscious didn't think so. my grudge had taken over. I wanted to talk to her now and free the air a bit. "The truth will set you free" and all that, right?

Maybe she'd understand.

Did she even have a choice?

If I was all she had left, it was unlikely she'd completely drop me as a friend. It might be awkward, but at least then there was no more dancing around each other. We'd finally be looking right at each other.

"Don't forget to take a pass!" Mr. Howard called to me as he walked to the next desk.

I realized I was already partway across the room, following the invisible path Mona had left behind.

I made sure to pause and snag a room pass off a hook on the wall before breaching the threshold into the hallway.

Brianna Rae Quinn

The halls sat empty with no soul in sight. There were still about ten minutes left in class, so I knew I had some time in silence to find Mona and talk to her.

Mr. Howard's awareness somewhat caught me off-guard. Turns out that spending your entire day reading the emotional musings of folks in a creative writing class makes you some sort of psychological master.

Emboldened, and inspired, I wandered down the open tile to the closest bathroom. It was a right turn out of the room and down at the corner before the turn into the second cafeteria.

The lockers on this floor were a deep plum purple to honor the school colors: purple and gold. Upstairs, they were all beige, I imagined because gold paint was a touch more expensive.

I recognized the plum lockers passing by in a blur, looking like a brush stroke on a canvas. I was walking a bit faster than I usually would.

Never Cried Wolf

The restroom door had come into view. It was closed, and I was suddenly unsure, again, of what I would do when I got there. What was I going to do? Walk right in?

What if someone else was already in there?

My pace slowed, and I could see the edges of every locker as I passed again.

The world around me stopped moving once I reached the door. My feet halted at the archway, fearing, again, what lay on the other side.

But I'd already decided to be fearless for the next ten minutes at least, so I pushed the door open a crack and called inside.

"Mona?"

"Yeah?" She replied very quickly. Her voice came much more evenly than I expected.

"Can I... uh..." I wondered about the least creepy way to ask the question.

"I'll come out." She said. Thank god.

I heard a rustle of a notebook. She must have picked it up from wherever she'd dropped it before coming back out into the hall.

The moment I caught a glimpse of her sunset orange braid, I reached out and hugged her.

She hesitated for only a minute before wrapping her arms around me in return.

I could tell we'd hugged a little too long, but neither of us released our grips.

Mona let out a deep, almost exasperated sigh. She didn't appear to be crying, nothing as I expected, but I couldn't say the same for myself. My nose burned.

I knew why I didn't want to let go. I didn't want to look at her when I said what I was about to say.

"Mona, I'm so sorry," I whispered in her ear. A little tear formed in my words and threatened to let out a cry, which I stuffed back down my throat, further making me sound like I was choking.

"I'm not your fault," she replied, which was probably the worst thing she could have said because now I had to say it.

And so I did.

"It is. It was me. It was all my fault," I held her so tightly. I didn't want to know the way her face was contorting. I needed to wait until everything was on the table.

"What do you--" her voice lilted in confusion, but no anger. I stopped her.

"It's me. I did it. I'm the one pulling your strings, and I'm so sorry, Mona."

The silence that followed was deafening. I waited for her grip to loosen. I waited for her to yell and hit me.

It never came, and to fill the sense of dread I felt in the silence, I simply spilled my guts.

"I told Leta something was going on with you and Oscar. I told Oscar you were spreading rumors about him. And I sent the tweet and told

Dante you had a less than pleasant history with men. I did it all. It's my fault."

I gripped her harder, letting a few tears escape my eyes and land on her shoulder and back, soaking into her striped sweater. I knew I was bracing for the blow-up, and then…

"Okay," she said.

That shocked me into pulling away. I looked at her face. She looked apathetic, numb.

"You're not mad." It came out as more of a statement than a question as if I'd only noticed.

"Can you fix it?" was all she said. She was looking right at me, but I didn't feel like she was really looking. Her stare wasn't vacant necessarily, but certainly not pointed. There was no focus, just a look. It was strange and unexpected.

"What do you mean?" I responded.

"Can you tell Leta it was a mistake? Can you tell Dante and Rafael you lied?" A pause flitted between us. "I don't care about Oscar." She noted.

It took me a moment to think, but I already knew the answer.

"They'll hate me, Mona. I can't."

I didn't think it needed any more explanation. If I confessed to everything I'd been doing, then my friendships with these people would be dead immediately-- if they even trusted me ever again.

"And there's no guarantee they'll forgive you either. They might think you're pushing me to say this or vouch for you. They might even hate you more."

Mona's dark eyes dropped to the tile at our feet. "You're right." She mumbled, punctuating the statement with a dry swallow. It sounded painful.

"I'm so sorry, Mona. I don't think I ever expected it to go this far," I still had wet streaks down my cheeks as I spoke. I went from trying to desperately avoid her gaze to wanting her to look at me and acknowledge me. I wanted to feel seen by her again. The only way I could fathom making this guilty feeling go away was for her to say she forgave me.

She hadn't yet.

"Can you forgive me?" I could hear the begging tone and the whine vibrating through my lips into the space between us.

Even if she didn't forgive me, she could at least be upset, or be… anything really. Why wasn't she reacting?

The silence reigned on, mirrored by a pensive, avoidant stare from Mona.

"If you don't forgive me, please just yell at me so this can be over."

I felt like an asshole-ish thing to say, even as it came out, but I didn't care. I needed to be absolved of all these icky feelings. I wanted to feel welcome, and like myself again, and no matter what I did, no matter what I was doing, nothing ever felt right. Validation, or vindication. Neither seemed to serve me.

This vigilante quest for justice wasn't me. This sniveling whiney child begging for forgiveness wasn't me. I didn't have a damn clue who I was because it all felt so fucking wrong all the time.

Everything was a show, and at this point, I didn't care how good of an actor I was, I wanted a break for a little bit. I wanted to know myself for more than a brief moment, and I still couldn't figure out how.

The bell echoed against the empty halls. My time alone with Mona was up as the space around us filled.

"I'm not going to yell. I just want some time alone, though. I'll see you tomorrow at lunch, okay?"

"You will?" I wondered.

"Yeah," She nodded and walked back down the hall to Mr. Howard's, presumably to grab her bag. I knew mine was in there too, but something didn't feel right about following her.

I stepped into the men's restroom next door and walked over to the sink to wash my hands and splash a little water on my face. I set my glasses on the edge and patted the water onto my skin. I glanced up at my reflection in the mirror. When I looked at my reflection, I recognized my face, but he still felt like a complete stranger.

CHAPTER TWENTY-NINE

Mona

He's all I have left. He made it that way. And I just couldn't decide if that meant I should forget about him and be alone, or if I should forgive him so I still had something keeping me in Kettlewood.

This all felt so reminiscent of freshman year. I could remember explicitly how hurt and upset I was to know Sam had betrayed me and completely put me on blast all those years ago. I can remember every comment, calling me names and insisting I was the problem. He was able to convince hordes of strangers that I was a villain.

He convinced my own friends that I was a villain.

And I knew, finally, with certainty, that it wasn't me.

And it still didn't make it any fucking better.

I still had the rest of junior year and all of senior year before I would be free of this place, and that meant getting comfortable at least, didn't it?

I slipped into Mr. Howard's room to grab my things. He sat at his desk shuffling through the day's worth of poetry he'd be grading. I chose not to say anything as I moved to retrieve my bag.

Sam's bag still sat in the chair at his desk. I knew he didn't follow me. I wondered what his game plan was, but I didn't care.

"Hey," Mr. Howard called from his desk, "I'm really proud of you for sharing your work today. I know it was hard."

Never Cried Wolf

I looked over at him and nodded with a forced smile, at least it felt forced. I could feel my lips unnaturally tight over my teeth. I was still tense, and I thought he could tell as well.

"You know," he began again, putting down his little green grading pen (because red pens "looked scarier"), "You don't *have* to stay in a situation just because you think it's more comfortable. Sometimes change is a good thing." His hands folded under his chin as he watched me collect my bag, and my one loose pencil on the desk. "Do you know what I mean?"

"Yes, and thank you," I said with a slightly looser smile.

I wandered out of the classroom with a half-hearted wave in Mr. Howard's direction, and he nodded before turning his attention back to his desk.

Sam wasn't anywhere I could see. If he was waiting for me to leave to come back and grab his things, that was a good move on his part.

At least he was self-aware enough to leave me alone right now.

I considered what Mr. Howard said.

Adults always thought the solutions were so easy. Nothing was ever as black and white as they made it seem.

Of course, I began wondering if he had somehow broken into my mind and figured out what was going on between me and Sam, or if he was subtly encouraging me to drop his class because I couldn't take a little read-aloud.

I sure hoped that wasn't it.

Strangely, Creative Writing always made me feel a little looser. Nothing ever went away, it seemed, but something felt good about putting a name and words to everything that was happening.

I wrote about how willing I was to be a marionette, and it turns out I already was in some wild reverse-Pinocchio situation.

Never Cried Wolf

Was I really willing to continue to be around Sam because he was comfortable? Or was it because there was no one left?

Did I even really trust him to stick around? I might have had all of next year, but he was a senior. He'd be checked out come June, and there I'd be, still stuck sad and alone until I inevitably stayed home on Prom night to avoid getting my house toilet papered by Oscar and his other shitbag friends. Or worse, Carrie'd with pig guts in some sort of cruel prank.

Was I really going to continue to call Sam my friend because it was easy?

It felt easy to just ignore everything and act like his little confession was a nasty joke, but I knew it wasn't. I knew he meant to hurt me, and he succeeded in hurting me, and now I was just about to… let it slide?

Experience had already dictated that even the closest of friends will slip away from you when they go to college. They'll meet new friends and get too busy to hang around you ever and start talking to you like an "almighty grown-up" who sees the world as black and white regardless of how much gray they've seen.

They'll tell you to avoid your "proximity friends" and only focus on real ones while they treat you with that same regard as if *you* were that proximity friend, and probably make new ones. Like Jae and Netta.

But maybe… *that* was the solution?

Maybe I needed to show up at Jae's door and then he wouldn't be able to tell me to buzz off or he's too busy. Maybe I should just be that proximity friend again. Maybe *then* I'd get my well-deserved Code Barbie and I'd come back fresh-faced and having a damn clue what to do.

State College was about two hours away, but I could easily make that trip and be back in one day if I had to, Mom would surely lend me the care, and it was just all the better if I could stay the night.

Fuck it. I had to try.

Never Cried Wolf

My feet operated on autopilot. I headed down the hall. I was not a skipper, but Racquet and Net Sports had become one of the worst periods of the day as I strategically worked to avoid playing with and playing against Rafael.

Part of me reeled at how much it sucked knowing that he hated me now and there was almost nothing I could do to fix it. Even if Sam explained all this away and Raf apologized to me, did I even want to accept his apology? He had been so nasty to me, it made him so ugly in my eyes. I couldn't unsee the hate when he looked at me, and it completely engulfed the image of him I used to have. His emerald green eyes were now muddy and slimy, and his teeth sure bothered me a hell of a lot more now. It gave him a supervillain-quality grin-- very Joker-esque.

I'd long since decided that Oscar could absolutely go fuck himself upside down and sideways, but what about Leta? I wasn't quite ready to let her go. Now when I thought of her, I didn't think of her being nasty or angry. I saw her hurting and all I cared to do was fix it, even if it wasn't my fault.

I didn't know how to do that without Sam's full confession though, and I knew he wasn't going to save me here.

Buzz. The message couldn't have been timed better. It gave me a reason to stop before entering the gym.

Jae

2nite!?!??! omg id loooooove plz do

I was definitely thinking Saturday night since I had to work the next morning, but it wouldn't be the first time I called out sick this week. Honestly, if it weren't for how horrendously short-staffed the coffee shop was,

I would have certainly been fired by then. Or perhaps it would have been a better move to just swap with someone. Most of my coworkers around my age would take a morning shift, even a Saturday morning, over any evening because it's more hours. Evidently, nine to four is much more desirable than four to nine based on earning potential alone, who would have guessed?

Mona

Yeah, fuck it. I'll leave after
school. Mom shouldn't mind. :)

Jae

YEEEEES BITCH!!! futon is urs
4 wknd!
ps. i got a union fundraiser ur
gonna help with on sun n imma
get u tix for a play netta and i are
gonna see sat night!
im dedass sooooo fukin excite
babe!!!!

Brianna Rae Quinn

Wow. I wasn't expecting all that, but damn it was fantastic to see Jae get so excited about seeing me. I hadn't felt so loved and appreciated in a hot minute and it was like having a giant weight lifted off of me. I could tell I was standing a little straighter and smiling a little brighter.

I pushed my way into the gym. The bell must have rung already, but I hadn't noticed.

"Miss Murphy, you planning on participating today?" my teacher called, recognizing my tardiness.

"Yes sir!" I called, with a light salute on my forehead and a fast walk into the locker room as I tapped out a simple reply to Jae.

Mona

Cannot wait!

As I shuffled into the little alcove that houses the entrances to the locker rooms, I noticed Raf exiting the boy's room as I was heading in. Eric looked a little too long as me, and Raf appeared to be turning his head away from me.

He looked so stupid with his nose in the air like that, acting all high and mighty.

I rolled my eyes and gave a petty little wave at Eric as I slipped into the room and dropped my bag on the bench to retrieve my gym clothes.

I could have skipped. I considered skipping, but absolutely fuck that. I'd already given Sam way too much power over me, and I'll be damned if I let Rafael do the same.

Besides, I picked this class for us, so if we're being petty, I'll just say it.

I was here first. I had the whole weekend ahead to run away from my problems.

CHAPTER THIRTY

Sam

Leta

Band party-- usual place!!

Saturday at 7, bring something

to share!!! <3

PS I invited Dante and Raf!

Sam

I'll be there! :)

Never Cried Wolf

I was thrilled on Saturday night to be heading back to the local party spot, "Leta's Basement." She had the coolest AV set up down there, complete with a projector, tons of couches, and floor space. It was perfect for hanging out as well as playing everyone's favorite party games.

If there was one thing I always found true about folks with any artistic talent, it was the weirdly sexual nature of any party that ever occurred. We'd probably last about twenty minutes before someone recommended Seven Minutes in Heaven and acted like it wasn't a socially acceptable excuse to get nasty in some place other than their own bedrooms where their overly nosy parents would absolutely catch them.

This was the first party in Leta's basement I'd been invited to in years, and I was dying for a little something to spice up my weekends. Someone always did something unbearably stupid which was the talk of the band for the next week, and I couldn't wait to witness it again!

I parked my car just down the road a bit and walked up, leaving a set of tracks in the inch or two of snow, marking my movement up to the house in shockingly untimid footsteps.

I had spent a shocking amount of time concerned about Mona since we'd spoken. I was practically overwhelmed with guilt as I went to eighth period. I couldn't look at Dante without thinking of Mona begging me to fix this.

Truly, I wanted to, but I wanted to keep my happiness too. I wasn't going to damn myself for her sake, even if I did feel sorry for her.

If anyone understood that feeling of being on the outside looking in, it was me, but regardless of how strong I felt now, I still wasn't *that* strong.

The house smelled like hot chocolate. I hoped that meant what I thought it meant.

The door creaked open and revealed Leta's kitchen island, complete with a hot chocolate bar. Classic Mrs. Schneider to be a fantastic party planner-- even if it wasn't that kind of party.

Thankfully, she and Mr. Schneider always went out for party nights, at least until midnight. I'm sure they knew exactly what went on at these parties and perhaps ignorance is bliss for some people on these types of matters, like, they knew, they just didn't want to hear it all going on.

I grabbed a little Styrofoam cup and began filling it from the large old-school office-style coffee pot which was intended to keep it warm. The cocoa-colored liquid steamed a bit, fogging my glasses as it fell in. I took a gulp almost immediately, ignoring the peppermint and cinnamon sticks, whipped cream, and variety of sprinkles and marshmallow toppings in favor of simply warming up as quickly as possible.

I shed my coat, draping it over a chair alongside a few others before following the subtle hum of chatter coming from the basement door.

When I opened it, the sound hit me like a wave. I imagined the Schneiders paid good money to make sure this room was sound proofed after having kids.

Leta's older brother, now long gone at college, used to have legendary ragers down here. On second thought, that might have been why Leta's parents always dipped out on party nights for Leta, because *nothing* she could do would ever top her brother's craziness. Maybe it was a reward for the trust she'd earned.

"Sammy!!" Leta cried from the couch, jumping up and running across the space in two long strides to give me a big bear hug. She wasn't drunk. She never needed to be. She was just that infectiously happy. It almost made me forget everything for a moment. Almost.

"You're just in time for the ga-ames!" She sang in two syllables. A smile broke loose from my lips and I laughed as another clarinetist I recognized from band glugged down the remaining sips of a mountain dew, let out a thunderous belch, and capped the dew for the first game.

"Spin the Bottle!" he called, dropping the bottle to the center of the room where a handful of partygoers were already ready to roll.

A cursory glance told me Dante and Rafael weren't here yet, but Oscar sure was. He was chatting with a girl on the sofa who seemed cordial enough, but she didn't seem quite as interested as he was. I think her name was Elizabeth or Ellen or something that started with an E. I couldn't totally recall.

The first few spins are full of forced oohs and ahhs per usual. The real fun only started when the people who resisted initially started joining. They're always either chancing it on their crush or really uninterested in the lot, there was never a real in-between. Except for me, maybe. I just liked the random interactions. It's not like I'd had a lot in the last few years. Well, real ones.

The door clapped shut up the stairs, informing the crowd of new arrivals, and to my sheer delight, Dante stepped down first, followed shortly by Rafael who was carrying a big bag of Doritos, presumably to share.

Hopefully to share.

He reached down to me as I sat in the carpet circle and slapped my hand in hello. Dante did the same and I felt a little shutter of electricity. I loved when he did that. I felt so cool and it always got me going.

"What are we playing here?" Rafael asked, taking a seat between me and the unfamiliar girl to my left.

"Spin the bottle!" Leta called. "Wanna spin?"

"I thought it was Angie's turn?" A trumpeter questioned from across the circle with an ugly snicker.

"It's fine. Go on!" Angie said in response. Evidently, she was not a big fan of the game so far.

"Okay," Rafael smirked, and the game picked back up. Dante stuck himself in between the person to my right and me, and the circle squished to give him some room. I felt like a Sam sandwich with ROTC bread, and I wasn't mad about it. It felt comfortable there.

The bottle spun smoothly along the carpet a few times before landing on a flutist a few butts down to the right of me. She blushed deeply as Rafael cross the circle to her, placed both hands on her cheeks, and left a light kiss on her mouth.

She looked positively smitten.

Raf must have known was he was doing, acting like prince charming. In a way, it almost bugged me because we all knew this wasn't that kind of game, and I knew he wasn't all that perfect.

She giggled a little and her friends pushed her to spin the bottle finally. After a little whiney over the teasing, she groaned a said, "Fine! I'm going!" Still, a smile decorated her face like pure sunlight.

It felt too long as the bottle spun, and I felt my stomach lurch a little as it slowed down. It looked like it was going to land on me.

And it did.

The fairly plain flutist leaned across the circle and planted a thick, slightly too-long kiss on my lips. I noticed her top scooped a little extra low. I wondered if she was excited to kiss me at all. She seemed like she'd be excited to kiss anyone, honestly. I wondered if she was hoping to pull a Rafael and get me all giddy because everyone seemed to think I didn't get that many girls.

It didn't matter. I wasn't as thrilled as I imagined she'd hoped.

I shook my shoulders loose and leaned over to twist the bottle. Just a little flick of the wrist and off she went, spinning once, twice, and landing on… Dante, right next to me.

My stomach flipped again, but it was a little different this time. Not so much anxiety, but maybe a little... anticipation.

I looked at him, expectantly. He looked back and shrugged, then leaned over and lightly pecked my lips.

I didn't expect that, exactly. I guess I was expected a little more, "Nah, man, I ain't gay!" from anyone with a plan for the military, but people always find ways to surprise you.

And there was one other thing for certain I learned at that moment-- it was that even a light peck on the mouth from Dante was better than a sloppy kiss from a flutist. It probably wouldn't even matter to the flutist.

He quickly darted his hand out to spin again, *sssssssssssssssssssssss* it slid around slightly then stopped in the most peculiar place... back on me.

We looked at each other again, this time in tandem. I looked over at Leta. She smiled.

"You know the rules, bro. Twice in a row means you add tongue." The same douchebag trumpeter chortled, high fiving with another guy in the circle.

"That's a stupid rule," Leta said, attempting to come to my aid.

"It's fine!" I called quickly and then hesitated, turning back to Dante. "I mean if it's fine with you."

"It's a party man, I don't care. We're supposed to do wild shit." He leaned over and before I really had the time to process the fantastic moment it was, his lips crashed into mine and I felt a velvety lick of his tongue swiping lightly behind my teeth. I barely had a moment to snake mine into the mix before he pulled away.

I sat a moment, letting his delightful flavor settle before glancing back down at the bottle. I avoided placing my fingers to my lips to ensure the moment was real. I could tell even then this moment would be replaying in my head over and over for the rest of the night. Hell, maybe even the week.

I flicked the bottle again. I didn't seem to go that hard as it made a single rotation and landed back on Dante once again.

"Oh come on," Someone groaned, rolling their eyes.

"OH SHIT. THREE TIMES." One of the douchebag trumpeter's friends squealed like a little girl in glee.

"Closet! Closet!" The trumpeter started to chant before Dante shut it down.

"Dude, I know it's a party, but I'm *not* gay. I'm not doing all that." There it was. He spoke with a certain absolution. He didn't sound defensive, just matter-of-fact. That made it sting a bit less.

It really shouldn't have stung at all.

I wasn't gay either.

"Damn, it was just a joke, man. I'm not trying to find gay where gay don't go."

Leta stepped into the tension and offered a solution. "Spin again, Sammy." She spoke with the gentle tone of an encouraging tee-ball coach. It was arguably a bit too sweet in tone, but I appreciated it nevertheless.

As the evening wore on, I found myself stepping away from the games and just watching everything unfold. Part of me still liked being the wallflower, listening and learning new little things about everyone.

An hour or so later, I realized I hadn't yet said much to Oscar.

I plopped myself next to him on the sofa, where he sat still chatting up the girl with the E name.

"Hey, man, what's going on?" I asked nonchalantly, waving to the girl like I knew who she was. It was easier than admitting I wasn't sure.

"Nothing really, I was actually just going to take Elena home. She's a bit tired."

Elena. That was close enough to Ellen. I'd call that a win.

"You sure? I haven't seen you off the couch all night, and we're still going to be here a while." I wondered why he would want to leave so early, especially with a girl who clearly wasn't that interested. It's not like she would be all gung-ho about playing tonsil hockey with him in the backseat of his car. She still didn't even seem all too excited to have him next to her on the couch.

"Yeah, man. I mean," He paused and leaned in to whisper, "She'll owe me a little something." He snorted and gave me a playful shove as if to ask, "right?"

My eyes narrowed a little. That sounded a little too familiar to me.

I saw Mona flash at the back of my eyes, and all the panicked texts she sent me. Wasn't this exactly what she said Oscar did to her?

I nodded slowly, almost imperceivably, before standing up.

There are some times in your life when the room seems to get impossibly quiet when you're talking about something you don't want anyone else to hear. In hindsight, I wasn't sure if it was really as quiet as it felt in the moment, but when it came out, it sure felt that way.

"You're kind of a creep, you know that?" I said a little bit too loud.

"What?" Oscar called back, his face contorting in sheer confusion.

"You heard me," I said, trying to emulate that finality of Dante's voice earlier. I wondered if I'd somehow absorbed a little bit of his boldness when we kissed.

That's probably what it was because I couldn't think of a single other time I'd ever say something so directly from my brain.

Maybe the hot chocolate was spiked, or the emotions of the week had caught up to me. It didn't matter. I'd said it, and I was ready to leave.

I swerved around the stairs and bounded up them two at a time, wishing I'd already had my coat so I could storm out.

As I twisted the doorknob, I hear light footsteps pattering behind me. I turned and saw Leta just two steps behind me. We were alone in the little alcove hallways that led upstairs.

"Are you leaving?" Leta asked, innocently.

"Uh, yeah. I think so." I spoke automatically.

"What happened with Oscar?" She inquired. I wanted to just keep walking, but I could tell by the intensity in her eyes, she was not just going to let me go. I imagined her stealing my keys out of my coat pocket and trapping me at her front door so I couldn't run. She was like that sometimes.

She would have been like that at this moment. I knew.

My brain shuffled through a variety of cue cards and mindless statements I could use to escape. I sighed and spoke, "I just don't know if

Oscar's been telling the truth lately." That's the phrase I'd settled on.

"About… Mona?" She asked. The mention of her name twisted my guts again.

I wasn't sure how much more swirling they could take before I positively threw up-- then it would really look like a rager in here.

"Maybe," I replied.

Her head bobbed up and down in a nod, and she looked down at her feet, her hand still resting on the handrail. I watched her grip tighten and loosen as she considered her next words.

"I have to go." I beat her to it. "I would see if Elena wants to call for her own ride though."

Leta's eyes shot up at me. They reflected a deep understanding that somehow made me more confused.

I wondered what she'd just discovered. Surely it wasn't me and what I'd done. No. Her fire wasn't directed at me, it was festering in the back of her gaze, waiting for someone else. She wrapped me in a quick embrace, "Thanks, Sammy. Drive safe." She smiled with her lips only, then turned on her heels to head back downstairs.

How funny that I was so excited to be here to witness the drama first-hand. Instead, I got to experience it.

What a twist.

CHAPTER THIRTY-ONE

Mona

Kettlewood Confessions

@KWHS_Confess

17 hours ago

"Graduation can NOT come fast enough. #getmeout"

"Oof," Jae groaned, sitting across from me in the State dining hall. "Never was there anything so real."

Never Cried Wolf

I decided to show him the Kettlewood Confessions Twitter account solely because I thought he'd get a kick out of all the high school drama he was certainly missing.

I stabbed at a pile of cheese fries I'd secured from the line of wobbly college kids.

We had gone to see a few of his friends in a musical. The songs were phenomenal, but the microphones kept cutting in and out of some of the leads, so I think I missed some major plot points in the lost dialogue.

It was nearing eleven and Jae had "swiped me in" to the hall with his student ID. He said his meal plan gave him a set number of meals every semester, and he always had a ton left over. Not to mention he said Saturday nights, like this one, were always the best because this particular hall stays open late and serves nothing but drunk munchies to soak up some of the alcohol the students were undoubtedly drinking before they got back to their dorms. The lines were stacked with cheese everything, carbs, fried foods, and warm sweets.

I was grateful to have something to nervously chew as I prepared my next words.

"Why were you so excited to leave?" I asked him.

I had been wondering that question since he left. Every time he bitched about Kettlewood or praised whatever got him out of that podunk town, I wanted to ask.

"What do you mean?" He shoved a bite of a suspiciously soupy risotto into his mouth. His dark eyes scanned my face, looking for an explanation.

"It just feels like you are so happy to be away from me and your family and everyone we know. You seemed fine when you were still in town. Was it really that bad?" My fingers absently reached for a braid of hair draped over my shoulder and I started picking through some frizzy ends that didn't appreciate being shoved in and out of an elastic to secure the plait.

Never Cried Wolf

Jae swallowed his bite hard as his brows wrinkled in the middle. He didn't look confused, but perhaps a little disappointed.

"You know it wasn't about you, Mona," he started. "I love you and you were the best part of that shithole! And we had the best times driving around all the country roads and walking through all the lake trails, but, it's just that… being happy only when I was with you wasn't enough." He explained.

My head made a swift, shaky nod, and my eyes averted down to my plate.

"Not in a nasty way, babe. I just mean you were the *only* person I felt like myself around. Like, I was one of, what? Three total Asian kids, not to mention gay, and even after I came out to my parents, I still felt like I was pretending to be the regular old straight son they wanted because, even if they didn't say it, they'd just, like… look at me different, you know?"

I looked back up at him, more in awe than anything. As comfortable as we were with one another, I didn't think Jae had ever been so honest or vulnerable like this with me. Code Barbies were constantly shrouded in mystery and wordless support.

"I mean, I knew you didn't get along with your parents all the time--" I began, but he cut me off.

"Or anyone, Mona. You're like the only person who didn't treat me differently or look at me sideways. It never mattered to you, even if I got mean or rude, you always tried to focus on what mattered and like, who I *really* was, not just the resident gay boy or the token Asian for diversity, which, I can't even possibly tell you how fucking grateful I am for that, but the times I wasn't with you-- I was just so *angry*. *All* the time."

Another nod from me told him to keep going.

"And like, not everyone was directly mean, but you can just feel when you're not welcome somewhere and I *never* felt welcome there. The stigma of it all just kinda made it worse. And the teachers are always like 'be yourself! But not if you're going to be a flaming distraction' and they'd like patiently wait to invalidate you or talk over you because whatever you had to say just wasn't as valuable as anyone else, or was like, too valuable because I happened to be in a math class and microaggressions in the Midwest are just, like, standard. Sometimes I would just say and do things to feel *powerful* or like I had some sort of control over *something*. But here, *everyone* is new, and *everyone* is different, and nobody *runs* this school. Even if they do, it's so fucking big, I can just run to the people who give a shit. The theatre kids, the Asian Student Union, hell, there's gay fraternities of people who just fucking *get it*. Finally, I'm not the only gay kid, or the only Asian kid, or even the only one who is *both*."

He sighed and looked around, seemingly searching for more words.

"I so love you for all the comfort you gave me for, like, my entire post-pubescent existence, but high school was only just the beginning of finding your place. Actually-- it's not even the beginning, it's just like… the exposition, you know? Just the background stuff and then you go away and start focusing on what really matters and what you really want to do and *that's* where things really start! In high school, you're still dealing with the same shit-bag kids that you've been dealing with for over a decade of schooling. This is a real, fresh start. You can really pick your people, and not just settle for whoever lives next door or deal with friends you've 100% grown out of just because you have some sentimental attachment or feel like you owe them something. And you're not limited by what the adults think matters because you *are* the adult. They have a club here just for nerds to sit around and play Dungeons and Dragons. Can you fucking imagine that in Kettlewood? And you know what, it's fun as fuck. I went once with a friend from my Comp class and I'm like a fuckin Orc or some shit. Still not a clue what it means, and I never went back, but just-- everyone has a place and can find their people. And to be fair, some already have their people, and for them, they're back home, and that's fine! It just wasn't like that for me."

He stopped to take another breath. I felt a stinging behind my eyes. I could tell I wanted to cry. Whether it was relief that Jae's vehement refusal to come home almost ever wasn't about me or if it was because his story just happened to hit me square in the chest, I wasn't sure.

"The people around you right now, Mona. Those are your *proximity friends*. They're in your life because they're *there*. Like, if you went on a month-long vacation to Europe tomorrow, how many of them would you try to text or call every day? Or even, like, remotely regularly? Seriously. Think about it."

I considered the question carefully.

"Leta, probably," I answered.

"See what I mean? Just one. And you're my one. Everyone else will fall away, and that's totally okay! That just means the best times of your life are ahead of you, and that's so cool. It's what keeps me going-- knowing tomorrow could be the best day of my life!"

I really hadn't seen Jae so happy or comfortable before. He was smiling, glowing even, particularly with the fluorescent lights reflecting off his shiny black hair.

"Things might be hard for you right now, but they get so much better after high school. Stereotypes and shitty people exist everywhere, but the world gets so much bigger too, so those things just seem smaller. The problems feel smaller." His words wrapped around my head and held them in an embrace. It was so comforting, and something about hearing them while I was actually here, away from Kettlewood made them hit a little harder, and stick a little easier.

A sad laugh hissed out of my nose as I smiled. I still fought the burning sensation behind my eyes as I decided to tell Jae exactly why I wanted to come here this weekend.

"Sam told me he tried to ruin my life," I started. "Well, he did, actually… kind of… ruin my life."

Jae tipped his head to one side. "Come again?"

"He, I guess, spread a bunch of lies about me and now no one's talking to me anymore. No one but you."

"Leta too?" He asked.

I nodded, solemnly.

"And Oscar, um, on the way home the other day, he like… Locked his doors and like, told me I owed him something for all the rides home I got."

Jae leaned in, and his dark eyes widened. "What!? Are you serious?"

"Yeah, I mean, he like, kissed me or whatever, and then he tried to get me to touch him, and I…"

"Mona, what the fuck!? Did you tell anyone?"

I stared back at him. "Well, no, I--"

"You *need* to! That's so fucking serious. He *assaulted* you, Mona."

"Well, I mean, he didn't hurt me, he just…"

"No. Stop." I stopped. He looked so serious, I had to. "Did you want to kiss him or touch him or whatever?"

"No, but I didn't stop it," I answered simply.

"It *doesn't matter*. Coercion is assault too. He can't just lock you in a space and tell you you have to over and over like you owe him your fucking body. That's YOUR body, Mona. Fuck him! You have to report him."

"To who?"

"Literally anyone! Like, call the police and file a report, and if you're too scared to, talk to your mom or a teacher or something. I'll literally call with you right now if you don't want to do it alone."

My hairs were standing up and I could tell I was on edge, which allowed the sudden buzz of my cell on the table to make me jump a little out of my seat (and possibly a little out of my skin.) It felt bizarre to hear these words. I was assaulted?

I didn't have enough time to process as flipped my phone over and recognized the name of the number which had texted me.

Leta.

"Leta just texted me," I said.

"What? What did she say?"

I read it out loud to him.

Leta

Can we talk tomorrow? About everything.

I pivoted the phone around on the table and slid it over to Jae for him to see.

"What do I say?"

"Say yes, dumbass. That looks like an olive branch to me." Jae stated, taking a sip from a large glass of coke in exasperation.

"That's all? I don't even know when I'm leaving tomorrow." I could tell I was stalling. Processing.

"Why not? Just go early. It's obviously important." He seemed confused as to why I was second-guessing myself.

I was too, but I wasn't sure anymore what Leta knew or thought she knew based on what had happened with Sam. I was terrified to make the wrong next move.

"If you don't send it, I will," Jae said, snatching my phone off the table and typing.

"Sent," he shrugged a little and tossed the phone back at me.

I quickly unlocked and read through the message he sent.

Mona

Of course! When and where?

She had already replied.

Leta

11? My place?

I felt a little sense of relief. This was real. I was going to talk to Leta, and maybe, finally, put this whole mess behind me. Or at least, a portion of it.

I replied in the affirmative and reread the message Jae sent again.

"I've never seen a text from you in full sentences with punctuation. Did you *try* to text like me?" I couldn't hold back a smirk.

"Obvi. Couldn't let Leta know we were conspiring. I'm much more discrete than that," he replied with a haughty smile.

I let out a laugh, and it felt so damn good.

CHAPTER THIRTY-TWO

Sam

Briefly, I considered sticking around just to keep an eye out, but I'm admittedly a bit of a coward in this respect. I considered myself a shout-and-run kind of guy.

Facing Oscar one-on-one in an actual, verbal dispute was way out of my pay grade, but when he sent me a text and tried to confront me, I didn't hesitate to engage in that discussion.

Never Cried Wolf

It was already late. I wondered if he'd sipped some alcohol before or after the party. I didn't see any while I was there, but the way he was texting, I wouldn't have been surprised to find out.

Oscar

Wtf is ur problem?

I snickered a little as I read the message. Thankfully, I had years of experience arguing with internet trolls on the blog to back myself up, and a little-known fact about me is that I always loved trolling them right back.

Sam

No problem here. What about you?

His response came so quickly, I was certain he was actively staring at the messages, waiting for my reply.

Oscar

Ur my fuckin problem bro

Oh, yeah. He was *mad*. I did not open the message. I didn't want him to know I'd seen the message yet. Instead, I chose to tuck myself comfortably into my nice warm car and take the long way home before sending another note.

It wasn't often I really felt like I was in control of a conversation, but I think I'd gotten fairly good at it in the last month.

Like falling into an old routine, I knew I had the upper hand, otherwise, he'd have run after me. Luckily, he was a coward too.

He had to be.

A soft vibration came through the soft wool of my jacket pocket rumbling against my ribs. I knew he'd double-texted and I couldn't wait to watch his head explode.

I couldn't imagine getting all worked up over one little criticism like that.

Never Cried Wolf

For years my blog posts were littered with people calling me a creep, but I don't think I ever thought to ask anyone what their problem was.

To be fair, I supposed none of those people were people I'd considered something of a friend (or at the very least an acquaintance.)

I let my mind wander as I twisted around the side streets, watching the even snowflakes melt along my windshield into droplets that were gently ushered off to the edges by the wipers and flung off by the force of the vehicle moving through the darkness.

I wondered if *I* should have offered Elena a ride home, but quickly shook that guilt off.

If she didn't want a ride home with Oscar, whom she at least knew a little, to drive her home, certainly a stranger wouldn't have been better.

Ostensibly, she might have had a clue about how weird he was being, insisting she got into his car specifically to get home.

But, if there was anything I'd learned in the last few weeks, nobody owes you anything, and that girl most certainly didn't owe Oscar, and frankly, neither did Mona.

Friends don't keep count. Friends don't bill you for every little gesture. Friends share Bosco breadsticks sometimes and don't expect anything in return. Relationships aren't transactional. Most of the time, they just *are*.

But even knowing this now and feeling like a better person for learning and recognizing that I was wrong-- I didn't really feel any better about everything that happened with Mona.

And I wondered if I was only doing all this now because of that guilt. Was I coming at Oscar to pay myself back, karmically, for what I'd done? Or did I actually believe Oscar deserved to be called out?

As I twisted my steering wheel into my driveway, leaving tracks in the white sheet which now managed to stick to the streets, I considered that maybe it was a little of both.

Evidently, I had a skill for ruining reputations-- perhaps I ought to use it for good, so to speak.

I shifted my car into park. The house was dark. Hannah was at the movies with some of her friends, I remembered. Mom and Dad, I think, were at some game night my aunt was hosting.

My phone sat, inviting me to pull it out of the cup holder to finally reply to Oscar.

How mean was I hoping to be?

I imagined him absolutely fuming, seething, and maybe a touch bit whining as he waited for me to reply.

There is nothing spurned friends like more than to be ignored, I thought sarcastically. *Maybe just give him another minute.*

I smirked to myself and pulled up my Notes app. I had to proof of it or any amount of certainty, but if he *was* sitting and watching the conversation for me to start typing, I didn't want him to know exactly when I'd seen it or started to reply. Especially if I wanted to make some minor edits for maximum impact.

Crafting the perfect roast I thought usually took some time, but this one came surprisingly easy for me.

A reaction to the original message, plus reminding him he lost out on a chance alone with this girl, *and* a little nod to calling him emotional felt like the right move.

I scanned the message for any typos, then copied and pasted it quickly into the conversation. I let it sit for a good thirty seconds so he might think I'd just thought it up and typed it at that moment before hitting send.

Sam

A problem with me AND blue balls? Must be a rough night for you.

From there, I clicked right back out of the conversation so I could continue making him play this little waiting game.

Another hasty response solidified my assumption that he was actively watching the chat, and also in such a blind rage that he couldn't say a single intelligent thing.

Oscar

FUCK YOU!!!!

It really wasn't that funny but I laughed. I could imagine steam bursting out of his ears like a pressure pot and his face turning redder than the flames of hell.

On the topic of hell, I instinctively thought of a snappy reply that I knew would not only get his goat but launch it into space.

Sam

You wish you could

I stuck around this time. I wanted to watch the speech bubbles show up and disappear and show up and disappear. I was not disappointed.

Waiting patiently, I turned the radio up and enjoyed the heat coming out of the vents, warm and cozy inside the metal walls of my car while the wind whirled snowflakes in spirals all around me.

His response was delivered quicker than I expected and read surprisingly measured. I wondered if he had someone over his shoulder with him, but I doubted that pretty seriously.

Oscar

Ur so fucking gay its not even funny. Say ur fucking sorry

Big talk for someone who thought toilet-papering a house was peak disrespect.

As a matter of fact, I thought to say so.

Sam

What are you going to do? Toilet paper my house? Nah. I'm good.

Within moments of sending that final message, I tapped his contact and blocked his number.

It was a surprisingly tough choice. Part of me desperately wanted to see what kind of lame unoriginal comeback he'd lob my way, but I'm sure it was better not to know. I could have played text tag with him all night, but as they say, less is more.

Maybe it was running again, but I didn't care. I got the last word.

He was a small, little man trying to make himself feel big and important. If I kept replying, he might think he was worth my time, and I couldn't risk him thinking that.

A quick look back out the car window reminded me of how cold I would be when I stepped out of the oven I'd made for myself in the driver's seat. I decided to stall a little and let the song on the radio finish.

I scrolled through my phone, heading over to my blog. It had been a while since I'd spent a good chunk of time checking up on my engagement.

I tapped into my analytics, scanned through, not paying too much attention, and then navigated to my inbox of direct messages.

I had a few unopened messages from memorable accounts that I'd interacted with so much over the years. The people I'd once considered my lifelines to communication now were only a piece of my social puzzle.

And it was strange how much I relied on the internet to fill my social need, but in a way, I sort of missed it. Feeling like I could say exactly what I meant all the time, and never have to worry if anyone understood. Someone always would.

Even now, with Leta, and Dante-- even Mona-- and invitations to parties, and small talk becoming the norm for me, it didn't quite feel as comfortable as it did.

The act I was so proud of weeks earlier had exhausted me. I craved the freedom behind the screen, and the ease of communicating through the written word, especially after a night like this.

As the song rounded out, I quickly shifted my keys back and opened the door so I wouldn't get sucked into another. I kicked my legs out of the car, feeling a subtle burn where the frosty air finally touched my warm jeans. I quickly slammed and locked the door, hustling inside to get back into the warm air.

I finally swung the inside door closed and stood, breathing out the air I could no longer see wait for a few extra moments before banishing the darkness with a flick of the light switch, and I made my way up the stairs and into my room to find my computer still open and ready for me to browse.

There was that craving again, urging me to just sit down and engage with my people like I used to.

It was familiar and warm, comfortable, and easy.

I'd spent so much time in the last few weeks trying to escape this digital world and break out into the open again, but I wondered now if being alone was so bad after all.

Did I have to run from something that brought me joy just to assimilate with everyone else? Did it even matter if I assimilated if I still felt like I was putting on an act?

Tired. That's all I could say to describe myself after this week, and I just needed a little recharging. Then maybe I'd settle enough to fall back into this same routine again on Monday and face Mona again fresh.

Really, I needed a little time apart from her too, and I believed it served me well.

CHAPTER Thirty-Three

Mona

I gave Jae a big hug the next morning. He had walked me to the front door of his dorm, decked out in his fleece pajama pants and a bright tie-dyed rainbow shirt.

His embrace was so warm, it felt like it stuck on my skin as I stepped out into the light snow to drive home.

"The roads don't look too bad but drive safe anyway!" He called from the cracked door.

"Of course, I promise," I replied with a little wave as I slug my pack over my shoulder. It was stuffed with all my warm sweaters from the weekend, so it looked stupidly full, but it was still light.

"I love you, babe!" Jae called once more, blowing me a kiss through the cracked door before closing it. It had fogged up from the heat inside just like the windowed doors in the frozen section of the grocery store.

"I love you more!" I called in response, waving and blowing a kiss as his blurred figure through the glass.

Squelching in a sopping pile of dark snow, I turned on the heels of my boots and quickly shuffled along to the parking lot across the main road where I was able to leave mom's car. It was still early, and the sidewalks were perfectly empty with nothing but tiny blades of grass poking through a subtle dusting of snow on either side of the walkways. They were definitely frozen over. When the light breezes came, they didn't move.

By the time I made it to the car, I was already shivering, and my rearview mirror reflected a soft flush over my cheeks. Everything felt so light and airy like I was floating along on the wind.

I felt refreshed after my weekend with Jae, it was like a dream, going back in time and spending time together for real, like we used to, but regardless of how fantastic it was, it was time to get back to reality a bit.

There were about one hundred and twenty minutes between this moment, sitting in the parking lot at State College, and meeting Leta for the first time in weeks.

I wondered if I ought to text her and let her know I was driving in from out of town, just in case. I didn't want to get caught in traffic on the way and end up late.

My GPS informed me the trip would be exactly two hours and one minute, and it was

8:54. Realistically, I would be a little early for our eleven o'clock date, but I wasn't feeling like being particularly risky.

Part of me wished I felt a little worse about second-guessing a text message to my best friend. I think a week ago it would have crushed me to think about, but now it felt standard. Everything was walking on eggshells, but if you walk on eggshells enough, it just becomes a habit.

Maybe I should have felt better when things were getting easier for me, but I didn't want to be complacent about not having her in my life. I wanted to fix this still, and I imagined the best way to do that was simply to treat her like I always would.

So I sent the message at 8:55.

Mona

Hey, I was out of town. I'm

driving back now. I should be

there a bit before 11 but just

wanted to let you know in case I

hit traffic.

I realized the bubble at the bottom of the message screen immediately popped up as Leta replied quickly.

Leta

That's cool. Bring a coat. I don't
want parents to overhear.

So I replied quickly as well. Matching the energy.

Mona

Can do.

The drive was long but easy. I hopped right on one highway, about an hour in switched to another and it led straight back into town.

I didn't tell mom I was coming home early to talk to Leta, then she might have wanted the car back to run some errands or something first, and I didn't know how long this conversation would take.

Ten minutes? An hour? Two?

Certainly, if Leta and I wanted to, we could have easily filled two hours chatting together, at least, that was true once. I wasn't so sure we could do it just then.

I swapped through radio stations, listening for anything good. Mom only had a CD audiobook of Hamlet within reach. I didn't know how many times she could possibly have listened to this to make it worth it, but I didn't want to know.

The rapid shift of the music between stations kept my mind occupied. I didn't want to let my mind wander if I didn't have to.

Arguably, I needed to distract myself more.

Never Cried Wolf

Leta asked me to talk, which means she had something to say. That meant I needed to walk in prepared to listen, not explain or defend myself again. No matter how badly I'd want to.

And if I spent any amount of time trying to rehearse myself before walking in, I knew it would only make things worse.

Just talk to her the way you always do I reminded myself.

Be there for her because she needs you.

With those words in mind, I rounded out the trip with a little deep breathing to keep my heart rate down. Honestly, I didn't need to. The cold I experienced the moment I stepped out of the car slowed everything down for me really quickly.

I jumped back in the car and sent another text at 10:58.

Mona

I'm here. In driveway.

Brianna Rae Quinn

I hadn't even hit send when I caught the garage door moving out of the corner of my eye. Leta was already wrapped in a coat and hat, revealing her pretty pink puffer jacket inch by inch as the door pulled itself up.

She stepped out into the driveway. It had snowed a little more in Kettlewood than down at State. The grass was fully coated, but the driveway was completely clear, and a big blue snowblower sat covered in ice crystals just on the left side of the garage. Obviously, her dad or brother had blown all the snow off early. Mama Schneider hated the snow and would rather drive right through it.

I stepped back out of the car and tightened my coat around my chest, tying m scarf up a little tighter, and slammed the door behind me, but not in an aggressive or intimidating way, just enough to close it. I was terrified that any move I made would send the wrong message.

Leta waited at the top of the driveway for me. I did an awkward, bundled-up penguin run to her and let out a deep breath.

We both watched as the icy smoke from the hot air blended back out into the wind and waited a moment.

It appeared as though neither of us wanted to be the first one to speak.

"How are you?" I finally blurted. The silence was more awkward than whatever we were about to say, surely.

"I'm okay," she replied partially nodding, partially shrugging.

"What's… going on?" I hesitated again, not wanting to say the wrong thing.

She looked over her should to the inside garage door, presumably checking for her mom.

I prepared. I could feel a wince coming on for whatever she was about to yell at me.

But she didn't.

"Not too long ago, um," she started. She swallowed. "Oscar drove me home from mini golf."

She stopped for a moment. I nodded. *Listen. Don't speak.*

"We were driving along, and he said something stupid about how gas prices have gone up, and I just kinda laughed because that's so stupid." She paused again. "And he turned the wrong way down Third Street to get back. He started like, driving off to this little alcove along Millionaire Row, you know that neighborhood that leads to their little park trails? We used to go there to, um… mess around when we were dating, I guess. And he just parked the car and started trying to kiss me, like we weren't broken up and that nothing happened."

My jaw didn't drop but slightly loosened as my eyebrows raised. I kept my mouth shut, one, to listen to my best friend tell her tale, and two, to keep my shit together.

"I asked him what he was trying to do, and that we broke up because we both just weren't feeling it anymore, and I still definitely wasn't feeling it, and he just kept talking about-- fucking… Gas prices? He said I owed him for the trouble." Her arms crossed over her chest, and she looked away from me. She hadn't yet looked me in the eyes, but now she'd fully turned away.

"And," she started again, stopping to let out a long, shaky breath. "Is that what he did to you?"

I sniffed. I could have easily blamed it on the cold, but that would have been a lie. "Yes," I answered. My lip quivered. Again, it could have been a shiver from the cold, but Leta and I both knew what was really going on.

We'd been taken advantage of. Oscar had preyed on me when I was alone and preyed on her too.

"Did he… I mean," I paused to consider my words, which felt so foreign and unfamiliar to me. "Did anything happen?"

She looked back in my direction and finally met my eyes. She didn't need to say it. She opened up her mouth to speak but didn't get any words out before I cut her off. "You don't have to tell me." I reached out and wrapped my arms around her. I don't know if it helped, but I tried everything in my power to will the warmth I'd gotten from Jae into her, so she'd feel better.

I knew, though, it wouldn't be enough.

I couldn't say how long we stood there, silently sobbing into each other, letting our tears freeze on our faces and blowing broken, hot, smoke breaths into the air behind us. After a while, I wondered if just the idea of separating would have sucked because of how cold it was.

Again, I couldn't totally blame the cold.

We needed this. We needed each other.

"I'm sorry I didn't believe you," she finally said in the silence between two whistling winds. "I should have known. I never doubted you before. I don't know what happened."

I did, but I didn't tell her. She was dealing with enough.

"It's okay. I know. Shit happens, and I'm sure if I were you, I would have questioned it too."

She pulled away a bit.

"I just kind of realized last night. Sam basically told Oscar in front of a whole group of people that he was a creep when he was trying to offer Elena a ride home, and it just kind of clicked."

My eared perked up.

"Sam said that?" I asked.

"Yeah." She sniffed while I processed. "I just don't want anyone else to get sucked into this, you know?"

A loud ping came from her pocket as we stood there, wiping our faces clear of snot and tears.

"Sorry," she said, grabbing her phone out of her pocket. "I had it on high so I'd know when you got here." She flipped it over to turn it down.

"It's just the confessions page anyway."

"Anything good?" I joked, falling back into my old habit of distracting myself instead of dealing with issues head-on.

She tapped the notification and showed me.

Kettlewood Confessions

@KWHS_Confess

Less than 1 minute ago

"Dalia Rayne, prom!? <3"

I read through the message once, twice, and then again.

"You know," I started, developing a slow, malicious grin. "I know first-hand how quickly information can get out with this account."

I decided maybe it was time to take a page out of Sam's book.

Leta grinned back. She seemed to have the same idea.

Never Cried Wolf

I watched as she toggled into the account and tapped the link in the bio. We found ourselves as a simple submission page.

Kettlewood Confessions
Submissions
Submit your confession here! Keep an eye out for it to be published on @KWHS_Confess!

Click, click, click the keyboard went as I observed Leta typing out our little message.

"Oscar Moreno begs girls
to get with him when he offers
them rides home. STAY AWAY."

She hit submit, and we read the submission confirmation thanking us for our contribution.

"Really, it was our pleasure," I replied, verbally.

Leta reached down and grabbed my hand.

"I love you. Thank you for being here with me, especially after everything."

I smiled and have her palm a squeeze, trying once more to spread a little warmth her way.

"I wouldn't take on the world with anyone else."

CHAPTER Thirty-Four

Sam

The week had been quiet, and shockingly so. Mona had been cordial, but distant. She was evidently eating lunch elsewhere, or so she said when I asked in Creative Writing.

There seemed to be no issue. It was like a minor scuff in our relationship, but somehow, after telling her the truth, she came alive again. So on Wednesday, I finally asked.

Brianna Rae Quinn

"You seem happy this week." It really wasn't a question, but it was certainly prompted by curiosity, so I classified it as a question.

"Maybe," she replied, finalizing a line of poetry before looking over at me. "I saw Jae last weekend and it was kind of exactly what I needed."

"Oh," I acknowledged her words and found myself bobbing my head as I remembered Jae's existence. "How is he?"

"He's doing really well, actually. College is treating him great. He says he's finally starting to feel like himself. Like the world is bigger now."

I made a face and glanced back down at my paper, primed for writing with dark slashes of graphite dividing words in half. The wrong words, of course, but I always thought it made the page look messy, even if it was both satisfying and faster to just cross them out.

"People are always saying college is going to be so much better, but I'm tired of hearing it," I finally mumbled, poised to begin writing again, but never actually touching the tip of the pencil to the paper.

"I thought it was comforting," she said plainly, also maintaining her look in the direction of her desk. "I can't change the way people see me here, but I have a fresh start built into my life as soon as I'm out. I could try and fix everything and redeem myself, or whatever, but by then I might be leaving." She took a pause. "Takes way longer to build trust back up than to destroy it."

I couldn't help but look at her, and when I did, I noticed her eyes on me as well, dark, and wide, opening a world of new questions.

"Come on, Mona. You have at least twelve more weeks of junior year and then all of senior year. You should at least try. I couldn't possibly just ignore all the bullshit for that long."

"Hey, watch the mouth! Channel all that rage into the writing!" Mr. Howard called from the inner circle. He was currently working with the kid who slept through an entire test a few weeks ago. The kid seemed alive and well, which was out of the ordinary.

"Sorry!" I replied with an uncomfortable grimace.

A few kids snickered but went back to their work pretty immediately.

"I guess we're just different in that way," she shrugged.

I shook my head in disbelief.

"I'm not totally giving up, you know. I'm just not worrying about it anymore," she continued, writing in a few more words in her notebook.

A scoff escaped my lips. She looked up at me through her reddish-brown eyelashes with a partially raised eyebrow.

"I'm sorry, but I just don't believe it's that easy. If it was, I think I would have been a lot happier the last few years," I admitted.

"I didn't say it was easy, Sam. I just want to set my sights on the future instead of wallowing in my own self-pity."

Never Cried Wolf

Her voice sounded so condescending. It was like nails on a chalkboard. It was hard not to feel as though her words were a personal attack on me for everything I'd done to her. Not that I didn't think I deserved it, but it certainly still bugged me.

It was nice, I'd say, to feel like I was being candid with her again. I didn't quite realize how tense everything had been for me since I started my little charade. Now, it wasn't just that words came easy, but they felt easy too. This little honesty trip between us had been so cathartic for me. Even though I still had to keep up appearances with Dante and Rafael, I felt lighter when I spoke to Mona about all the real stuff, even if we were both being a bit snide and passive aggressive. In a way, I think we both needed it.

So why not tack on a bit more honesty?

This time, I chose to whisper. "I'm afraid of leaving this place and everything I know behind. Starting over, for me, sounds so fucking intimidating."

Mona dropped her pencil and leaned her head on her palm to look at me again. "Things change whether you want them to or not. World keeps turning. We can stop walking but it'll keep going. It's up to you what you want to do. You can stick around in community college and keep hanging out with your people here, or you can go to college and try to find new people who let you feel more like yourself. That's what Jae did, and that's what I want for me."

I didn't bother replying. Just flexed my fingers a little bit. Even after all this time, talking about college still sent waves of panic through me. I knew Mona was right, but that didn't make it less terrifying.

"I haven't even really found my people here. Twelve years in this stupid district and I still don't know who my people are, and I don't even think I'm really myself around the people who made it kind of close," Twelve years, and no people. How can I possibly do that in four?

College isn't going to magically change me, or you, or anyone."

"You're right, but the people around you will change, and they're going to be just as lonely as you. Everyone's starting over, just with more life experience and social skills…I mean, hopefully." Her lips curved up in a light smile. She reached over to my flexing fingers and held my hand for a moment.

I don't know if I really felt better, but our relationship operated in strange ways now. Even if college still felt threatening, at least the situation between us had settled for now.

"Ten minutes until we start our peer review! Remember, we want to thicken up the skin a bit before we start doing whole class critiques, so be constructive and keep your minds open to what your friends have to say. Whatever they say will be a whole lot nicer than what the strangers will say, for sure." Mr. Howard was now across the room working his way around the outer circle. Mona and I would be last in his check.

We both exchanged a quick "Oh shit" glance and refocused on our writing. I only had three, uninspired lines and a couple of crossed-out words. I decided to start over with a not-so-subtle rip off the page and crumpled it up.

"Bold moves coming from the right side of the room," I heard Mr. Howard joke in response to my dramatic display, but I didn't care. I had to write quickly before it all left my head.

I wandered in the dark
For hours, seeking a way out
In a room with velvet-covered walls
And no doors that I could tell.

The darkest corners of the room
Sent shivers down my spine
And shadows crawled along my legs
Leaving goosebumps in their wake.

Never Cried Wolf

My arms reached out in a desperate
Grasp for any ounce of sun.
Though my eyes adjusted to the void
I still longed for color again.

An outstretched arm reached the end
Again, and pressed into the velvet wall.
I balled the velvet in my fist and saw
Streaks of light peak in.

I twisted, turned, and yanked, and pulled
And found the strangest thing.
The velvet walls were curtains
And could finally let light in.

When I finally looked away, Mr. Howard
was only a few desks down, and Mona was
doodling in the corner of her paper.

I was suddenly exceptionally excited to
share what I'd written, and my impatience won
the battle between waiting for Mr. Howard and
slipping my paper over to Mona immediately.

"I think I'm done. Are you?" I wondered
aloud.

"Mhm," she replied, nonchalantly.

"Do you want to just trade now, and we can trade back when Howard gets to us?"

She shrugged. "Sure," we did a quick rotation of our pages and her notebook replaced mine in front of me.

I looked down at my backpack, presently bursting at the seams, and considered pulling out a pen to write comments when Mona's hand shifted into my peripherals.

A quick glance informed me she had already pulled out a pen for me. "We don't have all day for you to fish something useful out of that thing," she teased.

I smiled and snatched the pen out of her hand and turned my attention to her piece. She had titled in, underlined at the top.

Never Cried Wolf

<u>Shooting Star</u>

She flies in the space between

Planets and stars and

Shoots over heads so quick

You might miss it.

She burns white hot,

And pushes so hard

To get where she's going

As fast as she can.

She knows that

Soon she'll feel the gravity

And twist with intention

Toward the pull.

She'll sore through speckled

Celestial skies, and glide through

Another atmosphere.

Brianna Rae Quinn

To land square on a planet
which welcomed her
And finally, find her place.

I found that I was smiling. I loved all the different synonyms she'd used for flying. It made the piece feel less redundant. I scribbled that along the bottom of the paper and continued to pull out things I liked and didn't.

I've never been much of a fan of varying stanza sizes. I liked the uniformity. I also thought it made the rhythm and cadence of the poems flow better. Maybe that was personal, but I wrote it anyway.

I ran my fingers through my hair, wondering what else I could say. I peeked over at Mona without moving my head to see if she'd written anything yet. She seemed to have underlined something in the first stanza. I was already itching to know what she put.

"Mr. Tafelski!" Mr. Howard called from above my head. I snapped prompt to attention and watched as he awkwardly scooched between the chair of the inner circle behind him and the front desk before him.

The student behind him hopped a little to pull the chair forward and Mr. Howard let out a deep sigh as if he'd been sucking in the entire time.

"Whew, thank you," he said, crouching down to get on my level. I briefly wondered how long it would take him to fall over like a log compared to someone as petite as Mona, but I refocused as he started talking.

"Is this your work?" He asked, recognizing the pen in my hand and the handwriting that most definitely was not mine.

"Oh, no." I turned and Mona was popping a dot at the top of a comment on my poem. She quickly capped her lime green Bic and picked my notebook up to hand it back to me.

I grabbed it and traded it with hers.

"Thank you," I half-whispered, half-mouthed.

Once again, the desire for instant gratification won out over my patience and I turned my attention to Mr. Howard, right in front of me.

"Can I read what she wrote really quickly?" I asked.

He shrugged. "Sure, maybe she'll give me some ideas for what to say!" He smiled in the way he always did. Half joking, maybe half serious.

I followed my eyes to the first line of blue pen I noticed near the bottom. She'd circled the word finally, written in the last line of my piece, just as hers was. Just below it, she added a note.

I'm so happy you've opened your curtains.

My head bobbed up immediately to see if she was watching me read.

She was.

Never Cried Wolf

And finally, Mona and I could really see each other for the first time.

EPILOGUE

Sam. 2 years later

I kicked a rock down the sidewalk on my way over to the student union. State College looked amazing in the spring, right when the leaves started to reappear on the trees. Waking up every morning and seeing a few more buds and greens poking out after the winter really got me excited.

There was a patch of daffodils outside of my dorm room that had already bloomed. The snow came back a little too late into the season and covered all the sweet, buttery-yellow petals with frost and ice, but they didn't seem to die.

They kept growing through it. I loved those flowers, every year.

"Hey!" A voice echoed across the central oval of campus.

On the other side sat a thin young man with bleached blonde hair, longer on top, resting on a bench and snacking on a bag of pretzels. He wore a maroon hoodie with the State logo screen printing across the front. He wore shorts with an inseam that may be slightly too small, but I certainly didn't mind. I was mostly wondering how he wasn't cold. Spring may have sprung, but it was still a bit breezy.

I smiled and waved, picking my feet up and little higher and faster to meet him across the oval as soon as physically possible without actually running. I popped myself into the seat beside him on the bench. I could feel my grin widening as I bumped my shoulder into his. I felt a little jolt of electricity where they met. I always did with him.

"Did you bring the flyers?" He spoke to me before I could formally say hello in response to his call.

I slipped my arm into my new shoulder bag and pulled out a stack of neatly organized flyers for the event we would be promoting today.

"Oh, shit," he snatched the stack out of my hands. "They look *so* good. You even used fancy cardstock!" I could tell he was teasing me. "And no ripped or folds? Wow? Did you clean out your nasty ass bag just for me?" He batted his eyelashes at me in a faux damsel-in-distress sort of vibe,

I rolled my eyes and grabbed them back. "I got the cardstock from the education center. No one ever checks to make sure you're an actual education major when you get there." I tapped my stack on the edge of the bench to straighten the flyers back out and put them back into my bag.

"Real talk, though, the colors on that look *amazing*."

I gave him thanks before asking, "Are you almost done snacking so we can go inside? I have no idea how you're not freezing."

"We're a little early, and I only signed up for one hour of table duty," He reminded me. He emphasized one hour absently while crunching down on another pretzel stick.

"Come on, doofus. I'm not waiting. You can watch *me* set up if you don't want to work so badly." I stood and held my hand out to him to pull him off the bench.

He rolled his eyes, zipping closed the blue and green lock on his pretzel bag before finally reaching up and placing his hand in mine.

That familiar, comfortable jolt of electricity warmed me up pretty quickly, but I definitely wasn't going to let him know that.

He rotated himself around to stand on my left, beside me and laced his fingers in between mine. We didn't even think twice as we walked into the student union to the event tables. Three tables in was our empty table, with a paper on top noting which organizations had it reserved for today. I assumed it was ours, anyway, as every other table had already been fully taken over with banners and balloons, and bowls of candy designed to draw passing students into a minute-long spiel about various campus events

I stopped in my tracks as I noticed a familiar frame standing at the next table. A petite shape leaned over the table, signing a piece of paper from what looked like members of an arts fraternity. There were some Greek letters on the table that I could fully read. (Almost two years into college and I still knew nothing about Greek life, even with Greek housing lining the route around old campus.)

A mass of red hair was thrown over the shoulder closest to me, though it was a little shorter than I remembered, and a familiar apricot sweater vest topping a collared shirt. It couldn't have been anyone but Mona.

Never Cried Wolf

Once I went away to college, we fell out of touch. Against what I thought we all odds, she was right. I did find my people in college, and I found myself.

Then it all came flooding back. I'd convinced myself I loved her. I wanted our friendship to be love so badly that I'd funneled every insecurity I had about myself and my sexuality into that one rejection—onto her. I thought since she'd rejected me, that made my gayness more real, and it was her fault. I'd attacked her to make her feel as uncertain as I did. That was who I had been.

But at this point in my life, I was a totally different person, almost completely unrecognizable to myself, yet I wondered what she would see when she looked at me.

Someone who hurt her? She moved on once. maybe it was all behind her again.

"Mona?" I half questioned, half called to her. Just as I imagined, her shoulders lifted, and she turned over that hair-covered shoulder to look to me. Her jaw relaxed in a not-quite jaw-drop before she fixed a smile on her lips.

"Sam! Hi!" She replied. I noticed her eyes flit down to where my hand intertwined with another man's.

I turned to look at the man attached to that hand. "Eddy, this is Mona. We went to high school together."

"Hello," Eddy took the lead in his own introduction, holding a hand out to shake Mona's. She reached her arm out to shake, pushing the sleeve of her oversized button-down out of the way. "Eddy Vale, the best thing that ever happened to him." I felt myself smile and blush a little. It had been a while since I'd blushed like that. I wondered what made me suddenly so bashful and embarrassed.

"Mona Murphy, um…" she hesitated, "Probably just *a* thing that happened to him." Her joke felt awkward and forced, but Eddy laughed anyway.

"Yeah," I continued, "Eddy's my… boyfriend." I threaded my hand back into his as it returned to his side.

I recognized Mona's eyes soften a little and her smile appeared a touch more genuine. "That's awesome, Sam. I'm so happy for you,"

I quickly jumped into another topic. "I didn't realize you came to State?" The words were a statement, phrased as a question.

"Yeah," she said, looking over her shoulder to wave her goodbye to the fraternity member she'd spoken to and stepped over to really speak with us. "I mean, I don't usually hang out down here by the union. I'm kind of a hermit in my dorm room. I have this online job where I proofread and edit quality assurance reports, so you're probably the twelfth person from high school to say that when I finally show my face in the daylight," she chuckled softly.

"Wow, do you like doing that kind of work?" I wondered aloud.

"Yeah, I just have to be sure I look away from the screen every now and then, lest I turn out like Forest Jenkins." Her chuckle was half-hearted.

"I totally forgot about him!" Forest Jenkin, the infamous creator of Kettlewood Confessions who revealed his secret identity minutes before walking at graduation imaging he couldn't be punished by administration then. He failed to recognize the wrath of the student body was undoubtedly more powerful.

We waded through our nostalgia, stagnant for a moment, before Mona pushed the current forward.

"It seems like you're doing well!" She noted, passing the conversation back to me.

"I mean, yeah," I looked over at our still-empty table. "We were actually down here to promote this big show our organization is putting on."

"Oh?" Mona asked. "What kind of show?" Her curiosity was genuine, I realized I hadn't thought about her much in the last few years, but being with her now, I sort of missed how genuine she was.

"It's a Drag Show," Eddy flipped the flap of my satchel up and pulled out my immaculate stack of flyers. "We're raising money for the LGBTQ+ Student Union Banquet at the end of the semester. We want to be able to recognize all the fantastic work our peers have done to make State a positive and inclusive environment for people of all sexualities." He pushed the top fly out of the stack and handed it off to her.

"You should come!" he called.

"Oh my god, this sounds so fun!" She chirped, scanning the details on the sheet.

"It most certainly will be. You'll be pleased to know I'll be headlining as Bi Felicia," Eddy made a motion like he flipped his hair over his shoulder.

I gave him a playful shove. "That only works if you have a wig on," I snorted.

Mona's eyes brightened as she watched out interaction.

"Whatever. I'm going to set up the table. You two catch up, or whatever." He waved me off, but added one more aside, "I'm finally on the clock." He smirked as he walked off to claim our little table.

I couldn't help another small laugh before turning to Mona.

"He seems fantastic," she said with that bright smile I always remembered her wearing.

"Yeah, he is. It's so good to see you," I noted.

Her smile fell a little sadder and more sideways. "You too."

I wasn't certain she meant it. I wondered if she was struggling to keep back all the negativity too.

My eyes dropped to my feet before looking back up at her. The odds of me seeing her again after then were slim, so I imagined if there was ever a time to say it, it would be right then.

"I'm still really sorry about the way things went with us you know. I think I was just so frustrated feeling like I couldn't really be myself in that town, and I was just… angry. I'm not proud of the person I was in high school."

Mona nodded once and tensed her lips in a sort of "what can you do?" style grimace. "I don't think anyone likes who they were in high school." She looked over at Eddy and then back to me. "I told you college wouldn't be so bad."

"You were right. Not just about that, but," I paused, and sighed. "A lot of stuff, I guess." I shrugged a little, following her gaze to look at Eddy too.

"We did the best with what we had. And who we had. You weren't too bad of a proximity friend, you know."

I could tell she wanted me to feel a little better. I didn't really. Thinking about high school always made me a little bitter and upset. Partially at myself and partially at the people who surrounded me.

"You either," I finally decided to say.

The silence between us felt miles wide but filled infinitely with could-haves and what-ifs. We didn't say any of that. He decided to leave the past in the past and focus our attention on what was ahead, for once, and continue living happily in our separate worlds.

"I'm gonna go, Sam," she broke through those miles and reached me again. "It was good seeing you though… really." That last word hit me in the gut but in a good way.

It felt good to be wished well. It felt good to want her to be well. I knew we were both exactly where we needed to be now, even if that wasn't with each other.

"You too," I spoke, holding for a moment. "Really."

She turned and head off in the direction of the cafeteria. I wondered if she was going to grab something to eat or if she was going to run back to her dorm.

It didn't really matter.

Never Cried Wolf

Nothing ever does.

It may not be happily ever after, but it was happy for now, and that was enough for me.

ACKNOWLEDGEMENTS

This time around, I'd known this story was somewhere inside of me. Before I wrote *Fake It Till You Make It*, this is what I thought my first novel would be. Incidentally, I fell in love with the idea of *Fake It* before I had the nerve to write this one down. The reason I had such a hard time was that certain parts of the story, again, were very personal.

There is something about writing what you know that's scary because the people from your past will know who these characters are meant to represent, and some of them might not appreciate being portrayed as a villain. But something I've found even more since I've started writing is that even some of the people in my life who, at the time, I saw as villains, I had such a hard time writing them as villains constantly, because there was a time I really, truly loved them.

Not every story's villain is a bad person, and they have the potential for growth. I know I have been the villain of many stories. That's why I made sure Sam got his happy ending, and also why Mona never really had hers written in. Sam deserved a redemption—and to my real-life Sam, I hope you're doing well and that you know I still value the good memories. You're also the reason this story exists, and one of the many people who helped me fall in love with creative writing. Thank you for that. And if you ever read this, you know who you are.

Writing this novel was also a struggle because, as much as I was writing what I know, I also wrote a lot of what I don't know. I wrestled a lot with what qualified me to write from a male perspective, let alone from the perspective of a gay male. Those are two experiences I have simply never had. Half of this book is a blind assumption, and I greatly feared tackling that challenge at the risk of criticism. But then again, I published three others books, and I have absolutely been criticized before, I knew now I could take it. I also know that writing this has been therapeutic for me, so at least getting this frustration out will make some space for more frustration to come!

As always, I'd like to thank my beta reader squad! Kaleigh Ceci and Gabrielle Dendinger, who read every few chapters and gave me feedback as I wrote; and Rachel Craft and Kaitlyn McClure, who read the full novel's draft (unedited I might add!) after it was complete!

I'd also like to thank my top two hype people, who provide nonstop support, Chrissy Margevicius (my real-life Leta!), and Nick Kemper (my real-life husband!). Also, my family for their undying support, even the ones who don't read, but always buy! It means a lot!

Never Cried Wolf

One shout out also goes to Amanda Sizler, my colleague who gave me the fun challenge of somehow fitting the word "affront" into my novel. I'm not sure I did it justice, but I just needed her to know I didn't forget! And another shout out to Sari Whims who literally saved my book cover.

Finally, my editor—Monroe Brackey – you're doing God's work! Making my stuff readable is no easy feat, and of course, all of you, for I know sometimes reading my stuff is no easy feat. You deserve thanks and applause too.

Until the next one! If it goes my way, it'll be a fun turn into the left field!